What People Are Saying About

Vatican Daughter

Vatican Daughter: So many skeletons bang on the closet doors, wanting to be set free, from this troubling tale of fiction based on disturbing, little known facts. This one is brimming with history, reality, and intensity — a story that will keep you on your toes all the way to the end.

Steve Berry, *New York Times* best-selling author with 25 million copies sold

VATICAN DAUGHTER is vibrant! Blending speculative storytelling and daring fact, Iraci compels, questions, and captivates — with all of Italy as her mighty backdrop. Told with the pace and verve of a feature film, this novel offers a deep dive into the world of a mother and daughter threatened by the secrets of the Church and the lengths men will go to silence their own mortal sins.

Afia Atakora, award-winning author of *Conjure Women*

A fascinating multilayered story about family, intrigue, love, and murder — with all of it set in and around the Vatican! Slick and exciting, *Vatican Daughter* races along at a breakneck pace that will keep you happily turning pages.

Tom Santopietro, author of the best-selling *The Sound of Music Story*

T0343536

Vatican Daughter

A Novel

Also by Joni Marie Iraci

Reinventing Jenna Rose

978-0999137048

979-8986407029 (2023 reissue)

Vatican Daughter

A Novel

Joni Marie Iraci

ROUNDFIRE
BOOKS

London, UK
Washington, DC, USA

CollectiveInk

First published by Roundfire Books, 2025
Roundfire Books is an imprint of Collective Ink Ltd.,
Unit 11, Shepperton House, 89 Shepperton Road, London, N1 3DF
office@collectiveinkbooks.com
www.collectiveinkbooks.com
www.roundfire-books.com

For distributor details and how to order please visit the 'Ordering' section on our website.

Text copyright: Joni Marie Iraci 2024

ISBN: 978 1 80341 778 3
978 1 80341 798 1 (ebook)
Library of Congress Control Number: 2024932630

A CIP catalogue record for this book is available from the British Library.

Design: Lapiz Digital Services

UK: Printed and bound by CPI Group (UK) Ltd, Croydon, CR0 4YY
Printed in North America by CPI GPS partners

We operate a distinctive and ethical publishing philosophy in all areas of our business, from our global network of authors to production and worldwide distribution.

Contents

For Joe, always and forever.
And for Karen, my 4:00 a.m. keeper.

But please remember: this is only a work of fiction. The truth, as always, will be far stranger.
– Sir Arthur C. Clarke, *2001: A Space Odyssey*

Chapter One

Joseph Morris stood in the "Crying Room" just beyond the Sistine Chapel, thinking the room was aptly named. He felt his teeth chattering as the cardinals placed the papal garb over him. His arms lifted mechanically to receive the garments. The conclave of cardinals from around the globe who'd traveled to Vatican City to elect the new pontiff gathered nearby. Cardinal Roselli, the epitome of the church's hierarchy, stood off in the distance watching the scenario unfold with envy in his heart.

"Would it be alright if I spoke with Cardinal Roselli for a moment before we proceed?"

The cardinals tending to Joseph Morris bowed respectfully and gestured for him to take his leave.

"I need to speak with you in the confessional," he whispered to a stunned Cardinal Roselli.

This unusual circumstance filled the cardinal with apprehension. He escorted Joseph Morris away from the conclave and off to a side chapel near the papal apartments. He entered the confessional, an old-world type where faces remained unseen. Cardinal Roselli stiffened in his seat. He usually used time in the confessional to catch up on his sleep, but this confessant was atypical, and he didn't know what to expect. Perhaps the odd request was an overreaction sparked by the anxiety one naturally experienced when they were faced with a sudden life-altering event, and this was merely a formality meant to seal the door to the past as the confessant approached elevation to the highest of earthly realms. The cardinal anticipated hearing the usual mundane offenses. He didn't want to waste this historic moment listening to the frivolous sins of a nervous newly elected pope.

"Your Holiness, it isn't necessary for you to confess anything to me or anyone else. I'm sure you are in a state of grace or this wouldn't be happening to you."

Cardinal Roselli's statement pleased Joseph, but didn't dissuade him.

"I need confession, please."

Cardinal Roselli sighed and hoped he wasn't about to hear what were referred to as "venial sins": envy, anger, gluttony, even the occasional mention of coveting someone else's goods, or the rare homosexual fling. The latter, however, went on more than it was ever acknowledged.

Cardinal Roselli leaned into the screen separating him from the confessant. Pope Joseph Morris recited the rote, "Bless me, father," greeting.

"Please continue, Joseph, we don't have much time."

Still reeling from the shock of what had transpired over the past few hours, Joseph Morris hesitated and cleared his throat. His nerves were getting the better of him.

"I've been living in sin."

"Go on," Cardinal Roselli instructed.

"I had an affair with a young woman in Rome. She's about to give birth to my child. She's a journalist for Sky Italia."

Cardinal Roselli stopped listening after hearing Joseph refer to the woman's profession. He asked her name, gave absolution, and waited for Joseph to exit the confessional.

Joseph rejoined the waiting conclave and they resumed the preparations.

"Remove your shoes, Your Holiness," Cardinal Giordano, a member of the Vatican Curia, instructed.

Joseph removed his scuffed brown shoes; they were an old pair of Gucci loafers his mother had sent from the United States. He remembered laughing at the time. He hadn't had the heart to tell her she'd essentially sent the shoes back home to their place of origin.

The red shoes, signifying the power bestowed upon him as the first American Pope, rested on a small wooden chair. Cardinal Giordano placed the shoes on the floor and Joseph slid his unworthy feet into them.

His mind was elsewhere. He wondered what it would have been like to have a child, be a father, a husband? He'd feared his own father when he was young. But marriage? His parents' marriage had been mundane, growing more and more so over the many years they'd been together, until his father died and his mother soon after. There was no glory in marriage. His father, during his regular occurring fits of anger, would rage, "I am the head of this family." At the time, the words had resonated with Joseph, sending shivers of fear down his spine. But what did it matter now?

Off in the corner, the Archbishop of Armagh was in a heated discussion with the recently appointed British cardinal. Joseph moved closer and strained to hear.

"An American elected," the Irish cardinal said lowering his voice, "I can't imagine God had a hand in this."

The British cardinal frowned but didn't respond. It was his first conclave. He was intimidated and it showed.

"Whose will is it then, Cardinal McMahon? Any ideas?" Joseph asked the stunned cardinal.

"I meant no disrespect, Your Holiness."

Joseph walked away hoping his response would demonstrate, to those in doubt, his readiness to assume the power his papal duties would require of him.

Joseph looked around for Cardinal Roselli. He hoped the unbearable weight of guilt he'd been shouldering had been lifted by the Holy Spirit working through Cardinal Guilo Roselli in the confessional. Not that he truly believed in the doctrine, but this was destiny and he believed in that. Still, he needed the security of Cardinal Roselli's presence when he ascended to the throne of St. Peter. Cardinal Roselli maintained the status quo and kept the centuries old conventions intact for the most part. As the first American Pope, Joseph would be held to harsh scrutiny by the unyielding Vatican traditionalists.

Joseph moved towards the drapes. They would soon be pulled back revealing him to his people for the first time. The roar of the crowd filled him with an unfamiliar yet overwhelming sense of the power afforded only to those who were revered, those who held indisputable authority. He prayed he was up to the task as Cardinal Giordano placed the pretiosa on his head; it was surprisingly light for something so elaborate. Two Swiss Guards stood in attendance holding back the drapery. Pope Joseph stepped onto the balcony raising his arms over his head blessing the waiting crowd as they chanted, "Santo Padre." Joseph was now the father to many, the "Holy Father"; he would bask in this glory and leave all thoughts of his former life behind.

He looked around one last time for Cardinal Roselli. His absence, at this most historic event, was palpable.

"Can anyone tell me where Cardinal Roselli has gone? Has he taken ill?" The gathered cardinals looked around at each other shaking their heads.

"We haven't seen him since you spoke with him," Cardinal Giordano answered.

Cardinal Roselli rushed towards the papal offices. If he was not beside Pope Joseph when he appeared on the balcony to greet the faithful for the first time as pope, it would arouse suspicion. He'd have to hurry.

"Pronto," he said to the man on the other end of the line. The instructions he gave were clear, "Trovala, find her."

The roar of the crowd could be heard long after Pope Joseph left the balcony. Cardinal Roselli was waiting to escort the pope to a luncheon in his honor.

"Were you ill, Your Eminence? You were missed."

"Si, I suffer from headaches. I went to my office for aspirin. I'm so sorry I wasn't at your side."

The quick and simple lie satisfied Pope Joseph. He turned to face his staff of cardinals who one by one came forward to welcome him.

Chapter Two

Twelve Years Later

A warm wind blew across the Grand Canal carrying with it Acqua Alta. The Venetian waters rose slightly at first, seeping through the pavement of San Marco. The platforms were readied, but they would prove futile if the water continued to rise. It was barely 8 a.m. The water gushed furiously behind the mask shop located just below the Rialto Bridge. The shop belonged to Maestro Lorenzo Mercuri, the kindly proprietor whose fame as master mask-maker drew many visitors to his small shop.

Sophia will be here soon, the Maestro thought to himself. She was the woman without a memory whom he'd befriended; the woman who traveled by vaporetto every morning to help him. He paid her a small stipend and instructed her in the Venetian art of mask-making. She took to it with ease and had a knack for painting. In the low season the Maestro would fill her head with stories of his clients in America. Many a Venetian tale was woven around the mystique of Sophia Mariana Travato. The people of Venice were quick to gossip as there was little else to break up the monotony of sameness.

Sophia lived with the Benedictine nuns at the clandestine convent of Santa Maria della Visitazione. From the palazzo and the esplanade along the lagoon that abutted the church, there was no sign of life, the church appeared to be abandoned. Sophia exited from a hidden back door into the alley.

She knew most of the merchants and many of the citizens in the small city. Her memory of life before arriving in Venice had been erased, the reasons were vague. Sophia, a captive audience to the locals and their nonstop chatter, had no story of her own to share. The shopkeepers offered strange remedies to her plight, "You must have been hit on the head, another blow should bring your memory back." Or they tried to ignite her memory by saying, "maybe you have a family somewhere, maybe in America." Sophia listened, widening her deep, almost black-brown eyes, shaking her head at their advice, answering, "Maybe I do, I don't remember."

Most Venetians couldn't comprehend Sophia's situation. They believed in luck, good or bad, and Sophia, in their estimation, had been a victim of bad luck.

If Sophia was Venetian, it wasn't apparent; she seemed most comfortable speaking English, she may have been educated abroad, but her Italian was flawless. She was an enigma. Shopkeepers passed the offseason conjuring up stories surrounding the origins of Sophia.

But Sophia didn't ask questions. "You were probably dropped off by boat; Reverend Mother found you in a heap at the convent door, you were nearly frozen, after being exposed all night long to the winds coming off the lagoon." One of the young novices recited the same story every time she passed Sophia on the pathway to the neighborhood church. Sophia knew this was something the young novice hadn't really witnessed but had been instructed to say. Sophia didn't question its validity; nothing prompted her to remember what came before — nothing. This story was as true a story as any of the others. Sophia was content for the time being, traveling freely through the palazzos and Calles of Venice. As long as the nuns allowed this, Sophia had no reason to doubt them.

Every morning, the café on the cusp of the vaporetto stop had a cappuccino waiting on the counter. Every morning at the same time, Sophia walked the plank onto the waiting waterbus, and traveled onto the waters of the Grand Canal and made her way to the Rialto Bridge.

When the weather permitted and the palazzos were dry, she'd walk home, over the bridges, past the Guggenheim Museum to the quiet part of Venice known as the Dorsoduro district. No one knew how Sophia came to be in Venice. If the nuns knew, they weren't saying.

The vaporetto came to a rocky stop at the edge of the Rialto Bridge. The clouds had dispersed and the sun appeared in the purple Venetian sky. The gushing water had turned to a trickle over the canal's edge and was swallowing itself back through the drains in the pavement. Sophia slipped her rubber boots off and put on her sandals.

"Morning, Maestro, I can watch the store if you want to sneak out for a cappuccino."

"I stopped on my way here — due," he said, holding up two fingers and tapping his portly belly with his other hand. His signature black, long-sleeved shirt and black pants held the evidence. A splatter of white cappuccino foam defaced his once pristine designer shirt. Lorenzo smiled when he noticed Sophia eyeing the stain. He ran his fingers through his slick black hair in an attempt to distract her.

"I put your mask on the shelf over there." Maestro Lorenzo enjoyed practicing his English with Sophia. It enabled him to hold his own with his British and American clients.

"Well, if you want another let me know," Sophia smiled. "There's still room on your shirt for a bit more foam."

Sophia had grown comfortable with Maestro Lorenzo over the years, she enjoyed their playful banter. Her life with the nuns was formal and devout. She feigned believing their beliefs. She found their life to be a hardship. Talk amongst the sisters consisted of reports on their daily routine, work, and more work inside and outside the walls of the convent. They found joy in work, and needed little in the way of worldly goods. Sophia longed for more, which had prompted her to jump at the chance to work in the Maestro's mask shop.

The shop's exceptionally small size proved problematic during the height of the tourist season. There was no room to observe the Maestro. But it was "riposo" time between noon and four which gave her the opportunity to practice her budding artistic flair. For now, the bridge was filled with gullible tourists who didn't get the memo — merchants along the Rialto were rip-off artists. It was mostly true, yet Maestro Lorenzo's shop was here and he was the consummate old master. He'd been there long before the gold merchants set up their shops hoping to lure unsuspecting tourists showing off the glitz of their wares while the masses were under the spell of the medieval Venetian ambience.

A line formed outside, and tourists took turns entering and exiting. A few bought small masks and put them on once they were outside and back on the bridge. Sophia and the Maestro rolled their eyes at this, in a simultaneous what can you do look.

A well-dressed man perused a catalog before he placed a substantial order for large animal masks. He wanted them shipped to his estate in California. The man seemed well aware of the Maestro's reputation. Maestro had created masks for many of his colleagues.

If the man didn't already know this, Maestro was sure to tell him, Sophia thought smiling. The men were distracted, chatting, while filling out paperwork as the flow of tourists continued in and out of the small space.

Sophia moved her folding chair out of the doorway and onto the still wet pavement. A woman, with a baby and a child of about three in tow, stood waiting for a turn to see the Mask Man. As they inched closer to the doorway, the three-year-old, a girl with a mop of brown curls, tumbled over her untied laces, scraped her knees, and started screeching.

"Would you mind holding the baby for me for just a minute?" the unnerved mother pleaded with Sophia. She thrust the baby into Sophia's arms without waiting for an answer and attended to her wailing daughter.

Sophia looked into the dark eyes of the baby girl. As if on instinct, she pulled the infant up towards her cheek, and took in her scent. The baby seemed so familiar.

"Nevaeh," she murmured.

She handed the baby off to her mother. The shop began to dim, disappearing in a haze. Another realm appeared as if it were unsealed, finally. It was the past returning. Memories were coming back to her mind as if someone had borrowed them and were returning them, little by little, to the shelves in her memory bank.

The faint sound of some kind of music was playing; she squinted, straining to hear. It was religious music, *Salve Regina*. In her mind, she saw herself looking out over tiled red rooftops while listening to the church bells ring out. Her head was starting to hurt. "Roma," she said, remembering something vague. She couldn't seem to breathe now — but all she was doing was breathing. She looked for the Maestro. He was there in front of her, he was saying something. She couldn't hear him. The vision returned — she was in a car, a taxi, the driver's face was not the same as the driver's picture. A baby was in the back seat. When Sophia turned to look again, the baby was gone.

Sophia screamed, "Nevaeh!" before she collapsed onto the floor.

Chapter Three

"Stay down, Bella, my doctor is just on the other side of the bridge, he'll be here shortly."

"Allora, I think I need to eat something. I'm okay now," Sophia told the Maestro who looked at her with eyes full of concern.

Her memories reappeared in an instant, flowing like the deluge that plagued Piazza San Marco when the canal rose over its banks. She hesitated to mention this to Maestro Lorenzo, she wasn't sure she could trust him. She'd have to wait, mull it over before deciding what her next step would be. She'd have to be cautious, methodical; she was dealing with powerful men who had sought and almost succeeded in destroying her.

"I'm better now, Maestro. If you don't need me I think I'll go home now and get some rest."

Instead of boarding the vaporetto, Sophia walked through the damp streets along the canals, up over the bridges to the isolated convent she'd called home for the past twelve years. Sadness overwhelmed her, but she couldn't let it, there was too much at stake.

Chapter Four

The cold marble steps burned Nevaeh's bare legs as she crouched out of sight in the wing of the sacristy. It was forbidden for her to be there, but she was cat-like curious. She slipped away from the convent to spy on the parades of visiting pilgrims. She wasn't sure what a pilgrim was, she'd only heard the sisters referring to the mass of people entering the church grounds as pilgrims. What she saw were families with children strolling hand-in-hand touring her city. How strange they looked to her dressed in colorful clothing while she was forced to wear white dresses. Her collection of sweaters, lace veil head coverings, and the shawls the pilgrims left behind in the pews of the Basilica were kept hidden from the sisters, only taken out during the quiet time in her room after vespers.

She was an orphan and forever being told how to behave according to the laws of God. She was reminded to show gratitude towards the "good sisters" who cared for her. Yet, after twelve years, her many questions remained unanswered. "It's God's will," she was told. But she was growing up and wasn't content with dismissive answers. She knew she was different somehow, she sensed things.

In the world within the confines of Vatican City she remained sequestered, yet she envisioned herself latching onto one of the families whom she watched as they worshipped at St. Peter's Basilica.

"Why are you hiding there, my little Popessa?" Cardinal Alfonso's voice startled her, "Come, Nevaeh, you'll catch cold."

Cardinal Alfonso Aleo had been assigned to oversee the education of Nevaeh Sophia Mariana. These days, he'd been schooling her in the lost Gospels of Jesus. No one could ever find this out. It was forbidden, a sacrilege, at least according to the laws of the Church, which for all appearances were designed by men. But Cardinal Alfonso knew this was the right way. The true path was contained within the hidden words of Jesus and the scrolls that had been found in the desert, yet these truths were not in keeping with the traditional teachings of the patriarchal Church hierarchy.

"Why is God's will the opposite of my will, Papa Alfonso?" Nevaeh asked. Her tone broke his heart.

"Be patient, child," he told her, but his response was not from his heart.

She has so many questions for a young child, he thought. Her innocence was childlike, but the questions she posed to him regarding the scriptures he'd taught her were remarkably astute coming from someone her age.

She was presented to him six years ago when he was instructed to begin schooling her as a normal child would be schooled out in the other world. Before that, who knows. He recalled seeing a child playing when he walked in the Papal Gardens. He assumed, at first, she was related to the papal gardener. But it looked to him that the sisters were in charge of her care. He wondered at the time, why was a young child frolicking about the outskirts of the convent? He knew better than to ask questions. The only remnant of a past outside of the confines of the Vatican was a necklace she'd always worn. Initials NSMT were inscribed on the back of the rare medal made of pewter. If anyone knew what the T stood for, they weren't saying, but the symbols on the front of the ancient amulet were what troubled Cardinal Alfonso. He recognized the symbols, which he identified as offering blessings of love, wealth, health, strength, and protection to the wearer. But he knew the origin. Its root was clear; it was Gnostic and a symbol of the myth of Sophia, the goddess of wisdom who was considered the earth mother. The innocent nuns who'd always cared for her would have no way of knowing the meaning of the symbols. Cardinal Alfonso believed it was beyond the scope of their education.

But if one of the cardinals or a member of the Curia spied the necklace, it would be cause for alarm and Nevaeh would be in danger.

"Remember, my dear," he often reminded Nevaeh, "keep your necklace close to your heart, do not expose it to the air. It's a very old piece and may be damaged."

This was not the reason, but it would have to do for now. As the Bibliotheca of the "Vatican Library and Archives," the cardinal was part of the Church hierarchy and bound to the Pontiff. As such, Cardinal Alfonso harbored many secrets; he spoke six languages fluently and comprehended many more including Aramaic. He didn't know where Nevaeh had come from, but he sensed she was special.

Chapter Five

Chris DeMarco was the only journalist working for *In Conversation Magazine* who spoke fluent Italian. It was the first time in his thirteen years as pope that Pontiff Joseph Morris consented to be interviewed and Chris jumped at the chance to return to his beloved Rome. He was the obvious choice to interview the first American Pope. He knew His Holiness, Pope Joseph I, knew him personally. He'd met him while on assignment in Rome when Joe was first ordained. Upon becoming pope, Joe kept his given name, raising some eyebrows. No pope since Marcellus in 1555 had done so. The Curia would have to keep a close eye on Joseph Morris. Americans were mistrusted. Historically, American Catholics were known to bend the rules of the Church to suit their lifestyle. Joseph Morris was not only an American, his ancestors had been settlers; they came to the shores of the new world on the Mayflower, and they were Protestant.

Joe had been a friend of Chris' older brother. Chris introduced him to his former colleague and friend, Sophia Travato. The three had spent time together mingling with the natives of Rome. Joe was nearly fluent in Italian, thanks to Sophia's lessons, and was far from holy back then. Joe fast-tracked it through the Church hierarchy and was the youngest cardinal at the age of 35. At 42, he was the youngest pope to have been elected in modern times.

It wasn't until Chris returned to Rome that he learned Sophia had vanished. Chris had his suspicions, but everyone said she'd run off with someone she'd met while on assignment in Europe.

Chris' job as a human interest writer was cushy and meant to give him a well-deserved reprieve after his stint as an investigative journalist behind enemy territory in Syria. He was bored with this assignment, and intended to use his time in Rome to get to the bottom of Sophia's disappearance.

Chapter Six

"Pronto," Maestro Lorenzo answered after the first ring, "Buongiorno, Bella." It was Sophia. As expected, she wasn't feeling up to coming to the shop.

Sophia wasn't suffering any physical aftereffects, but her emotional state was a different story. She was up most of the night. She needed to remain calm; she needed a plan and needed to execute it carefully in order to find what she was looking for. Her twelve-year-old daughter was either sequestered somewhere in the confines of Vatican City or she was dead. Sophia had no one she could turn to.

The small group of nuns she lived with spent the daylight hours out of the convent. Some worked as nurses, some as teachers in the Catholic school on the opposite side of Venice. She would be alone for most of the day, she had to work fast.

"I'm feeling unwell," she'd told the Reverend Mother after early morning prayers. She'd have to miss mass and needed to go to her room to rest, she'd told the elderly nun.

"Yes, go and rest, you seem out of sorts today. We all feel that way sometimes. It can't be easy living here with all of us. You'll recover your memory someday, I promise."

The Reverend Mother patted Sophia's hand before walking off towards the church entrance.

Sophia returned to the convent and headed straight for Reverend Mother's office. In the desk drawer, she found stationery with the letterhead of the convent and wrote a letter on her own behalf. She signed the Reverend Mother's name and sealed it with a hot wax stamp as they'd done since the 15th century. She took euro she found in an envelope in the desk drawer. She closed the door behind her and headed for the laundry. She found a freshly cleaned habit. The Benedictine nuns wore a simple one, it had changed little since the

6th century when the order was founded. The simple black robe would fit her perfectly, and the white head covering meant to fit snugly over her head and neck would serve the purpose. The habit would be her ticket into Vatican City where the International Communion of Benedictine Women were having their meeting.

Chapter Seven

Maestro Lorenzo had been nothing but kind to Sophia so, after a sleepless night spent in the chapel asking the God of the Benedictines for guidance, she decided it was best to confide in him. She went to the café for her morning cappuccino in an attempt to keep her routine intact. She skipped the vaporetto and walked through Venice to give herself time to build up courage.

"Buongiorno, Bella," Maestro Lorenzo stood at the door to his shop, struggling with the keys.

"All this dampness causes the keyhole to rust. So many problems we poor Venetians have living in the water."

Sophia didn't answer.

"Allora, everything okay, Sophia?"

"I need to go to Roma, today, right now."

"Roma? For what purpose, Bella?"

"Will you help me? My memory has returned. I have a child, a daughter and she's in Roma and she could be in danger. I need to go now."

"What do the sisters say about this?"

"They don't know my memory is back. I can't tell them, I can't tell anyone."

"You can tell me, Cara. What is it you remember?"

Maestro Lorenzo locked the door to the shop, he reversed the sign on the door to "Chiuso." He would keep the shop closed until Sophia said what she needed to say.

He was fond of her, and he unfortunately considered her to be the daughter he'd never had.

Sophia sighed hard to avoid the tears that had been rising to the surface since her memory returned. She began, "I think I'm an American, but I have no family. The story I remember being told was I was found in a church when I was around five

18

years old. My mother or whomever left me there with a note attached indicating my name, and this strange amulet ring on a chain. I was raised in a Catholic charities orphanage. A wealthy donor in town paid for my education; he or she chose to remain anonymous. I was in Roma years ago working on a story. I worked as a journalist. It was my first real assignment, but I'd spent time there while I was in college and I spoke fluent Italian. I had an affair with a powerful man."

Sophia stopped to wipe her eyes, she stared out the window and watched as the gold merchants made their way up and onto the Rialto Bridge. She seemed far away.

"You can tell me, Sophia. I love you like my own daughter. If you need help or protection, I have people for that. Slow down, just talk. I'll start a new mask. You keep talking."

Sophia's memory flooded back in waves with more specific and vivid detail coming through as she spoke.

"*Salve Regina* was playing, I heard it ring out from the church bells that morning as I looked out from the Intercontinental Hotel. I remember the rooftops below me. An August-like haze hovered like a film over the city even though it was late September. The baby stirred on the bed; surrounded by pillows she looked like an angel resting on clouds. I picked up the plane ticket and looked it over. I'd been ordered via email to return to the United States. It wasn't safe for me to remain in Italy. I had to protect the baby and myself. He'd apparently arranged for me to go to his brother outside of New York City. I believed him."

"Who, Sophia?"

Sophia didn't answer, she continued, "The phone rang, it was the front desk informing me my cab was there. They sent a bellhop to retrieve my two bags and the baby's car seat. I wrapped the baby in a light blanket and went to the lobby. The driver was an unsavory-looking man, unshaven, and not entirely clean; he had the same film over him that hung over the city. He wore black leather gloves, which I thought odd at the time. I dismissed those thoughts, chalking it up to the early morning hour, and tended to the baby. I secured the car seat in the back and when I slid in next to Nevaeh, that's my daughter's name, the driver told me I had to sit in the front because there was only one seat belt in the back. I told him it didn't matter, but he insisted so I moved to the front seat."

Sophia looked up at the Maestro with tears in her eyes. He put his arm on her shoulder, "You can stop now if you want to, Cara. Tell me more later if you'd rather take a break."

"I've had over a twelve-year break, I have to remember, I have to find her."

"Continua, Sophia," Lorenzo shook his head from side to side. It was a habit he'd had since childhood. This tic of sorts manifested itself whenever he was nervous. This story of Sophia's was unraveling now and may have no good end. Lorenzo started to worry, he regretted being involved.

"The driver took an unfamiliar route to the airport. I just assumed he was avoiding traffic and didn't pay much attention. The baby was asleep. I tried to relax, but then I noticed the driver's identification card. The picture on the card didn't match the face of the driver."

"What did you do, Sophia?"

"I told the driver I was feeling car sick and asked him to pull over. He ignored me and continued driving, passing the signs for the airport. We were in the country heading north. When we got off the Autostrada and took a narrow road, I began to struggle with the driver, but I didn't have the strength. He pulled off the road to an isolated spot. I remember him injecting me with some drug. I gathered up all my strength for the sake of my daughter and hit him hard with my fist before the drug had time to take effect. He hit me harder, dragged me out of the car, hitting me again. My head hit the ground or a rock or something.

I didn't pass out right away. I remember him making a call and saying to whomever answered, 'It's Severino Poverelli, I need to speak to Cardinal Roselli now.' I'd heard that name mentioned before. I vaguely remembered Joseph speak of him, referring to him as being a powerful member of the Vatican Curia."

"Oddio, Sophia." Severino Poverelli was a name Lorenzo hadn't heard for many years and he feared getting more involved with Sophia would mean Severino would be back in his life.

"When I woke up, I was in the convent in Venezia. I had no memory until that woman asked me to hold her baby. It just flooded back." Sophia stopped, she wore a sad smile. "The scent of the baby was so familiar, it was only then that I remembered. It was like a portal opened up and everything was back, not everything yet though, it comes in waves. Someone has her, someone needed to keep her hidden so the world wouldn't find out about her."

"Who would do something like this? And why, Sophia? Why?"

"Who would do this, you ask me, but you may not believe me if I tell you."

"This story you tell would be hard for even the most creative mind to conjure up. I don't have any reason to doubt you. But if you want my help I have to know what or who we're dealing with. Who is this powerful man you talk about? Who, Sophia? Tell me. You can't manage this on your own, look what happened the last time."

Sophia knew he was right. What she didn't know was Maestro Lorenzo had powerful connections.

"I can't help you if you don't reveal more information. Exactly who is it you're talking about?"

Sophia whispered as if she were afraid to say the words out loud. She knew the truth, but saying it and putting it out into the universe made it all too tangible — all too real. She didn't want it to be real. She wanted it to be a tale she'd conjured up, but it wasn't and it all had ruined her life and maybe that of her daughter. She had to find her.

"Sophia, what did you say, again who is it?"

"Pope Joseph! It's Pope Joseph or the Curia of the Vatican who took her."

Lorenzo sat down on the small stool reserved for days when he was too tired to stand. He sat stunned. He wasn't one of those devout Italians who dismissed all the goings-on behind the closed walls of Vatican City. Dealing with this situation would not be without its difficulties.

"Joseph Morris was a friend of my colleague Chris. We were inseparable. Joe was on a fast track through the Church hierarchy, but he was far from chaste. He fancied himself after Father Ralph."

"Father Ralph?"

"Yes, Richard Chamberlain's character in the movie, *The Thorn Birds*."

"Joe thought he could have it all. I fell for him hard and fast. When I got pregnant, I told him, but he said, 'It wouldn't be possible for me to have the baby.' These were the hypocritical words of a so-called holy man. I could do no such thing. By the time the baby was born, he'd been elected Supreme Pontiff. It was all reminiscent of the behavior of popes during the Middle Ages. Their scandalous activities were flaunted; now the pretense of superiority and the holier-than-thou arrogance is the cover-up for so many untoward activities. I don't know exactly who took my baby, but I know she was taken by order of someone at the Vatican. I suspect Severino Poverelli, he was employed by Cardinal Roselli to get rid of me. I assume my daughter is in Roma. He could have taken her there. I was in an unconscious state, 500 km to the north. He must have brought me here to Venezia."

Lorenzo nodded, but said nothing.

Chapter Eight

Joseph Morris never dreamed he'd have this life. The vows of poverty, chastity, and obedience he'd taken as a young priest hadn't sat well with him. He'd had a wild side then, he thought with a tinge of regret, but still he missed those days. Now he found himself surrounded by an opulence he couldn't have conceived of in his former life. Joe Morris had a far from poor background; his family had landed in America long before it was independent. They were settlers and signers of the Declaration of Independence and Constitution. Joe wanted no part of his heritage, yet now he too would have a place in the history books.

He wasn't a particularly religious kid. His father had converted to Catholicism before marrying his devout mother. As the eldest son of a religious Irish mother, Joe had been groomed from childhood for the priesthood.

Joe lay in bed and looked around the room where every pope as far back as the 17th century had resided; some had died in this room. Despite recent renovations, the ten-room apartment complex still had the musty aroma of an ancient dwelling. Joe rose and walked over to the desk on the opposite side of the large room. He glanced quickly at his appointment book and read: 12 p.m. luncheon meeting with journalist, Chris DeMarco. Joe felt a flutter of panic. He and Chris went back far enough for there to be trouble. He knew that Chris had been more than fond of Sophia, their mutual friend. But Joe and Sophia had been more than friends, much more, and Chris knew that. *But Chris wasn't the only one,* Joe thought sadly. Joseph was privy to what had transpired, but he kept it deep inside. His priority now was to get Mother Church in order. The Priory was wary of him. Being an American was not an asset within the secretive hidden world of Vatican City, he had his work cut out for him. He was playing a role. He hated donning the same

23

white garments every day. Despite being well into his forties and set in this coveted position, he often longed to be one of the masses, wearing jeans, drinking unholy wine or beer, prowling the streets of Rome after hours. Those days were behind him forever. Keeping the status quo intact here in the Vatican was his priority and now he had the added worry Chris DeMarco would be snooping around looking into the disappearance of Sophia Travato.

Ah, sweet, beautiful Sophia, he used to say she'd bewitched him, but Joe knew that wasn't the truth. She'd been a young, impressionable ingenue spending that year working in Rome; she'd never returned to the United States after she was snatched up by Sky Italia to do research and prepare scripts for Roman historical documentaries. Her fluency in Italian added to her charm and had been an absolute asset to both Joe and Chris as they struggled with the language. Sophia had tutored them both, but after Chris had taken an assignment out of the country, Joe used the opportunity to linger after the sessions ended. He stayed late into the night, raising more than one eyebrow in the rectory in Lazio. He made the excuse, "I'm the confidant of a fellow American, a young woman away from home who needs my counsel." It was a lie and it spiraled out of control. Like an untended wildfire, news spread Joseph Morris was a gifted counselor who had a rapport with young people.

Joe's handsome dark, good looks and charming presence fueled his celebrity appeal. It energized him and his ego soared along with his popularity. The cardinals soon got word of the then Monsignor Morris' good works.

Sophia knew the truth and Chris DeMarco knew a version of it, enough to ruin Pope Joseph Morris. Joe had a few hours to mull over possible scenarios surrounding the upcoming lunch meeting with his former friend. He had to be on guard. He'd insist on meeting him alone without his secretary present.

The world had him billed as a quiet, prayerful pope who spent his time in solitary reflection. The truth was he had no idea what he was doing, what he stood for, or how to deal with the traditional conservative Curia who'd been setting the tone of Church doctrine for centuries.

Chapter Nine

Sophia was waiting outside the mask shop when Maestro Lorenzo arrived. She was leaning against the damp stone façade. She stared into the canal and then skyward as if looking into another realm for comfort.

"Buongiorno, Bella," Lorenzo said in his characteristic booming voice. But Sophia seemed not to hear. Lorenzo approached and tapped her lightly on the shoulder.

"Everything okay, Sophia?"

"Oh, yes, sorry. I guess I'm distracted," Sophia answered while bending down to retrieve a large duffle-like bag.

"What have you got there?" Lorenzo's concern was that Sophia was going to march over the walls of Vatican City in a headstrong manner, making outlandish albeit true remarks that would cause an international sensation and land her on the psych ward.

"I have some necessities to tide me over in Roma."

Sophia neglected to tell the Maestro about the stolen habit and the euro. She needed to be cautious. She'd been betrayed and didn't know who she could trust.

Lorenzo pulled a high stool over to the work bench, he placed another next to him, and gestured for Sophia to sit.

"Sophia, what I'm about to say to you I say out of a deep affection and concern, as well as from the experience I've lived through. I do believe you, but I caution you not to be hasty in attempting to rescue your child. You must be very cautious. Here is what I propose…"

Sophia listened as Lorenzo laid out a plan she realized he must have given a great deal of thought to. As anxious as she was to get to the bottom of the whereabouts of her daughter, she knew the Maestro was right. She'd have to be careful, she'd have to be patient.

"I have connections in Roma, I will make arrangements for you as soon as I can," Lorenzo told her.

"Don't be in a rush to leave Venezia. I suggest you begin acting forlorn as early as today. Eat before you return to the convent, refuse their food, remain in your room, don't speak, and answer when spoken to in a soft barely audible voice. This will raise some concerns. After a week has passed, we should pick a date and time, leave the convent before sun-up, float your clothing in the lagoon and walk, don't take the vaporetto. Cover yourself, but walk, come meet me at the Piazzale Roma. I'll be waiting in my car. By the time they realize you're missing, we'll be nearing Roma."

Sophia tried to pay attention. She fingered the ancient ring that hung from a pewter chain around her neck. It was her only true possession — a remnant of origins she had no recollection of. The inside of the ring was inscribed, *Sophia Mariana Travato, the bearer of light*. As Sophia looked out over the Grand Canal, half-listening to the Maestro's calculated plan, her thoughts were of Nevaeh, the child she'd lost, the child who was given the medal that matched Sophia's ring. Sophia hoped the medal still remained where she'd placed it twelve years before.

Chapter Ten

Nevaeh sat in the Papal Gardens; her long white dress pulled up to her knees, she dangled her feet in a fountain. Cardinal Alfonso walked towards her. He was stunned as she seemed to be bathed in light. A dove had landed softly on her shoulder, a doe appeared and sat at her feet. Alfonso left Nevaeh undisturbed, but stood at a distance watching.

"It's okay, Papa Alfonso, you can come closer. I've told them about you, they aren't afraid."

"Nevaeh, how is it there is a doe in the Papal gardens? I've never seen one before in all my years, only parrots and a few cats, never deer."

Nevaeh shrugged, "I guess I woke it up."

"Shall we have a lesson, it's time."

"Yes, but let's stay out here, it's so peaceful."

Cardinal Alfonso hesitated. He hated to refuse Nevaeh, she'd asked so little of him, but he'd been instructed long ago to keep the child out of sight and away from the crowds of tourists and gardeners. But this child was clever and smarter than anyone suspected. She'd often prowled the nooks and crannies of the Basilica and was adept at slipping passed the guards who stood watch in the Vatican museum. Cardinal Alfonso often found her engrossed in a book she'd swiped from one of the other cardinals. Cardinal Alfonso thought she was blessed with a touch of the mystic.

"Perhaps we can move to the other side of the gardens where we'll have privacy."

He'd hoped Nevaeh would comply without too much of a fuss. If they stayed put, they would be in full view of the tour bus that regularly took visitors for a bird's-eye view of the pope's gardens.

"Okay, Papa, but it's Wednesday, no tourists today."

When Nevaeh stood up, the creatures left quietly as if they'd been dismissed for the day.

Much of the 57 acres of the gardens were ornate, filled with statues and areas designated for quiet devotion. Nevaeh and the cardinal walked the acreage and found an area undisturbed by marble statues. It was formally treed, and the hand of man was evident in the design of the plantings. Nevaeh seemed to savor nature, no matter how it came to be. Alfonso sat on a stone bench, Nevaeh plopped herself down on a grassy knoll at his feet.

"Papa, I have some questions regarding the scriptures." She looked up, staring directly in his eyes, "I've located other gospels that I've studied and I'm confused by the difference in the accounts of Jesus that His Apostles have told. I've read it all carefully. I read Paul's works as well and I came to a decision."

"What is it, Nevaeh?"

"Based on what I've been reading, I don't believe Catholicism, as we know it, was designed by Jesus. I think Paul created this religion to suit his own purposes and to diminish the words of the Apostles. Perhaps Paul was jealous since he'd never seen Jesus in the flesh, only in a vision. It seems to me that much of our religion was created by men, not God. Didn't the God of the Jews ban human sacrifice? Then how is it He sent His son to die on the cross as a sacrifice? It seems to me that we celebrate His death over and over by kneeling in front of the cross; we are not focusing on the resurrection which was the point, wasn't it?"

The cardinal was astounded to hear the astute questions and hypothesis posed to him by someone so young. Scholars had debated such things for centuries. How could he answer her?

"Yes, Nevaeh, you're quite correct in your thinking. Let's just say that one must have faith that the hand of God is at work in these matters, and our collective beliefs are a result of His will."

He knew she was too intelligent to accept this response, but he had no choice, he had to be dismissive. If he taught her any other way at this stage he'd be charged with heresy.

Nevaeh didn't respond to the cardinal; she looked off into the distance for a time before speaking. "Papa, why is it Jesus said, 'My kingdom is not of this earth,' yet His followers live in palaces? Perhaps none of this," Nevaeh waved her hand over the surrounding area, "is the way it's supposed to be."

"All this, my dear, is fuel for the mind. Things to contemplate and discuss at length, but remember there are no clear-cut answers to your questions. It's as I said before, a matter of faith."

Cardinal Alfonso left it at that, but he knew there'd be more questions. He had studied the same writings in depth. He too felt the weight of doubt, the undeniable evidence of something sinister and ill begotten hidden deep within the origins of his wavering faith.

Chapter Eleven

Cardinal Guilo Roselli stood in front of his office window. The glorious day he looked out on gave him no cause to rejoice. All he saw, was that wretched child, the constant reminder of his failed mission to safeguard the reputation of the Holy Catholic Church. She was getting far too chummy with Alfonso Aleo. "The gentle one," they called him, yet despite his meek demeanor, he was a brilliant scholar and could comprehend, analyze, and interpret the ancient writings contained within the Vatican Library with ease. He had been the obvious choice to teach the scriptures to the youngster, but lately Cardinal Roselli observed Nevaeh doing the talking. Alfonso merely gave short responses to the child's lengthy diatribes.

Cardinal Roselli would have to deal with her sooner or later, she couldn't remain sequestered here forever. Something had to be done with her and her denying father. He simply couldn't risk losing all he'd worked towards. This pope and the popes before him had been puppet heads of the Church. Cardinal Roselli had called the shots for the 30 years he'd lived within the walls.

I'll bide my time. All good things come to those who wait. I won't fail next time. The opportunity to be rid of this menace will present itself, Cardinal Roselli thought to himself before being summoned by Pope Joseph.

"Cardinal Roselli, I'd like you to meet one of my dearest friends, journalist Chris DeMarco. He'll be conducting a series of short interviews."

"How do you do?"

Cardinal Roselli hesitated without responding. He stood at the far end of the room with an odd look on his face. Chris walked towards the cardinal and extended his hand. Cardinal Roselli took Chris' hand as a gesture of feigned friendship. He had not expected friends of the pope, old or new, to show up at the Vatican. He'd been assured by his minions that Joseph Morris had no friends or allegiances to anyone with the exception of that vile woman, and she was no longer a concern. He'd heard she suffered from amnesia, and until he'd heard otherwise he'd leave her be. But now a journalist was in their midst, prowling around. He'd have to look into Chris DeMarco and find out exactly what he knew about the American pope.

He cursed the wretched Curia for electing this troublesome man. The glowing Christ-like reputation Joseph Morris had presented to the world had been a deception. The desperate times the Church was faced with gave him easy access to this powerful position. Their guard had been down and the Church hierarchy, Cardinal Roselli included, reluctantly decided they'd needed someone who'd distract the world from the scandals plaguing the Church. Joseph Morris fit the bill and provided the necessary distraction as the first American to be elected Supreme Pontiff. The Cardinal hoped Pope Joseph's scandalous past would remain there and not come home to roost. He'd do everything in his power to make sure of it.

"Good to meet you too. I was unaware of His Holiness having past acquaintances. This is indeed a nice surprise. I'll leave you to your interview. Should you require my assistance, I'll be in my office. Shall I send your secretary in?"

"No, that won't be necessary. This is an informal meeting. We'll meet again for a more detailed discussion on Church matters."

Cardinal Roselli closed the door behind him, wishing he'd bugged the inner offices as he'd wanted to. He'd been afraid of American ingenuity and of being found out. Since that fateful day, when he'd learned of the child, he'd dealt with it, but since then he'd kept a low profile only tending to Church affairs.

Chapter Twelve

Sophia spent her last night in Venice staring out the window at the church courtyard. The view resembled a bygone era. Aside from the erosion of the stone façade caused by the barrage of wind and sea water coming off the lagoon, little had changed in the landscape since the 14th century when the church had been built. Sophia wondered if her life would have been easier had she been born in that earlier time. She imagined herself married to an older, wealthy Venetian merchant who would have doted on her shamelessly. She pictured herself dressed in a gown made of rich fabric, her neck and ears adorned with jewels. She'd always had a sense of déjà vu when it came to her Venetian home, but she knew she'd been raised in the United States. Still, Venice was in her blood and had always been oddly familiar.

Sophia dressed in the dim light. She was prepared physically for her trip to Rome. She'd taken a cloth grocery bag from the convent kitchen and put the clothes and shoes she'd planned to float in the Venetian waters inside. Emotionally, she was riddled with anxiety. She feared the worst: her daughter may be dead. She had to find the truth and this was the first step.

She crept out of her room and tiptoed down the dark corridor towards the back door of the convent. It was barely 3 a.m. Hopefully, the streets of Venice would be empty. She made her way to the Grand Canal, over the stone bridges, and up to the Fondamenta Della Case Nuove. It was a long walk, cold and damp at this hour, but it was away from swells of tourists who may be out lurking in the Venetian shadows trying to savor its Medieval charm unencumbered by the foot traffic of the daily hoards.

Sophia reached the grassy knoll and sat on a bench overlooking the lagoon for a few minutes to gather her thoughts. She threw her clothes, a cotton dress and its sash, into the beckoning sea. She then placed a pair of sandals on the stone pavement and walked away in the direction of her new life. She threw the bag in one of the rare garbage bins and walked slowly towards the Piazzale Roma where the Maestro would be waiting. Sophia thought about him and all their chance meetings when she'd first recovered and had been permitted to walk the calles and palazzos unescorted by one of the novices. There he was having his first morning cappuccino at the Laguna Caffe near to the convent. She'd often see him sitting in the piazza feeding the pigeons when she was first allowed to go shopping at the Coop for the Reverend Mother. It was there when he first spoke to her.

She remembered the scene vividly for the first time since that day: he tipped his hat in her direction, oozing the charm of an older Venetian man who was unaware of the new ways of addressing women, "Signora, or is it Signorina? I have seen you walking about on many occasions, but always by yourself. I'm wondering what is wrong with the young men of Venice who seem not to be smitten by your beauty."

Sophia had just stared at him. Surely, he'd heard tales of her, the young woman ward of the sisters who landed on their doorstep, a gift from the sea. He worked his magic and had won her over, months had passed, her memory had not returned, he took pity on her and offered her a job as an apprentice of sorts.

Now Sophia wondered about the chance encounter. *Why was the Maestro appearing on the other side of Venice?* Now it occurred to her that *he'd sought her out, befriended her with intent. I'm just being paranoid,* Sophia thought, *he's offered to help me, take the time to drive me to Rome when he's a busy man.* Sophia rid herself of these dark thoughts and was relieved to see the Maestro standing by his car when she arrived at the Piazzale Roma at exactly 4:30 a.m. just as they'd planned. His hair was wet, evidence of a quick shower, a rare gray curl brushed his collar, and dripped droplets of water down his shoulder. He brushed them off, taking Sophia's bag with his free hand. Sophia noticed his watch, a Rolex, expensive and genuine, not like the ones sold in bins by street peddlers. His jacket flew open in the morning breeze off the canal and Sophia got a flash of the label, "Ermenegildo Zegna." She raised an eyebrow without meaning to and her suspicions resurfaced.

"Buongiorno, Sophia, let's get moving so we can avoid some traffic."

When the car pulled out of the lot and finally entered the Autostrada, Sophia tried to relax for the first time in weeks. As uncertain as her future seemed, at least she held the reins from now on. She could be decisive, keep her options open, and find her own way if she had to.

"How long a ride is it to Roma, Maestro?"

"Call me Lorenzo," the Maestro said, patting Sophia's knee.

Sophia grew more alarmed wondering if the Maestro's intentions could be sinister, something she'd not considered before now, but Lorenzo continued speaking unfazed.

"We'll be traveling together for a few hours and then we'll be in Roma. I've secured a residence for us in the Lazio area not far from Vatican City. It's best if you refer to me by my given name to not draw too much attention. Try to relax, you look tired, get some rest now."

Sophia nodded, she dismissed the forward gesture as a sign of old-world Venetian male behavior and looked out the window. The farmland gave way to mountainous terrain. She wished she'd had a different life, but she needed to stay focused. She'd need all her strength to get to the bottom of her daughter's disappearance all those years ago. If Nevaeh was still alive, what would she say to her?

"Nevaeh will be a teenager soon if she's still alive."

"Try not to dwell on what may not be the truth. We'll find out, I have powerful friends in Roma."

Sophia wondered who these powerful friends could be and why a Venetian mask-maker would have influential people in his circle. Sophia realized she knew very little about the background of Maestro Lorenzo, but she was too tired to think about all that now. The monotonous landscape provided little stimulation and Lorenzo was a quiet companion. He kept his eyes focused on the road, his hands securely on the steering wheel, and he preferred to keep the radio off. Sophia soon gave in to the fatigue that had plagued her since she first got in the car. She fell asleep to the sound of the whipping winds coming off the hills.

When Sophia woke up the car had stopped. They needed fuel, and Lorenzo was out of the car and on the phone. Sophia opened the window to get some air. Lorenzo looked upset; Sophia strained to hear his conversation.

"Allora, Severino, I need assurances. I'm not turning her over until you make certain promises. I don't want her harmed."

All Sophia's fears came to the surface, her instincts had been correct. Severino was an unusual name, and not one often heard. It was too much of a coincidence. For Sophia, it meant Lorenzo had been part of this. He could have been the one who brought her to Venice. He'd probably been hired to keep watch over her all these years. Hired by Severino at the behest of Cardinal Roselli, the name she'd heard at the time she'd been taken. All this was supposition on her part but the pieces were starting to come together.

Lorenzo returned to the car, Sophia opened her eyes and stretched, trying to remain calm.

"Where are we?"

"Another four hours or so to go."

"Mind if I use the restroom and get something to eat. I didn't have my usual café this morning. I was too anxious."

Lorenzo nodded. "Of course, my dear, I'll wait here, I have some calls to make. Grab me an espresso, would you?"

"Sure, I need my bag from the back, lady issues to deal with."

Sophia grabbed her bag, she entered the Autogrill, and found the ladies room. She changed her clothes quickly. Two girls came in laughing. They nodded in her direction and began to discuss their travel plans, "Do you think he'll take us all the way to Rome?" a girl with purple hair asked her companion, an equally wild-looking girl with spiked short hair. Her face held several unseemly piercings. She struggled to speak. Her tongue was pierced with a thick metal ring. Her eyes were a mesmerizing shade of emerald, which was her only endearing feature.

"He said he's only going as far as Perugia."

"Ah, c'mon, you can work your magic and get him to drive us all the way, can't you?"

"I can't and you know why? No euro; we've got nothing left, we can't pay for fuel. We can't pay for anything else. We agreed to pay for everything when he picked us up in Verona."

"I have money," Sophia told them. "I need to get to Rome, my travel companion is a letch, and I have to get away from him now. I'll pay for fuel, food, and whatever you need if you just take me to Rome. Go talk to your driver. I have to leave now before my companion gets suspicious."

The purple-haired girl stayed behind, she reapplied makeup to her already laden face, while the other girl went to seek out their driver.

"I'm Zara," she said, extending her free hand to Sophia.

"Sophia, nice to meet you. Grazie, for agreeing to help me."

"Our driver's a cranky guy, he's young too, I don't know what his issues are. You'd think he'd be thrilled to have women companions and ones who drive at that. But no, he barely says a word, just grumbles one word responses."

Sophia wondered if this had been a good idea, maybe the driver was a drug runner and she was going from one bad situation to another. She feared for her life now and that of her missing daughter, but this was her only hope.

"Gina, this is Sophia," Gina stood by the door and nodded at Sophia.

"So?" Zara raised her shoulders and gestured with extended arms and with her palms up.

"He wants to see the money."

Sophia didn't blame him. After all his two traveling companions had reneged on their agreement.

Sophia opened her purse, took out her wallet and removed 150 euro. She kept the remaining 650 euro in the lining of her bra. She feared being robbed on top of her litany of woes. She would need euro when she got to Rome now that Lorenzo's true intentions had made themselves known.

Sophia held the euro in her hand and followed the girls out to the waiting car. The driver was twenty tops with unwashed blond hair; it had been cut to lay straight across his forehead. He wasn't a bad-looking sort, but his demeanor indicated a past riddled with hardship. Along with Sophia's memory a sense of heightened awareness and intuition seemed to have surfaced.

"I'm Sophia Travato," Sophia extended her hand, but the driver didn't return the gesture. Instead he looked at her through beady eyes, "Show me the money." He had a Germanic accent, which reinforced his brutish disposition.

"Can I at least know your name before I hand over my cash?"

"We aren't going to be friends, I'm not driving a school bus. I agreed to take these two to Rome on the condition that they pay the way. Now, I have one more female who wants in and I need the money upfront."

"I'll give you 150 euro — that should cover the rest of the trip for the three of us." Sophia got in the back seat, sat behind the driver and thrust 75 euro over his right shoulder.

"Oliver, my name's Oliver."

"There's only 75 euro here." Oliver turned around to face Sophia.

"You'll get the other half when we're safely in Rome."

Oliver grumbled something in German and started the car.

"Where are you from, Oliver?" Sophia asked, but Oliver, no last name, didn't answer.

Sophia looked out the back window of the car as they pulled out of the Autogrill and onto the Autostrada. Lorenzo was leaning on his car, he was still on the phone. He was probably making the arrangements to turn her over to whomever he worked for. Sophia leaned her head back in the seat, she let her shoulders drop, unclenched her jaw, and tried to calm down. Zara and Gina were discussing their plans to attend a rock concert in Rome the next week. Sophia wondered how they planned to do so since neither of them had euro. She wondered about the back story of these three and how they managed to get together in the first place. The girls were young and frivolous, and Oliver was rigid and seemed old beyond his years. It wasn't her problem, Sophia decided, she had more important matters to deal with than the antics of her young travel companions.

Chapter Thirteen

It was nightfall before the nuns realized Sophia had gone missing. The Reverend Mother was sitting at her desk; she'd opened the drawer to retrieve stationery when she heard alarming cries coming from the hall.

"What is it? What's happened?"

"It's Sophia, she was ill this morning but she's not in her room and her bed hasn't been slept in. I've phoned the Carabinieri. They gave me distressing news."

"What is it? Tell me now, Sister."

"They said women's clothing was found on the banks of the Laguna right at the water's edge, and shoes were floating near the shoreline. I asked for a description. I think they were Sophia's clothes."

The young novice, barely out of her teens, let out a gut-wrenching sob alerting the other nuns who came running. Reverend Mother often felt like a den mother to these young women. Most were too young to be making such a severe life choice but that was out of her jurisdiction and in God's hands.

The Reverend Mother, formerly known as Maria Jilani, now Sister Rosa, was one of the rare native-born Venetians. Attending the University of Bologna to study education had been the only time she'd left home. She'd traveled by train, making the grueling three-hour commute, four days a week. She'd returned to Venice proper and earned a master's degree at the Ca' Foscari University and finally her PhD in linguistics. After graduation, she joined the order of the Benedictines. Maria took the name Sister Rosa after her maternal grandmother. Her parents had vehemently disapproved and threatened to cut her off both emotionally and financially. Maria took her final vows alone, without the presence or support of her parents. She knew she'd been overqualified to teach elementary education and so did the bishop. After a few years of teaching the next generation of Venetians how to read and write, Sister Rosa was given a position at the International School of Venice. Every morning she took the train to Mestre. Her flair for and fluency in several languages along with her gentle composure were assets to the secular school. The students were from all parts of the world; if Sister Rosa didn't know their language, she'd make the effort to learn at least a part of the student's native tongue. This endeared her to not only the children, but the parents as well. When word reached the bishop, he'd selected Sister Rosa to be Sister Superior of the convent Santa Maria della Visitazione. Sister Rosa did not wear the title well. She'd preferred to be called Reverend Mother. She would be superior to no one.

Her role as Reverend Mother had been an easy one, and except for dealing with the chronic repairs the convent required, she'd had no complaints. There were only a handful of nuns under her charge and they were dutiful, of high character but young. Her loyalty to the Church was steadfast, so it was without question she'd agreed to harbor the young woman suffering from a head injury when Cardinal Roselli called requesting her service. Two of the sisters were nurses and would tend to the patient until she regained her strength.

Sister Rosa had difficulty concealing her alarm that stormy night when a man dressed all in black showed up on the dock with the unconscious woman. He'd carried her under the cloak of darkness from his rickety boat. Her head crooked over his arm, she was limp as a rag doll.

"She should be in hospital," Sister Rosa told the man. He'd ignored her, and walked into the alley and entered the convent from the back.

"Where shall I put her?"

"In here," Sister Rosa, accompanied by Sisters Angelica and Bernadette, led him to the spare room located behind the kitchen.

"What happened to her? Who is she?"

"Enough with the questions, do as you were told. It's your duty."

"I know what my duties are, Signore, but we need to know what we are dealing with so we can properly care for her."

"She fell from a car and has a head injury. She has no other apparent injuries."

Sister Angelica pulled up the young woman's eyelids to check her pupils. "They're equal and dilated. It's a good sign."

"Can we at least know her name?"

"It's Sophia Mariano Travato." The man brushed the rainwater off his jacket and headed out the door. "I'll be watching her. Keep her here. If she recovers call me, here's my card."

"I thought he looked familiar," the Reverend Mother whispered to Sister Bernadette.

"Who is he, Reverend Mother?"

"He's the mask-maker from Rialto. I can't imagine why he's involved with this poor girl but we have to look after her. We have our orders."

It took three days for Sophia to regain consciousness. Sister Bernadette had smuggled IV fluids from the hospital, hooking them up with makeshift support hangers off the side of the bed to keep her patient from dehydrating. Sister Bernadette rarely left Sophia's bedside; she'd kept the Reverend Mother apprised of Sophia's progress.

"She was assaulted by someone, there's no doubt in my mind," Sister Bernadette informed the Reverend Mother. "The gash and hematoma on the back of her head are a clear indication of an attack with a blunt instrument or a rock perhaps, but she's suffering from exposure to the elements as well. There are no visible cuts, bruises, or broken bones which would be evidence of a fall."

Sister Rosa had many suspicions but Sophia soon became part of their small community. Once recovered, she'd spent her days working for Lorenzo in his shop on the other side of Venice where tourists outnumbered the locals. Reverend Mother had concerns regarding this arrangement but her hands were tied. The young woman was in her care but not one of her charges. Sophia was respectful of their beliefs, she'd bow her head during evening prayers but she'd never expressed an interest or desire to learn about their vocation. Sadly, she had no history to share, no childhood memory to relate. But she'd listen intently as the young sisters spoke of their early years playing in the palazzos of Venice pretending they were maidens in ancient times drawing water from the cisterns erected in the 15th century that now were covered with graffiti. Sister Rosa, as Reverend Mother, did not share in the banter. She'd kept her former life confidential; she'd chosen not to reveal the shame she'd caused her family to anyone. Both jobs, her teaching role and her position as Abbess, required discipline and devotion.

Over the years, Sister Rosa had refused to allow their convent to become a hostel for the tourists of Venice to use as cheap accommodations. Cardinal Roselli provided the convent with the funds she'd needed to keep the roof over the heads of the nuns and young woman in her care. The arrangement had been an unspoken one, making Sister Rosa uneasy but her options had been few.

When the rumors surrounding Sophia's disappearance and probable drowning reached the convent, they'd blossomed and taken on a life of their own. Much arguing went on, everyone had their theories. "Her memory probably returned, she had a shameful past, maybe killed someone, so she committed suicide. Or someone raped her on the waterfront and threw her in the lagoon. There are unseemly types here now that the borders are open." The sisters in the convent joined in the gossip. "Suicide — never. Someone hurt her."

Reverend Mother had known better. She'd called Lorenzo when Sophia went missing that morning. He wasn't picking up.

His shop had been closed for several days before the Reverend Mother became aware of his absence. She'd considered calling and notifying Cardinal Roselli. She'd opened her desk drawer to look for his number and had discovered 800 euro was gone from the strong box. When Sister Angela informed the group that one of the habits had disappeared, Reverend Mother smiled. *Sophia has found herself again.*

"Let us pray for Sophia before we say grace. May she find peace wherever she may be."

The other sisters looked up, stunned. "Do you think she's still alive, Reverend Mother? Do you have news of her?" Reverend Mother kept her head bowed, she didn't answer.

Chapter Fourteen

"He's an odd one," Chris told Pope Joseph. He was referring to Cardinal Roselli.

"Yes, well, he's not too fond of me. He'd prefer the old school type. He's not interested in change even if it's for the better. He's very suspicious. He doesn't believe I've got the best interest of the Church at heart. I guess he's afraid I'll usher in some radical transformations."

"Will you?" Chris was genuinely interested. He'd love to have the inside scoop on what exactly this probable renegade pope had in mind for the future.

"Yes, I'll make some adjustments. The Church has stagnated and lost members because of their failure to acclimate to modern times. Archaic practices and mindsets have not served us well."

"May I quote you? I don't know what you have in mind or if you're willing to share your ideas at this time, but I'd be anxious to learn of your plans when you're ready to share. I'm sure you'll get a lot of resistance no matter what you plan to do."

"Remember, I'm infallible when it comes to Church doctrine."

Chris raised an eyebrow, he wasn't so sure about that. Infallibility had always been a cause for skepticism on his part. All of this was designed by men anyway. He knew Joseph Morris, knew all about him and his past behavior, and believing he was infallible in any circumstance was a big pill to swallow.

"Any chance you're going to allow women to become priests? After all there were women followers of Christ. They might help the Church repair her waning reputation."

"We don't need women complicating matters. The women who followed Christ were handmaidens, nothing more."

"You don't know that for sure." Chris knew he was being snarky, but he couldn't help it. He added, "I've never heard of a pedophile nun."

"How about we keep this informal for today? How are you, by the way?"

"Well, I did some reporting in Syria. That was a rough patch. I'm working for a magazine now, we do mostly human interest stories. It's a reprieve from hard journalism."

"How secure is your job? Aren't magazines passé with all the online journals?"

"We're good and well-funded. It's not going anywhere. I'm free to stay put in Italy for as long as it takes." Chris returned to the subject he'd been hired to ferret out of the pope.

"And how are you doing? Are you adjusting to the old guard here?"

"I'm trying to maintain my authority without causing too much disruption."

Joseph didn't want to give away too much inside information. In the company of his old friend, he'd felt the pangs of that other life pulsate. He longed to tell Chris everything, but he kept silent. He couldn't risk it. The Vatican secrets fortressed behind these walls were many, and while Pope Joseph's personal secret paled in comparison, it made him vulnerable. Too many people were involved in keeping it out of the limelight. And to make it worse, he had no idea who they were. If it ever got out, it would be one more scandal and could conceivably be the one that launches the fall of the Roman Catholic Church. For now, he was at the mercy of Cardinal Roselli. For decades, Guilo Roselli held the power behind the scenes at the Vatican.

"Shall we have some lunch now?" Pope Joseph asked in an attempt to keep things light.

"Yes, I hear you have an amazing garden. I've only seen it through the window of the tour bus. Is it possible to have lunch out there?"

"The gardens are closed to tourists on Wednesdays — what a wonderful idea."

Pope Joseph summoned his assistant and arrangements were underway to have lunch set up in the garden.

Chapter Fifteen

"Pronto," Cardinal Roselli answered on the first ring. It was Tim Daniels, the administrative assistant of the papal offices, calling. Cardinal Roselli had hired Tim, a layperson, after Cardinal Amaro's asthmatic condition had suddenly worsened. The slightest exertion rendered the old man weak and winded. He'd been advised to take a leave. Cardinal Roselli used the opportunity to place his own staff, someone he could trust to keep him apprised of the goings-on within the inner papal offices. Pope Joseph was thrilled to have a fellow American on board.

"Your Eminence, His Holiness is requesting lunch be set up in the garden; the journalist will be dining with him."

"Grazie, Tim."

"There's more, Your Grace, the girl is having her lessons outside today. She's with Cardinal Alfonso. It would be wise to bring her inside."

Tim hated being in collusion with whatever it was that Cardinal Roselli was up to, but the job offered him many advantages he'd never have found on his own. He was in the midst of the most valuable art collection in the world, his salary was tax-free and padded with a substantial stipend, albeit bribe, courtesy of Cardinal Roselli, and the modest apartment within the walls of Vatican City cost a trifle in comparison to Roman housing. His free time and excess cash afforded him the opportunity to study online. For all this, he would bide his time, turn a blind eye and remain a loyal servant to the man who'd given him a huge leg up in life.

Timothy Daniels had finished his year abroad, studying Roman art history, when he'd decided to stay. He'd found the Italian lifestyle more to his liking than the stressful frenzy of his native New York. It was sedate in comparison, but living in Rome had not been without its difficulties. It had been impossible to find a suitable job in his field. Art historians with PhD's had flooded the tourist trade. Tim held only a BFA, he didn't have a shot.

He'd worked the bar scene in Manhattan as an undergrad, so bartending had been the obvious second choice. Tourists frequented local bars. The bar where Tim had worked attracted mostly young men and the occasional older, distinguished gentleman who'd arrive with an abundance of cash, making him a target.

Tim had generated the most tips; his outgoing persona and knowledge of all things Rome combined with striking good looks, and a tall stature, fueled his appeal. Keeping customers at bay proved to be his chief complaint as time went by. He'd made enough to live on and had managed to save enough to do some traveling, but this didn't satisfy his passion. He'd longed to be in the midst of ancient Roman artifacts, sharing his wealth of knowledge with those who toured his adopted city. Fighting off the nightly barrage of unwanted advances of touring men had been wearing on Tim. He'd had enough saved, but was hesitant to quit. The last thing he'd wanted was a quick fling with someone who'd give him a few days of their time, only to disappear forever afterwards.

It was five years earlier when, on one of his monthly visits to the bar, Cardinal Roselli had made his move towards Tim with intent. He'd had his eye on Tim Daniels for quite a while. Now, the time had come for him to make a move.

Guilo Roselli's longevity as a member of the hierarchy in the Vatican afforded him the opportunity to hire and fire employees at will. He had the funds on hand necessary to provide the adequate bribe he'd needed to suit his purposes. Having staff beholden to him had served him well in the past. Once he'd realized the likelihood of Joseph Morris being elected Supreme Pontiff he'd firmed up plans to fortify his team of subordinates.

When the papal secretary announced he'd need time off for an extended sick leave, Guilo Roselli put his latest plan into action. An administrative assistant was needed to temporarily fill in for the ailing Cardinal Amara. Cardinal Roselli doubted the old man would be back, and he had just the person in mind for the job.

The bar was unusually quiet when Guilo Roselli entered from a side door in the alley that afternoon. He'd always been discrete — he'd dressed in layman's attire and used the pseudonym Antonio Mecelli for these purposes.

"Buonasera, Tim, how's it going?"

"Buonasera, Tony, it's slow but it's early, should pick up later when I'm long gone. I'm on the early shift for a few weeks. Probably a punishment for taking a week off last week."

Tim had dabbled in archeology in an attempt to keep his hand in art history. He'd been a volunteer on a dig in Urbisalvia. He'd been instrumental in unearthing a Roman cistern and part of an aqueduct. If he didn't need money, he'd have stayed behind. It had been a thrill being part of something important. Being in the thick of history was his passion and had become a nagging desire. The bartending job had been a dead end leaving Tim antsy and frustrated.

Tim remembered thinking it odd at the time when Antonio Mecelli addressed him. He'd rarely if ever engaged Tim in conversation, and he'd usually come in later when the crowds were thick with touring young men. "You seem out of sorts, Tim," he said, "You're not your usual jovial self, anything wrong?"

Tim had hesitated, he'd made it a habit of keeping his personal life close to the vest, but he'd grown lonely and tired of waiting for his life to start. Antonio had been an acquaintance, nothing more, he seemed harmless, and Tim had no reason not to confide in him.

Against his better judgement, Tim had told him, "I'm discouraged, I guess. I've been at this job for two years now, can't save enough money to pursue my career as an art historian or to go back to school. I am here day after day doing the same boring job getting nowhere fast."

"I may be able to help you," Antonio had said without a moment's hesitation. Tim realized all this in retrospect, mulling the whole scenario over in his head during sleepless nights.

It came as no surprise to Tim when Antonio Mecelli revealed his true identity. Many a "holy man" frequented the bar. They wore regular clothes that did little to conceal their truth. He could usually pick them out with bull's-eye accuracy. It had been a sport of his to pass the monotony.

Now Tim suffered pangs of guilt and uncertainty; deep down inside he knew there was something seriously amiss within this sacred office. His phone rang snapping him back to reality.

"Pronto."

"Tim, delay the lunch, say the chef had a kitchen mishap. Give me an hour to get the child out of the garden." Cardinal Roselli hung up without another word.

On top of everything else that plagued Tim's mind, now he was expected to lie to the pope. He liked Pope Joseph. He found him charming and surprisingly irreverent for a pope. Tim's stomach began to churn, he felt nauseated. Trapped in a web of deceit, he feared he had sold his soul. He saw no way out. If he reported his suspicions, no one would believe him. Tim wondered about the child, the girl dressed in white who lived with nuns whose only task was to pray for the Pontiff, tend to his linens. *Where had she come from?* Cardinal Roselli had dismissed all Tim's questions regarding the girl, "She's an orphan of one of our guards, her parents were killed in a car accident. She had no other relatives, we raised her here."

If this were true, why the secrecy, why did she have to be ushered out of the Papal Gardens and remain hidden from visitors?

Chapter Sixteen

Cardinal Roselli's cell phone buzzed in the pocket of his cassock. He ignored it, rushed out of his office, and walked past Tim who was on the phone. He gave a slight wave. Tim gestured for him to wait, "Your Eminence, there's a Severino Poverelli on the line, he's asking for you and won't tell me what it's about. He says it's urgent."

Cardinal Roselli rolled his eyes, and with a hint of disgust in his voice said, "I'll take it in my office." He rushed back inside, shut the door, and picked up the phone.

Tim held the extension quietly to his ear; he'd hoped to learn something that would give him leverage against this powerful man if he should become an adversary. Tim noted the date and time of the call and the name of the caller in a notebook he'd kept locked in his desk drawer.

"Haven't I asked you never to call me at this number, to only call my cell phone, and only after hours?"

"Si, Cardinal," Severino answered, "I tried, no answer, and this is a bit of an emergency. The woman has recovered her memory, Lorenzo agreed to escort her to Roma, but she's escaped."

"Fools, the lot of you. What do you mean escaped? Why would she escape from Lorenzo? I thought he'd been her confidant all these years. What happened? Never mind, deal with it."

Cardinal Roselli slammed the phone down. The secrets he'd worked so hard to keep were seeping out. He regretted having given in to the pleas of Joseph Morris.

"Don't harm her," Joseph begged, "find a way to keep her away but I don't want her harmed." When Cardinal Roselli told him that the young woman had an unfortunate accident, a fall, he called it, leaving her without a memory, the pope seemed relieved. "Let her be," he'd instructed Guilo Roselli. At the time,

Guilo saw no reason to eliminate her, which was proving to be his first mistake; bringing the child to the Vatican had been the second. Before he had time to consider the mother, he had to remove the child from the gardens before that journalist started asking questions. He heard the branches of the tree outside his window beat furiously against the glass; he grabbed his cloak off the hook on the back of the door, and walked out of his office. With his dark eyes, black hair, and his purple trimmed cassock and cape, he could have been mistaken for a character out of Hogwarts.

By the time Cardinal Roselli reached the gardens, Pope Joseph and Chris DeMarco were engaged in conversation with the child and Cardinal Alfonso. Nevaeh and the cardinal were engrossed in a child's card game. Nevaeh was explaining the premise to the two men. She'd learned it from the granddaughter of one of the gardeners who'd brought her to work with him one day last month.

"It's called, Go Fish," she told her captive audience, "Here's how you play."

Cardinal Roselli remained out of sight but within earshot. He'd have to move in fast to diffuse the situation in case the conversation turned into an inquiry as to Nevaeh's origins. So far, the talk was playful. Cardinal Roselli prided himself on his stern authoritative manner. He rarely if ever let his guard down, but even he had to admit that this child was mesmerizing. She had a luminous aura around her. *Enough sentiment, too much is at stake. She's becoming more visible. She has to go. She'll fetch a good sum when the time comes,* he thought to himself.

Pope Joseph and the journalist walked on. Joseph pointed out historic artifacts, showing off his knowledge by reciting the origins of each monument, and whom they represented. Chris had no interest, he was in awe of the child. Something about her was familiar.

Cardinal Roselli remained hidden until Pope Joseph and his loitering friend were out of sight. As he approached Cardinal Alfonso, he heard Nevaeh say, "Papa, if these cards were wishes, I'd throw them back until I could pick what I wish for."

"What is it you would want to pick, Cara?"

"I'd 'go fish' until I picked the right wish."

"What would you choose as the right one?"

"To have a different life than this one."

Cardinal Alfonso sighed, he'd once wished for a different life. As a young man he'd worked hard as a laborer in the Sicilian village where he'd grown up. There had been little monetary reward but he'd had a strong faith back then; he'd truly believed that he'd find his way to a better life. When his young wife and child were killed in a tragic accident, he'd turned to his parish priest for solace. Devastating grief led him to a life of service. He'd studied hard, making up for lost time. His former life had afforded him little time for scholarly pursuits. In his twenties, he'd become a devoted family man who'd struggled to make ends. Now in his seventies, he was a well-respected scholar and linguist. He knew desiring a change in one's life could be a potentially dangerous wish.

Cardinal Alfonso patted Nevaeh's hand but said nothing. Cardinal Roselli looked on and muttered under his breath, "She just might get more than she wished for."

Chapter Seventeen

Lorenzo had given Sophia more than the allotted time a woman would need to tend to her bodily functions, but he had no experience with such matters. He had been ill at ease since this whole thing started, and now he was in the thick of it with no way out. After an hour had passed, he'd gone into the Autogrill to look for her. She was gone, nowhere in sight. How could this happen? He'd been so careful. He knew that he'd have to call Severino in to take over and there would be no good end.

Severino was a shady sort who could both charm and repel people, and he relished this trait. It had served him well. He'd grown up no better than a street rat in Naples. His mother had died of an overdose when Severino was three. His father dabbled in dealing, and was strung out for much of his son's life. When Severino's maternal grandmother moved in to raise him, it was the last time Severino would see his father. When Severino was only ten his grandmother died. He was young but already well-versed in the ways of the Napolitano netherworld.

Lorenzo and Severino had been mates; growing up under similar circumstances they'd formed a lasting bond. Lorenzo's artistic talent had been recognized and championed by his teachers. Opportunities presented themselves. Lorenzo apprenticed with the finest Venetian mask-makers. He'd learned their trade, embellishing their tricks with his own artistic flare. Mask-making was a dying art, and while he'd become a master, it didn't generate the income he'd hoped for.

Severino, too, was on a fast track, but his talents were far from God-given. He was a master of deception, immoral, devoid of a conscience, and able to rise up through the criminal pecking order because of it. It didn't take long before he'd found himself following in the footsteps of his father, but only on the business side of drug smuggling, he'd never touched the stuff. Being on top of his game was the focus of his whole existence. Severino was feared but respected.

His contacts in Venice kept watch on his old friend, Lorenzo. The mask shop profited during tourist season, but the winter months were quiet with few tourists frequenting the dank, medieval city. Lorenzo rarely opened the shop.

When Severino approached Lorenzo with a proposition to sell his masks throughout Europe, Lorenzo was intrigued. A typical artist, his business sense and marketing skills were nil. Severino agreed to take control. "A gesture of friendship," he'd called it. He wanted nothing in return. Lorenzo didn't realize what had been going on until the shop flooded, soaking a box of masks that lay shoved in a tight corner waiting for Severino's toady — a wiry, muscular, unkempt youth of about eighteen — to show up. The kid hadn't shown up on time, *probably sleeping off whatever it was he was on,* Lorenzo thought at the time. He wondered why the kid would want to incur the wrath of Severino Poverelli.

The box had been soaked through and the soggy bottom separated. Bits of white powder seeped through the cardboard dripping into the rising lagoon water on the shop floor. A wave of shame flooded over Lorenzo; he'd been duped, he should have known better. He'd known of Severino's reputation and he'd let him in, let him manipulate him with the lure of money. Severino had charisma, he'd give him that much. Lorenzo had been trapped, and just like the toady, he would forever be under the thumb of his childhood friend; there would be no way out.

Severino had called on Lorenzo to assist with a few random jobs. Lorenzo was a big guy, ominous looking, and could pose a threat, albeit idle, just by his presence. He was often sent along with the toady kid, Andreas, to collect debts. Lorenzo didn't mind, Severino paid him more than enough to sustain him through the slow times in Venice. When the call came to befriend a young amnesiac, it was a dream job compared to the rest. He'd been at it for years now, had grown fond of the woman, and had been resting easy. He was finally out of the drug smuggling business.

"I'll have to hire the woman," he'd told Severino at the beginning, "and teach her mask-making so I can be with her every day." It had gone well for years, until that fateful day when her memory flooded back.

Chapter Eighteen

"Why are you slowing down? We've only been driving for a little over an hour."

Sophia perked up in her seat. She'd been in a virtual daze since she'd gotten in the car, formulating ideas in her head, in an attempt to figure out her next move. She should have prepared a contingency plan, a just-in-case-Lorenzo-turned-out-to-be-untrustworthy plan. She'd ignored her budding intuition by trusting a man she'd grown suspicious of.

"I'm stopping in Perugia, I have to see someone."

"Allora! You do that and I'm not going to pay you more euro. We can take a train from Perugia to Roma for a lot less euro."

Zara and Gina had been asleep for an hour. Startled by the sound of loud arguing, they woke up, "What's going on?" both of them spoke at once.

"He wants to stop in Perugia?"

Oliver had already exited the highway. He pulled off the side of the road — a rural spot a few yards from the Autostrada. He considered dumping the women there but he needed the money. He wanted to visit his grandmother in Perugia. She'd been sick for a few weeks, he needed to check on her. His parents had been killed last year and his grandmother was the only family he had. He wasn't about to share personal information; he'd enjoyed being mysterious. He had no desire to see any of these women again.

"C'mon, Oliver, you can't do this? We've been in this car for hours and hours, take us to Roma. Whatever you have to do in Perugia can wait, can't it?" It was Gina. Oliver watched her in the rear view mirror. Her eyes flickered, those dancing green orbs made her hard to resist.

Driving another two hours to Rome and back would add four hours to his trip, Oliver thought with disgust. *On the other hand, his grandmother didn't expect him and the 75 euro was easy money.*

"Okay, but do me a favor and shut up."

The women leaned back in their seats satisfied at having gotten their way. Sophia didn't want to lose any more time. She was anxious to get to Rome. It had been over twelve years since she'd been there and she wondered if the ancient city and her old neighborhood were still bursting with the enchantment that had captivated her when she'd first arrived. Her landlady, Lauretta Jenco, had been kind to her, offering her more space in her apartment building than Sophia could afford, treating her like the daughter she'd never had. It had been Sophia's only true home. She'd go there first.

Sophia didn't say another word until they were on the outskirts of the city limits. "Oliver, please drop me off in Trastevere."

"Driving over there is a nightmare, I can't access it easily," his tone was curt and adamant.

"Let me out at the Ponte Sisto Bridge, I'll walk the rest of the way."

"What about you two, any special requests for drop off?" Oliver smirked fully expecting to let the other two out at a youth hostel.

"Aventine Hill, Via della Fonte di Fauno, my father lives there."

"I'll drop you two off first, I assume you're leaving together," Oliver glanced in the mirror addressing the two younger women.

"Yup, two peas in a pod, that's us."

Oliver drove up Aventine Hill beyond Santa Sabina and into the wealthy residential area. Zara instructed him to pull up into the driveway of an apartment building that boasted a sprawling top floor with an expansive gardened terrace.

"This is us," Zara announced.

"What does your daddy do?" Oliver grumbled remembering the lack of funds Zara had claimed early on.

"Not much," she said adding, "Grazie mille, hope we meet again, Sophia."

They'd barely exited the door when Oliver pulled out, skidding in the process.

"Easy, Oliver."

The normal ten-minute drive from Aventine Hill to the Ponte Sisto Bridge took 45 minutes. Sophia didn't remember witnessing so much traffic in Rome, but back when she'd lived there she'd walked everywhere, usually with her head in the clouds; she wouldn't have noticed.

The delay wreaked further havoc with Oliver's disposition. He cursed in two languages without restraint.

"The bridge is up ahead, you can let me out here," Sophia told Oliver.

Oliver came to a screeching halt in the middle of the road causing the cars behind to slam on their brakes. Irate drivers opened their car windows raising fists in the air in Oliver's direction.

He was unfazed, "Give me my money." Sophia handed him the 75 euro, and Oliver took off without a word of goodbye.

Piazza di Santa Maria was unchanged. Its ancient crumbling, but vibrant pink and amber colored stone buildings still held terraces where flowering shrubs dripped blossoms down the sides. Sophia watched the young locals recalling how she too had once been one of them, carefree, enjoying the nightlife of Trastevere. She stopped, briefly took in the scene, breathed deeply, and stood in front of the dark green door of the apartment building she'd called home all those years ago.

Sophia held her finger over the buzzer bearing the name, L. Jenco. She hesitated, rethinking her options; a thousand what ifs flooded her mind; she needed a little more time and a lot more courage before she could face the daunting task ahead.

She walked back to the Piazza di Santa Maria, found a trattoria, and sat in the corner. She was famished — she realized she hadn't eaten all day. She ordered cacio e pepe and a glass of Lambrusco di Sorbara — a light red wine. It would take the edge off but she would still have her wits about her. She lingered over dessert, picking at the torta caprese in an attempt to kill time. Spying out the window at the hordes of college-aged kids and straggling tourists flooding the streets did little to allay her fears. Sophia longed to be one of them. Where would she be a year from now, would she ever recover from this assault on her life? She brought the cloth napkin up to her lips and subtly wiped off the bits of chocolate that had stuck to her teeth, paid the bill, and left. The wine had served its purpose, she was buzzed, not drunk. Walking the piazza and perusing the shops along the way rekindled her sense of belonging. This had been her home. Here is where she belonged. If Lauretta was still alive and lucid, she'd be the one to trust. Sophia walked back towards the bridge; she knew she was procrastinating but she needed more time to reflect.

The sun had gone down and the bridge was illuminated. Sophia felt surreal, like she was walking in the midst of a fairy tale. She hesitated on the bridge, leaned against the ancient stone railing and looked to the north out over the Tiber at St. Peter's Basilica. *My daughter is there,* she thought with hope in her heart.

The restaurant on the shoreline near the bridge was filled with tourists. Their boisterous laughter resonated off the river making it hard for Sophia to think. She meandered slowly back into the heart of Trastevere, placed herself once again at the doorstep to the building Lauretta had purchased after selling her father's home in Sant'Angelo. "I'm more a bohemian than I am Jewish, Trastevere is my idea of Utopia," Lauretta had told Sophia on one of the nights they stayed up late, enjoying a glass of wine and each other's company. Lauretta had never married, had no children, few friends, and no family with the exception of a cousin. He was an official in the Ministry of the Interior. The cousins were cordial but rarely saw each other.

Sophia held her breath and pressed the buzzer. It seemed to take forever for Lauretta to answer.

"Si, pronto, c'e, who is it?"

"Lauretta, it's Sophia Travato."

Lauretta didn't respond, the buzzer screeched welcome. Sophia let herself in, climbed up the marble stairs looking at the familiar cracks and crevices. Little had changed — the dim lighting had been replaced with LEDs but the stone railing held the same chips and crevices, and the paint still peeled in the same spots. The worn façade created ambience. Decay added to the charm, despite the havoc it made on the interior workings. When Sophia looked up, she saw an aged Lauretta with her mop of white hair hanging down. She was squinting through the open landing and filigreed balustrade to see if it was really Sophia returned from the abyss.

Chapter Nineteen

Sophia reached the second floor landing; she came face to face with Lauretta. She was afraid to step any closer. She'd known she had no right to go back to Lauretta even before she'd made the trip. She had thought about it fleetingly; there was nowhere else to go, but she knew this wasn't fair. She'd left all those years ago without a word. Lauretta had given her a home, taken care of her throughout her pregnancy, and Sophia had repaid her by leaving, and taking the baby without a word of goodbye. She'd left all her possessions behind, taking only a carry-on for herself and a few necessities for the baby to tide them over until they were safe in the United States. Her trust had been sorely misplaced back then. She knew that now. How would she explain the last thirteen years to this woman who'd shown her nothing but kindness? Sophia was inert, she felt limp; her life was a shamble all because she'd been young and reckless, allowing an older man, a man of God, to seduce her. She'd been a fool. Her irresponsible behavior just may have cost Nevaeh her life; it had almost cost Sophia hers. She was home now, but she hesitated, wondering if she should have found another way. A weariness was weighing heavy on her body and soul.

Lauretta was the first to make a move. She reached Sophia, and despite her frail appearance and unsteady gait, she pulled Sophia close holding her with a firm arm and a sturdy grip. She escorted Sophia with her arm linked through hers into the apartment.

Lauretta's apartment was more spacious than Sophia remembered, all the dark draperies had been removed, replaced by crisp white shutters. They were pulled open revealing the large, flowered terrace. The abundant bougainvillea dripped out of their terracotta pots down the side of the building. The fuchsia blossoms, vibrant against the golden plaster, attracted many a tourist hungry for a photo op. Even the locals never tired of their beauty. Lauretta prided herself on her gardening talents. Lemon and olive trees stood in splendor side by side thriving in the Roman sun, an herb garden was planted in low pots, and larkspur towered behind. The colorful spectacle mesmerized Sophia, taking her mind briefly off her troubles.

Sophia was startled when Lauretta touched her shoulder gesturing for her to move onto the terrace. The bistro table held a single dinner plate. A half-eaten chicken breast lay across the flowered dish.

"I'm so sorry, Lauretta, I've interrupted your dinner."

"It's nothing, Sophia. Have you eaten?"

"Yes, but please finish, Lauretta."

"Would you like some wine?"

The dinner wine buzz Sophia had experienced earlier had now worn off. She readily agreed to another glass.

"Sit, Lauretta, please let me get it."

"There's a bottle of Chianti, over there on the table."

Sophia opened the bottle, carried it and two glasses over to Lauretta, and sat beside her.

"Tell me when you're ready, not a minute sooner."

Sophia poured them each a glass, took a sip, and began to let her tale unravel.

"Sophia, wait, where is Nevaeh?"

Sophia put her head down on the table and let out a gut-wrenching sob. Lauretta rested her hand lightly on Sophia's head. Her touch was soothing. A warm breeze blew onto the terrace, rustling the leaves of the trees releasing a lemony scent in its wake. Sophia raised her head, comforted by the fragrance. She looked at Lauretta through tear-soaked, soulful, ebony-colored eyes. She brushed her honey-colored hair off of her shoulders, took a sip of wine, and began where she'd left off, "I left because I was told to. I was also told not to waver from the instructions they'd given me. I was not to speak to anyone, tell no one of the plans, take nothing but what was absolutely necessary for the trip. I couldn't say goodbye. I'd been so frightened, these were powerful men I'd become entangled with." Sophia hesitated, while taking another sip of wine.

"Is this the baby's father you are talking about?" Lauretta interrupted.

"I'm not sure; I assumed he'd been the one making arrangements for us but now I know it hadn't been. It was someone else."

Lauretta had only seen glimpses of whom she'd assumed was the baby's father. She'd had her suspicions about him. Shaded by the thick bushy trees that abutted Lauretta's walled terrace, she'd been able to spy on Sophia's suitor as he exited the building under the cover of darkness all those years ago. Lauretta had always been a light sleeper. The ancient plaster walls did little to muffle the sound of footsteps on the staircase, and the closing of the heavy wooden doors resonating off the cold marble would awaken Lauretta in the wee hours. She'd never lingered in bed, but would get up and tinker in the garden under the light of the Roman moon. *I'll rest enough when I'm dead,* she'd told herself.

She'd never been introduced to Sophia's love interest. He was older, wiser, and taking advantage of her beautiful Sophia. Lauretta knew this for a fact, she'd lived long enough to recognize the signs of a train wreck ahead. But she'd kept quiet. She didn't want to alienate Sophia, the girl had no one, and Lauretta wanted to be the one she'd turn to if she ever needed anyone. As the years passed, she'd often thought about Sophia; she'd never given up hoping one day she'd return with an explanation.

The sky was brightening when Sophia had finally finished recanting the story of where she'd been for nearly thirteen years. She'd barely come up for air and didn't realize it was morning.

"I'm sorry I kept you up all night, Lauretta."

"Pfff, sleep is for the young. Tell me who are these men who've taken your child? What was their motive?"

Sophia had kept Joseph Morris' name out of the story. She kept the facts vague, fearing she'd sound unstable. Even she, who'd lived through this nightmare, knew it would sound far-fetched and unfathomable to the listener. But Lauretta was perceptive, she sensed there were holes in the story, and she pressed for answers.

"Sophia, you've come here after all these years, talked all night but omitted something. Now let me tell you. I have no children, no family except for my big shot cousin, Alessandro. I considered you family, Sophia, and I still do. You need support, someone to trust. Tell me the truth, all of it." Lauretta's voice was strong, authoritative and oddly maternal, sounding a lot like a mother who was chastising a misbehaving child.

Sophia hung her head with shame. "I messed up my life by having an affair with a man who should have been off-limits. It was wrong from the start and I've incurred the wrath of the universe because of it."

"Cut the drama, Sophia. It's not the dark ages, things happen. Very little is taboo these days. Who was this off-limits love? Was he married?"

"No, he was a priest, now he's pope." Sophia blurted it out finally without restraint. It felt like a heavy fog had lifted. "The pope is Nevaeh's father. Someone in the Vatican took her, I don't know if she's dead or alive. I have to find her, but no one will believe this."

"Pff," Lauretta said again, raising her hands up in the air. "Sophia, you've been sequestered, you've been kept in the dark all these years. The Church is riddled with scandal, more now than ever before in modern times. Everyone will believe this. Come now, you need rest, we'll talk more later."

Lauretta took Sophia by the arm and escorted her down the hall to her old apartment. She took a ring of keys from her apron pocket, found the right one, and opened the door. Everything was the same as it had been since the day Sophia left. The furnishings had been covered with sheets to keep them free of dust, and her clothes remained untouched in the armoire in the bedroom.

"Lauretta, I don't know what to say. Surely, this apartment could have been rented out all these years."

"Eh, maybe, but I gave that up a while ago. Now I'm doing a VRBO."

"What's that?"

"I rent only to tourists, never for more than a month at a time. It's less of a headache, I get to meet people from all over the world, and it generates more of an income. I saw no reason to lease out your apartment. I kept it as you left it. It seemed like the right thing to do. Now rest, we'll talk later. I have something I need to tell you."

Sophia wondered what it was that Lauretta wanted to tell her; she was afraid she was going to say she was sick, maybe dying. *Not now, please,* she said out loud to no one. Lauretta had gone and left Sophia alone with her thoughts. She opened the door to her own gardened terrace a crack to freshen the room; the bed on the opposite corner with its crisp white bedding beckoned. Sophia lay on it, and fell asleep as the comforting perfumed scent of Trastevere blew in softly over her.

Chapter Twenty

Sophia was disoriented when she woke up late in the afternoon. Opening her eyes and looking around her bedroom, she had the sense she'd never left, that time had stood still. The feeling lasted only a minute before reality hit. She'd have to get on with her plans to find Nevaeh. It would be evening soon, she'd wasted another whole day. She took a shower in the white tiled bathroom; the warm water was soothing. She wished she had the luxury of lingering, the bathroom was luxurious when compared to the archaic, convent showers she'd grown used to. The convent plumbing never allowed for a leisurely shower with its trickling water barely offering more than a sprinkle at a time.

The aroma of Lauretta's espresso brewing wafted over her, bringing more memories to the forefront of her mind. *The human mind is a source of wonder,* Sophia thought, *the mere scent of something as simple as coffee can be a trigger bringing a long buried memory to the surface.* Sophia recalled the first morning after she'd moved in there all those years ago. Lauretta had arrived at her door carrying a tray of biscuits and what would soon become known as her famous cappuccino. Lauretta never revealed the secret flavor contained within the frothy treat, and no one, Sophia included, was able to figure out what it was.

Sophia opened the wardrobe and breathed in another familiar scent. The old pine cabinet held the musty odor of age. She chose a black pleated skirt from the wardrobe and a light pink pullover sweater, pulled her hair back in a pony tail and went in search of Lauretta.

"You slept the sleep of the newly released," Lauretta told Sophia when she greeted her at the door. "I used to sleep when I was young, now sleep eludes me."

"You don't look any worse for it."

"It's a side effect of growing older, one of many," Lauretta laughed.

Sophia's anxiety began to surface; she fidgeted with her hands and started to pace around the kitchen.

"Sophia, you're going to have to calm yourself if you want to find your daughter. You'll need help and a plan."

"I thought I had help, but that turned sour. I don't know what to do now. I'm not sure how to approach this, how to gain entry into the Vatican, I mean. I stole a habit from the nuns' laundry but it may not be the best plan. I have to think, I have to find a way."

"If you want advice from an old lady, I have a few suggestions. If you don't, I understand, but by telling me this story, you've invited me in. I can't very well unhear it now."

"Of course, Lauretta. If I didn't trust you, I never would have come here."

Lauretta sat beside Sophia taking her hand. "I think we should talk to my cousin Alessandro. He's a higher-up at the Office of the Ministry. He'll know what to do. You have to be careful, Sophia. The Church is powerful and Vatican City is not only its headquarters, it's a Sovereign nation with its own laws. I know they'll cooperate with Roman authorities on some matters but this is a scandal involving their Supreme Pontiff. It isn't going to be easy."

"Why would your cousin even want to help me? Why would he even believe that the Church would kidnap a child?"

"He'll believe it's the truth, because he knows they've done this in the past."

"What do you mean?"

"Allora! It's a story that my grandmother told us. She'd heard about it from her grandmother and now I'll tell it to you. But it's something that shames both Catholics and Jews alike."

Sophia sipped her caffé and waited for Lauretta to begin. Instead of starting the story, Lauretta told Sophia, "You'd better eat something because you're going to need wine while you're hearing this."

Loretta began, "In the 1800s before the unification of Italy, the pope reigned supreme over the papal states. Jews were marginalized and had to wear gold badges to be identified as such. This was God's will according to the pope as he was deemed earthly ruler of the one true faith. My grandmother lived in Bologna before she married my grandfather and moved to Rome as a young bride. The story I'm about to tell you is one she'd heard whispered about. She'd grown up in the neighborhood where this incident took place many years before. It's not spoken of today, but it's factual, you can be sure of that."

Lauretta paused and looked up at Sophia before continuing, "In the mid-1800s it wasn't uncommon for Jews to hire Christian young women as household servants. This enabled them to have the help they needed during the Sabbath when a Jewish servant would have been unable to provide services. The Mortara family lived in the Jewish ghetto of Bologna in 1859 with their children. As an infant, their young son had been ill with an undisclosed childhood disease said not to be life threatening. Their young, illiterate Christian servant observed the distraught parents keeping a bedside vigil and assumed death was imminent. She took it upon herself to baptize the child. Years later, the parish priest learned of the baptism and notified papal authorities. It was forbidden for a Catholic to be raised by Jews. Edgardo Mortara, at the age of six, was now considered a Catholic in the eyes of the Church. He was forcibly removed from the arms of his mother and taken to Rome where he was raised by Pope Pius IX."

"That's outrageous." Sophia was visibly upset.

"Is it any more or less outrageous than the story you tell?" Lauretta frowned. "The family did everything they could to get their child back. The Church resisted and when international pressure was thrust upon them, they spun the story with talk of his miraculous conversion. They told of Edgardo having been spiritually transformed and asking to be converted. Pff, all this at the tender age of six. Mrs. Mortara never fully recovered. Mr. Mortara made many trips to the Vatican. He was allowed to see the boy at first; it seemed clear to him his son was afraid of someone. Mr. Mortara never met with the boy alone. The boy was said to have been shamed by talk of the Jews having been the murderers of Christ. Mr. Mortara's business suffered as a result of his dedication to retrieving his son from the clutches of the Church hierarchy. It was to no avail, he faced ruin. The family was offered a bribe, their financial situation would be restored if they agreed their son had received redemption. When they refused, another solution was offered — they could convert."

"Oh my God, Lauretta. How is it this isn't common knowledge?"

"It was shameful for Catholics, although Pius IX has recently been considered for sainthood. But his nomination was withdrawn after much protest. It was shameful for the Jews to relive their vulnerability. Better to be quiet. This was the most infamous case but not the only incident."

"What happened to the young servant?"

"She had betrayed the Mortaras after they had been kind to her. Earlier, when she'd found herself pregnant, they supported her and paid for the services of a midwife who sheltered her until the baby was born. This was how she paid them back. That she had feared for the soul of the child was her defense. The story becomes more and more convoluted. The family's life was ruined. Prejudices ran amok back then. Catholics saw Edgardo as a martyr for his new faith."

"What happened to the boy?" Sophia was growing increasingly alarmed by this story.

"He was taken to the seminary. He became a priest at the age of 21. A special dispensation by Pius IX was given since technically the boy was too young to be ordained. The pope saw himself as the father of the boy. Interestingly, it was Pius IX who'd established the rule of papal infallibility." Lauretta frowned and nodded her head. "You see how powerful men can manipulate every circumstance to support their dominance?"

"That was deranged behavior."

"Perhaps, but they saw themselves as the ones who were enacting the will of God. It was their duty. It was the old-world thinking, medieval in a sense; the Church did not practice religious tolerance back then. When papal rule ended the priest who had initiated the taking of Edgardo Mortara was charged. Ecclesiastic privilege had been nullified. I'm presenting the highlights here but you understand now what power in the wrong hands can do? It wasn't the Nazis who first ordered Jews to be badged. As I said earlier, it was the pope. This case ushered in modernity. The Jews began to form united fronts. But only Jewish historians spoke of this. My grandmother's uncle had been a rabbi and a scholar. It was through him that this story lived on. She, in turn, kept the story alive."

Lauretta got up, walked over to the bookcase and pulled two relatively new paperbacks off of the shelf full of antiquated, faded hardcovers. She stood still for a moment staring at the bookshelf. She brushed her fingers lightly over the book bindings.

"I've inherited most of these books from my father. He was a reader, as well as a businessman. Here are two books about Edgardo Mortara. One was a bestseller written by an American professor, Pulitzer Prize-winning author and historical scholar, David I. Kertzer. The other is the unpublished memoir supposedly by Edgardo himself. The latter is dubious if you ask me. It sings the praises of Pius IX claiming he promoted the sanctity of one of his own. It attempts to discredit Professor Kertzer as he is said to have not referred to the archives of the Canons Regular of the Lateran. These archives documented the faithful devotion of Father Mortara."

She went on to say, "In my humble opinion, Professor Kertzer was correct in not referring to this propagandized account of Edgardo Mortara's road to piety. He was a young boy when he was taken, clearly brainwashed, it was a classic Stockholm Syndrome situation. You may have these if you'd like to read them."

Sophia merely nodded. Her mind was racing. *Nevaeh had just turned thirteen. Pope Joseph could easily give permission for her to become a nun. She would comply, the Catholic Church was all the child knew.*

"If Nevaeh is still alive she'll know nothing of the outside world. She'll know only what they want her to know. She'll only know the ways of the Church."

Sophia was frantic. She fingered the chain around her neck.

"Do you have a computer, Lauretta?" Sophia wanted to search for more than her daughter, she wanted to know the origins of the ancient ring she held.

She had thought it was of Gnostic origins; it was just a feeling, but now it had been verified by online research. If the necklace she'd placed around Nevaeh's neck all those years ago still remained in place, it may put her in danger. Gnosticism was still considered heretical by the Catholic Church. Religious intolerance prevailed even in these modern times.

"I nearly forgot to show you this." Lauretta moved over to her desk drawer and pulled a business card out from the clutter of papers shoved inside.

"This man came here looking for you a few weeks ago. I told him I hadn't seen or heard from you in many years. He gave me his card and told me he was staying in Roma indefinitely, and I should contact him if I had any news of you. He seemed sincere and nonthreatening. But I'm always wary of strangers who come calling."

Sophia took the card with the tips of her fingers. She was afraid, at first, it was Lorenzo who'd somehow located her former residence. But the timing was off. Maybe that cardinal whose name she'd heard the kidnapper mention or maybe the kidnapper himself had found her. Lorenzo would have notified him and Pope Joseph would remember the apartment in Trastevere. It would be the first place they'd look. Sophia started to shake uncontrollably. She feared for her life and that of her child.

"Sip some wine; this is strong, my neighbor makes it herself. It will calm you."

Sophia took a sip, then another; the wine was thick and syrupy. She took a deep breath and looked at the card in her hand. It read: *Christopher DeMarco: Journalist — In Conversation Magazine.*

"Chris," Sophia whispered.

She let her shoulders drop and felt relief wash over her. Chris would help her. She knew in her heart that he would be the one to help her find Nevaeh.

Chapter Twenty-One

It was Wednesday, the day Pope Joseph and Chris DeMarco had designated to have their ongoing interview. A late lunch in the Papal Gardens would be the perfect setting, this would keep the questions light as Pope Joseph had no intention of revealing any of his plans to his former friend. Their long time ago comradery was a distant memory. There were no common interests between them that would foster renewing a friendship that once was but could no longer be jumpstarted. Sophia, the link between them, had unknowingly set them up as rivals. It had never been addressed, but jealous rivalry had been there simmering under the surface. *Chris would have had to be blind not to have known about Sophia and me,* Joseph thought while preparing for his Wednesday morning meet and greet with the faithful. It was routine; every Wednesday, he would scoot around St. Peter's Square in the pope mobile waving to his devoted followers. He found it tiresome but still he relished his celebrity status.

Chris was waiting in the garden when Pope Joseph had completed his morning ritual. Chris was strolling through the massive labyrinth of greenery admiring its pristine nature. *What a waste all this luxury is; it must have been an exorbitant expense to establish and it clearly costs a fortune to maintain,* he thought as he walked along. He thought about the suffering he'd witnessed while on assignment throughout the world. He was sitting on a stone bench at the outskirts of the maze when Joseph approached.

"Afternoon, Chris, I hope you weren't waiting long."

"No, not long. I took a stroll in the labyrinth. There's a distinct smell of oregano and maybe thyme. Do you grow your food here? Must cost a bundle to keep it so flawless."

"Much of the fruit, vegetables are grown here, and there's an extensive herb garden. Yes, it's all meticulously maintained, but as far as the costs I don't handle the expense account. I wouldn't know. I leave it to the Camerlengo to sort out."

"Maybe you should know these things. There's so much suffering in the world, seems to me much of it could be alleviated by a redistribution of the Vatican's wealth and holdings."

"I can't imagine how the Vatican would begin to do such a thing. What would happen to the Catholic Church? The people expect to see magnificence when they come here to the Vatican."

"Well if they'd educate themselves on the history of their own faith they would understand the folly of it all. Why would a simple carpenter with rag-tag followers have had any of this splendor in mind when he set out? He was a rabble-rouser attempting to demonstrate the harshness of the time in order to show the way to bring peace and harmony to his people. His words were misinterpreted to suit powerful men who revised the story of the life of Christ into something it wasn't. The Church, as it is today, was designed by men who wielded power to manipulate the masses, keep them suppressed, and under their thumb. All this wealth is a side effect of centuries of power run amok."

"Chris, you are misguided."

"With all due respect, Your Holiness, I believe you are the one who is misguided."

"Speaking of power, what happened to Sophia? She disappeared just when you were named as one of the Papabile. Is she dead?" Chris let his anger get the better of him and he'd blurted out questions he'd hoped to have eased into slowly.

"I have no idea where Sophia is. She probably ran off."

Pope Joseph wasn't lying, he truly had no clue as to Sophia's whereabouts. Cardinal Roselli had recently informed him Sophia went missing from the convent in Venice. She'd apparently regained her memory. He didn't think much of it at the time but now he worried dust from his past was blowing up around him and may not be easily contained this time. *There's no way she can get to me,* Joseph thought. He smiled, thinking about what Chris had said about power. He was insulated by power, no one would believe he could be involved in anything sinister.

"Do you find something amusing in what I've said? I noticed you were smiling."

"These are not new thoughts you bring up, scholars have been mulling over all this since early Christendom. Let's just say it's a matter of faith and leave it at that. I'll take your suggestion to dispense with the Vatican's holdings under advisement," the pope said with a laugh.

Chris was not amused. He knew the pope was hiding what he knew about Sophia. He had no proof yet, it was just a feeling. He felt his phone buzzing. He stuck his hand in and switched the toggle button to silent.

"I have a busy afternoon and evening, I'm afraid we'll have to end for the day. I trust next time you'll have more pertinent questions for me. I'm sure your readers won't be interested in the antics of a young woman we were mutually acquainted with years ago. I'll see you next week, Chris."

Oh, but they will, Chris thought as he walked beyond the Swiss Guard who were standing at attention on the outskirts of the garden entrance. Leftover crowds still lingered in St. Peter's Square. It was late into the afternoon, the pope's rendezvous with the faithful was a distant memory, yet they'd stayed put immersing themselves in the atmosphere he'd left behind.

Chris felt relief as he passed back out through the Vatican walls and was securely in Rome. He had the distinct feeling he'd need to tread lightly on the subject of Sophia. He saw how Pope Joseph tensed up at the mention of her name. The pope held all the power Chris had mentioned, the power to put an end to the interview and possibly the power to put an end to Chris as well. His former friend, now pope was in a different realm. He was the ruler of the Catholic Church and the ruler of the tiny nation where he reigned supreme. Yes, Chris would have to be mindful of all of this to keep himself safe.

Chapter Twenty-Two

"It's me," Cardinal Roselli whispered into his cell phone, "any news on the missing woman?"

"No," Severino answered, his strong authoritative voice wavered, "Lorenzo retraced his steps, no one at the Autogrill remembered seeing her but he didn't have a picture of her to show them."

"Find her, we can't afford a scandal. Even if she's made to look incompetent, some fool will believe her. There's a journalist nosing around here, he may have known her; he's an old friend of the Holy Father."

"She must have some friends here in Rome. She probably sought them out. You'll need to ask the pope if he remembers anything — a former address, something to go on. Lorenzo's here now, we'll find her."

Cardinal Roselli hung up. He hadn't wanted to involve the Pontiff in this matter but now there was no choice. This had to be dealt with before he and the pope left the Vatican next month for their three-week long ecumenical visit to South America.

Cardinal Roselli found the Holy Father in the Papal Apartment. He was seated at his desk; his head was down. Pope Joseph was deep in thought, he was writing a sanitized memoir.

"Your Holiness." Cardinal Roselli had trouble verbalizing that title when referring to Joseph Morris. He was anything but holy in his estimation, and while Cardinal Roselli realized he wasn't one to judge, he deemed his own actions justified. They were for the good of the Church not for his own selfish purposes.

"I apologize for the intrusion, we must talk privately."

"No one else is here, Guilo."

"Yes, but we must be absolutely sure no one can hear us."

"I'm sure, what is it?"

"The child's mother is somewhere in Roma. I've been assured by my men they will find her but they need some assistance. If you remember anything that can help them please tell me."

"Why do you think she poses such a threat? Who do you think is going to believe a story like hers? Consider the source, Guilo, a woman who loses her memory suddenly regains it, recalls having a child, and outlandishly claims the Supreme Pontiff is the father. Come now, Guilo, be rational. She can't hurt us. Relax. Call your men off. Sophia's smart, if she's back to her old self she'll know it would be futile to pursue searching for her child. The Vatican is not governed by outside laws; her accusations will fall on deaf ears. People will think she's pazza! Calm yourself. Anything else? Are you ready for our trip? It will do you good to get away from all this worry."

Cardinal Roselli nodded in agreement. "Perhaps it would be wise to send the child away. It may arouse suspicion if people were to notice her here. Your journalist friend has already seen her."

"He won't be a problem. He seemed satisfied when I told him she was the orphan of one of the guards who'd been killed along with his wife. Don't worry so much, you'll be dead before your time."

The cardinal wasn't so sure no one would find the woman's story so unusual considering the morality of the inner sanctum of the Church had gone off the rails. The presence of a child, a girl, no less, inside the Vatican walls only compounded the problem. He'd have to distance himself should any of this come to light in the future.

"Thank you, Your Holiness, I'm sure you know what's the best course of action to take."

Cardinal Roselli left the apartment and headed to his office. He had a lot to think about. *Severino and Lorenzo had proven to be inept. They were low-level thugs who could handle things when everything went smoothly, but as soon as a slight blip occurred, chaos ensued. Sophia should have been dealt with years ago. There had been many opportunities back then, she'd been contained, now who knows where she was. He'd need someone more professional, less emotional and no nonsense to be waiting in the wings just in case. Someone who could take care of both Sophia and the girl without involving him. He wondered if he could trust Tim, bring him in on this. Tim was easily swayed by a dangling euro. But Tim was too mild, he had no violent tendencies. As much as the Church hierarchy had become disentangled with the Italian Mafia over the past few years, they would be the only ones capable of helping him and keeping it quiet. This burdensome task was put on my shoulders by that infernal Joseph Morris.* Cardinal Roselli walked into his office slamming the door hard, causing the window to rattle and a few books to fall from the shelf.

Chapter Twenty-Three

"Papa, look at this!" Nevaeh held a book close to her face, her hand was placed over the cover.

"Listen, Papa." Alfonso stood in front of her, smiling.

"What is it that has you so excited? Please read, I'm listening."

Nevaeh began, "The Kingdom of God is inside you/within you (and all about you) not in buildings/mansions of wood and stone."

"There's more, should I read it to you?"

"No, Nevaeh, tell me, where did you find this book? Let me see it."

Cardinal Alfonso took the book from Nevaeh.

"I found it in the convent, it was in a pile of old books. One of the sisters was throwing them out, I think. I thought this was garbage which meant I could take it, right?"

"Well, since you aren't really sure it was garbage you should have asked for it."

"I never ask for anything, Papa. I just take what they give me. They tell me to be grateful for whatever they give."

"Tell me, do you spend time with the sisters? Do they talk to you?"

"One of them is my teacher, like you are. She teaches me math and reading. Everything else I learn from you. You are more fun though. Sister Mariana is the sister in charge, she told me the sisters are here to pray for the pope, and to keep the linens; they take care of me because they were told to by Cardinal Roselli. Every few years new sisters come to stay but they are all the same."

"Do they talk to you at meal time?"

"I eat by myself in the kitchen. A plate of food is left for me for breakfast, lunch, and dinner."

Alfonso's heart sank. *This beautiful child deserved better than this. He'd make it his business to get to the bottom of all this secrecy. Why was she here and where did she come from? He didn't believe for a minute that she was the orphan of a Swiss Guard. He'd been living here long enough to know that wasn't the truth. Only one Swiss Guard had died during his tenure, he'd been murdered along with his wife. This occurred years before Nevaeh was born. The contrived orphan story was generated by Cardinal Roselli and Pope Joseph Morris.*

"Papa Alfonso, does this saying mean I was right?"

"Nevaeh, this passage is from the Gospel of Thomas, remember we spoke about him? This gospel is what is referred to as Gnostic and it's forbidden for those of the Catholic faith to read it or even consider it truthful."

"What is Gnostic?"

"Gnostics believed that humans were divine but stuck in this world. The world, according to Gnostics, had been made by an irrational, flawed spirit — the God of the Old Testament. Some believe that Jesus came to earth as a revealer of knowledge (gnosis). They believed Jesus was a perfect man, and he was infused with a spirit called 'Christ.' It's a very complex story of many gods having different roles in controlling the universe. But they also believed a female spiritual being, named Sophia, also fell from the heavens. Sophia means wisdom. She could be called the 'earth mother.'"

"Perhaps a revealer will come again. I think we are overdue for one. The Church doesn't want us to know the truth because power would be lost and all this glitzy stuff." Nevaeh giggled, twirling around while pointing to the expansive array of marble and gold around them.

Alfonso frowned, "You mustn't say these things. It will cause trouble and I'll be blamed. We must keep this between us. Promise me."

"I promise, I'm sorry. I didn't mean to upset you, Papa. It's everything I thought about right here written thousands of years ago. How could I know about this?"

Alfonso wondered the same thing. *No young girl, no matter how educated, would be so intuitive to surmise mysteries such as these. Despite the danger,* Alfonso knew *Nevaeh had a gift and keeping up with her studies was essential in order to cultivate those gifts.* He would speak to Pope Joseph but in vague terms so as to not arouse suspicion. He'd need permission to allow her access to the Vatican Archives. *Who knows what she'd be able to interpret? But he had to be cautious, he had to keep Nevaeh from revealing too much. He was far too old to be defrocked for heretical teaching; he'd have nowhere to go.*

"Do you know what else I think, Papa?"

"No, what is it?"

"I think Sophia, the wise Goddess, is my mother and maybe I'm a revealer."

"Why would you say such a thing?"

"Because I belong to the earth, I feel trapped in there with all those material things. Why do you suppose creatures come to me when I'm out there in the garden? Look at this, Papa."

Nevaeh took a small black case out of her pocket. She placed it on a stone bench while she ripped a small piece of paper out of her notebook. She wrote her name out in capital letters. She opened the case. A small mirror was on one side and a bit of peach powder on the other.

"Nevaeh, where did you get this?"

"I found it in the church; I go there at night when everyone is asleep. I sneak by the guards and I know where the cameras are. I find all kinds of things the pilgrims leave behind, sometimes I go out in the garden too. But look, Papa."

Nevaeh tilted the mirror up with the powder side resting on the surface. She held the paper up in front of the mirror and said, "See, Papa."

Alfonso bent down and knelt on the ground to get a better view of the mirror. There it was the reflection of Nevaeh's name as it read reversed in the mirror spelling out, "Heaven."

"I see, Nevaeh. It's wonderful and true, you are heavenly indeed. Just what we need around here."

The cardinal had little else to say about this, he remembered the last time in the garden — *he recalled seeing an aura of light around her before he'd approached her that day. He'd attributed it to sunlight but there was something special about this girl, more to her, much more, something that had to do with that medal she wore around her neck. He had to find out, for her sake as well as his own. Whoever knew the truth about this child aimed to keep it long buried like all the other suppressed truths behind these walls that had been eroded by layers and layers of untruths leaving little of what was once credible behind.*

Pope Joseph may be amenable to discussing the gifts this child may possess, Alfonso thought. *His open-mindedness had been recognized as soon as his reign as pope began. More than eyebrows were raised by traditionalists such as Cardinal Roselli as Pope Joseph began his crusade to modernize the Church. Church hierarchy had expressed outrage at many of the radical ideas proposed by or those that had been enacted without the advice of one more experienced in Church matters. Tolerance for the beliefs of the other were one thing but inviting the practice of earth worshipping rituals onto the grounds of Vatican City were quite another. Lately, he'd noticed a reticence on the part of the pope. Perhaps, Cardinal Roselli had his ear. He could be persuasive. I'll have to be cautious,* Cardinal Alfonso sighed wondering if the Church would ever be able to right itself and begin once again to follow a united path in the footsteps of the Christ.

Chapter Twenty-Four

Chris feared the elaborate lunch Pope Joseph and he had once shared in the Papal Gardens was a thing of the past. The prickly conversation Chris had initiated served as the catalyst to end the interview for the day. He'd been dismissed, sans lunch. Chris knew he'd hit a nerve, a big one; now he wondered if he'd ever be invited back to finish what he'd started. He'd gathered more than enough information to piece a story together. There was already plenty of hype written about this pope, but Chris had hoped to dig up a few tidbits of his own, an exclusive behind the scenes story on the daily life of the first American pope or at least some clandestine plan the pope had up his cassock he'd share with an old friend who happened to be a journalist. Chris knew he'd crossed the line; he'd ventured too far into the past inquiring about Sophia. It had been too early in the interview process. Now he'd just have to wait to see if this was pursuable.

Chris sat at a table for one at an expensive trattoria on the outskirts of Vatican City; he knew better than to frequent a known tourist trap but he'd skipped breakfast. He'd anticipated a lavish papal lunch which never materialized, and he was famished. The waiter, a distinguished gentleman in his fifties, came to take his order. Chris ordered in fluent Italian. The waiter was taken aback since most of his customers were Asians or Americans who'd attempt to order in Italian murdering the language in the process.

Chris took his phone out to write a few words in the note section setting. He noticed the earlier call, *Missed Call-L. Jenco,* the face of his cell phone informed him.

L. Jenco, who was L. Jenco? Chris wondered. He checked the exchange to see the location of the call.

"Ah, Trastevere," Chris said out loud. *Must be Lauretta, Sophia's former landlady.*

Chapter Twenty-Five

After spending a sleepless night reading David Kertzer's book on Edgardo Mortara, Sophia had a new worry. If Nevaeh was still alive, she may no longer be in the Vatican. She may never have been taken there, and could be anywhere. From what Sophia read, there was little evidence of any Christ-like behavior going on within the walls of Vatican City. Those who held the power, held on tight; they would stop at nothing to keep their secrets. Chris was her only hope but he'd yet to answer Lauretta's call.

Sophia had asked Lauretta to make the call; she'd felt uneasy reaching out to Chris after all these years. She was ashamed of her past behavior. She'd rebuffed him all those years ago in favor of the inappropriate Joe Morris. How could she face him now? Why should he help her? But he did come looking for her, so maybe he'd suspected something happened to her. She'd just have to wait and see.

Sophia took herself down the hall. Lauretta was preparing a late lunch; the table was set for three.

"Are you having guests? I don't want to intrude."

"Pff, don't be pazza. I've invited my cousin over to talk. Someone in authority needs to be made aware of your situation. It's a crime what happened to you. Another crime perpetrated in the name of religion. Sit now, have some wine, and try to relax."

"I'd rather stand out on the terrace. Your garden's perfume is intoxicating and will calm me down."

Sophia took a gardenia plant gently between her fingers and held it to her nose. The scent was familiar but she had no recollection as to how she knew of it. Lauretta had given her a tour of the plantings. Gardenias had been a new addition. Sophia looked out over the street. Trastevere seemed to pulsate, bubbling over with the palpable exuberance of its natives and visitors. Despite the constant commotion, its quaint ambience, reminiscent of a time long gone, provided a welcome respite for the weary traveler. Sophia would stay here forever if she could.

In the crowd of tourists wandering past the shops, Sophia thought she'd recognized someone, but the doorbell rang and she shook off the thought.

Lauretta buzzed the visitor in, and went to the door to welcome her cousin, Alessandro. Sophia felt relieved knowing someone with authority would be made privy to what had transpired. She sat at the dining room table and took a sip of wine.

"Sophia, oh my God, you're alive."

"Chris." Sophia rushed into Chris' arms without thinking. She sobbed on his capable shoulders. He put his hand on her head and held her tight.

"It's alright, I'm here now."

The doorbell rang again, this time Lauretta held the button down, "Chi e'?"

"Pronto, Lauretta."

Chapter Twenty-Six

Lorenzo waited at the trolley stop on the outskirts of Trastevere. He preferred the Metro but Trastevere was isolated, and the nearest working one was too long of a walk. His phone buzzed, *Severino*. Lorenzo cursed the day he'd gotten involved with this sinister man and his dirty dealings. Now he was trapped. He had to make good on his offer to find Sophia; he shuddered to think what would happen to him if he didn't. But what would become of Sophia and her daughter if he did locate them? Poor sweet Sophia, so many years he'd spent with her. He hadn't lied when he said, "I love you like a daughter." He'd been fishing at the time, attempting to ferret out information, trying to see what memories of hers were surfacing, but a part of him was sincere. Still, it was unfortunate for her that she'd trusted him; her memories had flooded over her suddenly like the waters rising on the streets of Venice. He had no choice now, he had to find her and hand her over to Severino. He'd have to put all emotion aside.

"Pronto, Severino. Si, I followed him to Trastevere. He entered an apartment building owned by an L. Jenco. He's still there. Another man arrived a few minutes later but I'm not sure whom he was visiting. It's a small building with a few apartments. No sign of Sophia."

"I'll look up the name and call you back."

"Lorenzo, L. Jenco runs one of those VRBO establishments. Perhaps our journalist has tired of hotel living. He's probably looking for an apartment. Go back tonight and see if he returns or if there's any sign of the woman."

Lorenzo was tired of his role as Severino's lackey. He had too much talent for this, he was a master mask-maker. He missed his shop, he was pining away for Venice, despite her flaws and watery woes. To him, she was majestic; to him, she was home. Rome made him uneasy. He was unused to traffic. Several times he'd walked without thinking into the road and had nearly been run over by a motorist. He lacked Severino's bravado, he wasn't cut out for this life. He'd told this to Severino many times over the years, but he'd been dismissed. "You're in it now," Severino had told him. If only Sophia hadn't remembered, he could have remained cloaked in his role as her savior, maybe married her despite their age difference. Now it was too late, Sophia was in danger, she may be wandering the streets of Rome where there was no one to help her.

Lorenzo felt his heart aching. If he could find her first, he could send her away, keep her safe, but she'd never trust him again. She must have heard him on the phone with Severino. Why else would she have run off? He'd been so stupid. He should have turned Severino in years ago when he'd first called him regarding the injured young woman. He'd never believed she'd fallen from a car. She'd been attacked, probably by Severino himself. *What have I done?* Lorenzo whispered to himself.

The trolley approached but Lorenzo didn't board. Instead he walked away from Trastevere through the streets of Rome, cautiously this time, avoiding the alleys where the sidewalks were so narrow they made walking in the road a necessity. Lorenzo's wanderings found him at Via del Babuino section. High-end shops lined the roadway leading to the Piazza del Popolo. He glanced in the shop windows and wished Sophia was at his side. He imagined her wearing the latest fashions.

On the cusp of the Piazza del Popolo, a local bar beckoned. There were two establishments side by side. He gestured to a waiter at the first bar who pointed to an empty table facing out. The young host, a teenage lad, not quite a man, flirted shamelessly with a group of Japanese women while attempting to lure them to a table. They spoke neither Italian nor English, and left the young man little choice but to attempt to communicate in their native tongue.

"Sayonara," he said shamelessly. The women giggled, took a few photographs and walked on. Lorenzo shook his head with disgust. *Men,* he thought to himself, *what we won't stoop to in order to have our way.*

"Una grappa," Lorenzo raised one finger in the air in the direction of the waiter. He didn't really like the taste but he ordered the vile drink; he needed something strong. To his right was Piazza del Popolo.

A group of twenty or so German tourists lined up along the perimeter of the bar, blocking Lorenzo's view. The guide spoke in Italian through one of those robotic interpreters. *Nonsense!* Lorenzo thought; he couldn't help but hear her. As an Italian native, Lorenzo knew the guide was incorrect and the piazza was named not for the people but in honor of the poplar trees that surrounded the Santa Maria del Popolo — one of the three churches aligning the square. Looking out at the crowd of people gathering around a local street performer, Lorenzo concluded that the gist of the title remained the same but their purpose had been altered. It hadn't necessarily evolved, he thought, looking over at the Michael Jackson impersonator, who was singing off key to the crowd of tourists around the ancient Egyptian obelisk in the center of the square.

Lorenzo finished his drink, flushed his mouth with ice water, and paid the check. He'd walk back to Trastevere to wait in the shadows of the evening crowds for Chris DeMarco to surface.

Chapter Twenty-Seven

Alessandro Jenco was younger than Sophia expected. He was late forties — maybe — had salt and pepper hair and a thin build. He was off duty. He wore a crisp black blazer over khaki pants, yet he exuded authority. Sophia tried to relax.

"Good to meet you, Sophia," Alessandro said, taking Sophia's hand in his and kissing it lightly.

His dark eyes seemed to look right through her into her soul, "Laura is very fond of you and was very distressed when you disappeared. I hope I can be of some help to you."

Sophia nodded, "Mr. Jenco, this is my former colleague, journalist Chris DeMarco. He is on assignment in Rome."

Alessandro and Chris shook hands, engaging in small talk while Sophia and Lauretta put the finishing touch on lunch. Alessandro, as it turned out, was Lauretta's first cousin once removed, which explained the age gap between them.

"Pff, a cousin is a cousin," Lauretta said as she guided the men to the outdoors.

"Let's move to the terrace, it's not too noisy on the streets this late in the afternoon, and I heard there's a concert outside of the Coliseum. That will keep the crowds out of Trastevere tonight."

The four of them sat at the stone table on Lauretta's gardened terrace. Sophia wrung her hands attempting to compose herself. It was all becoming too much for her: she feared she was about to unravel. She had to hold it together, she had to be strong.

"Go on, now, Sophia. No one is here to judge you. Have some wine and tell them what you've told me. It's going to be alright."

A conspicuous silence hung in the air after Sophia had finished relating the story of her lost and now restored memory.

She told what she'd remembered about her missing child, and who she'd suspected was involved.

Alessandro was the first to speak, "Severino Poverelli's a shady character. Are you sure his was the name you heard?"

"Yes, I'm sure."

"Severino's a fixer. He's hired to fix things for the powerful elite who have gotten themselves into serious scrapes but don't want to get their hands dirty. I'm going to put a guard here, you already know what these men are capable of. They will stop at nothing to find you now that your memory has returned and you are out of their clutches. Even though Severino Poverelli may turn out to be the easiest one to deal with, I'm not taking any chances."

Sophia hung her head, "What do you mean, Alessandro?"

Alessandro took Sophia's hand, "My dear, the Vatican is an independent state, a monarchy, if you will. The Holy See is located within the walls of Vatican City, and it's the governing body for the universal Roman Catholic Church. Pope Joseph Morris, whom you lay claim as the father of your child, is the supreme ruler of this small nation and in essence is the Holy See himself. There's currently no process, legal or otherwise, where a pope can be accused of a crime and removed. Since the establishment of the Holy See, there have been staggering evidences of the Church turning its back and choosing to ignore the suffering in its midst from the persecutions during the inquisition, to the kidnapping of Jewish children, to colonialism, to slavery, to Nazism, and right up to the current sexual abuse of children by Catholic priests. According to canon law, the pope's authority is given by divine decree and it can never be dissolved. It passes from one pope to the next."

Alessandro took a sip of wine. He looked sympathetically at Sophia before continuing.

"The pope's status is sealed by the Vatican Constitution. He has full legislative, executive, and judicial power. His priority, above all else, and at all costs, is to preserve and protect the reputation of the Roman Catholic Church. The Holy See has come under fire in recent years after they not only failed to protect children from egregious abuse by Catholic priests, but they impeded secular criminal investigations by relocating abusers to remote third world countries. International lawyers have argued with canonical lawyers regarding the status of the Holy See as a sovereign state and how that position translates to its obligation to comply with international law. The UN recognizes the Holy See as a state which exists separately from the Vatican State, but the pope reigns over both entities. It's a convoluted system designed to confuse the secular world. But you see, my dear, accusing the Supreme Pontiff of a criminal offense such as you describe, despite mounting evidence in favor of your case, would be futile. Pope Joseph would be both judge and jury. He cannot be tried nor convicted."

"So, am I supposed to give up? Pretend I don't remember what happened? Forget about my daughter?"

"No, of course not. If there were a way to appeal to someone in the Church hierarchy, perhaps someone in the College of Cardinals who may be privy to what has happened, the pope may be pressured to relinquish custody of the child. But their first and foremost task is to safeguard the reputation of the Church. Nothing will stand in the way of their duty so convincing them to expose the pope will be a daunting task. We'll need hard evidence."

Chris DeMarco was eerily silent during Alessandro's disheartening discourse.

"Chris, what do you think? You haven't said a word. Don't you believe me?"

Sophia was frantic. Lauretta got up from her chair, moved behind Sophia, and put both hands on her shoulders to try to comfort her.

Chris lifted his wine glass with shaky hands. He breathed heavily and felt faint.

"What's the matter? Are you ill?" Lauretta asked.

"No, I'm okay, it's just that I've seen her."

"Who?" Lauretta asked while Sophia and Alessandro looked on.

"The child, I've seen the child."

"Where did you see her? Are you sure it was her?" Sophia stood in front of Chris, and leaned her face into his, demanding answers.

"Please, tell me," Sophia sobbed.

"She's okay, calm down, Sophia. I think I can help."

"How? Alessandro made it all sound so dire."

"It's true I'm here on assignment. But it's not what you think. I'm freelancing for a human interest magazine called *In Conversation*, and I'm here in Roma indefinitely to not only interview the pope, but to do my own freelance investigation of his agenda. I meet with him every Wednesday. Two weeks ago, I met the child, I assume is your daughter, Nevaeh, in the Papal Gardens. She was with Cardinal Alfonso Aleo. I think he's her teacher. I looked him up. He's the Bibliotheca of the Vatican Library but he's essentially retired. When his family was killed in a tragic accident he became a priest. He's known as 'The Gentle One.' I think your daughter's safe with him as her guardian. I was with Pope Joseph at the time, the child seemed not to have any relationship with him, and he appeared quite aloof towards her. Perhaps a charade put on for my benefit. But there was something I recognized about the girl. I couldn't understand how I could have known her or anything about her, yet she seemed so familiar. When I inquired as to who she was, I was given the dismissive explanation — the child was the orphan of a Swiss Guard who had been killed along with his wife. There is no recorded incident of the death of a Swiss Guard in Nevaeh's lifetime. I was lied to."

Chris sighed hard, looking up at Sophia, "Sophia, I don't entirely agree with Alessandro's assessment. While Pope Joseph wasn't completely forthcoming with me as of yet, he did reveal that he's mistrusted by the old powers that be in the Vatican. There's a Cardinal Guilo Roselli, a traditionalist who is seemingly his nemesis. I met him as well. If there's anyone to fear, it's him. But, there's something else," Chris tried to remain positive. "I may have overstepped during today's session."

"What happened?" Sophia was becoming increasingly agitated.

"I asked about you. But I did so in an accusatory manner, which I see now was dead on. I haven't been dismissed yet, so I'll show up as planned next Wednesday. I have an idea but let me set the stage first before I run it by you."

Alessandro interrupted, "I'm sure your journalistic skills are exemplary but we're dealing with forces here that may as well be alien in origin. I'm not sure what you have in mind but as I stated before the pope cannot be held accountable. Whatever comes to light as a result of this scandal, the Vatican will handle it as they see fit in order to protect the Church's standing in the world as a universal spiritual leader. We must tread lightly. Sophia, I suggest you move in with Lauretta; you too, Chris. It's best to have you all under guard."

"I've been a prisoner long enough, I won't live like one anymore."

"Allora!" Alessandro sighed. "Okay but I'm putting an armed guard on all of you. He'll be undercover. I hope you're in agreement, Lauretta. I didn't mean to be presumptuous but you are all in danger now, by association."

"Don't you think you are overreacting just a bit, Alessandro? Who's going to harm me?"

"Laura, whomever was desperate enough to hire Severino Poverelli will eliminate anyone who stands in the way of their agenda. Trust me, I've dealt with him before."

Two guards, not one, a man and a woman, arrived an hour later. With suitcases in hand, they looked more like tourists than undercover law enforcement officers from the Ministry of the Interior. The woman was assigned to escort Chris to his hotel where he would check out and retrieve his belongings. He thought all this drama was overkill but he complied with Alessandro's wishes. He'd move in with Lauretta and Sophia, but he would continue with the papal interview as planned no matter the consequences. He didn't need or want an armed escort.

Chapter Twenty-Eight

Trastevere was oddly quiet for a warm evening. Lorenzo was ill at ease, he felt the eyes of the locals on him as he lingered on the corner across from Lauretta Jenco's building. He walked over to the nearest trattoria. From there he could still observe all the comings and goings without drawing attention to himself.

"I'll start with the Jerusalem artichoke," he told the young waiter, "Oh and vino della casa, per favore, una caraffa."

He was halfway through the appetizer when the door to Lauretta's building opened. Chris DeMarco accompanied by a young woman exited and walked towards the outskirts of Trastevere.

"Cameriere," Lorenzo shouted. "Il conto per favore." The flustered waiter appeared with his arms flailing.

"Signore," the waiter raised his hands up in a questioning fashion.

"Conto, la urgenza."

Lorenzo dropped a 100 euro on the table, put the carafe of wine on top of it and ran off in search of Chris DeMarco. He spotted the woman and the journalist as they were about to board a bus. Lorenzo dodged the traffic, waving his hand in front of the window of the bus as he ran in front of it.

"Pazzo," the bus driver yelled while he opened the door to Lorenzo.

Lorenzo shrugged and took a seat within eyeshot of the journalist. Something struck Lorenzo as odd; the two sat side by side without speaking, and the woman was dressed in business attire. *Maybe she's a colleague,* Lorenzo thought. He tried to avoid looking at them. Severino was more equipped for these cloak and dagger assignments. Lorenzo was jumpy and on the verge of panic. He took a deep breath and tried to remain calm. After all, neither Chris DeMarco nor his female companion knew they were being followed. Neither had ever seen him before, Lorenzo reasoned.

Twenty minutes later, the couple got up, waited for the bus to stop, and stepped down onto the Via Veneto. Lorenzo hesitated a moment before following. Once off the bus he stopped and pulled out his cell phone in an attempt to look like a lost tourist. When he glanced up, he found himself staring at the façade of Santa Maria della Concezione dei Cappucini. He shuddered and felt his blood run cold as he recalled the last time he'd visited the spot. He'd been no more than ten when one of his artistic mentors, a macabre older man named Vincenzo Tempesta, decided that Lorenzo's talent needed broadening. He took Lorenzo on a weekend excursion from Napoli to Roma by train. First stop, the crypt under the Church of Santa Maria della Concezione. The crypt's walls held the unburied skeletal remains of Capuchin friars. They had been relocated in the 1600s to this current locale, and had remained as an adornment to remind the living that death comes to everyone. Young Lorenzo shook with fear as he descended into the crypt all those years ago. Without warning, and after his eyes had adjusted to the darkness, he found himself facing the pile of skulls that were stacked along an interior wall nearly reaching the ceiling. The memory of Vincenzo's firm hand on Lorenzo's back as he pushed him towards the ghastly site could still be conjured up in the nightmares that plagued him ever since.

By the time Lorenzo finished reminiscing, the couple were two blocks ahead of him. He caught up to them just as they were entering the lobby of the Baglioni Hotel Regina. *They must give journalists quite the expense account,* Lorenzo thought. The hotel's lobby was posh but people-free; its bar was to the side with an entrance on the Via Veneto where no seat was available that would afford a view of the goings on in the lobby. Lorenzo waited outside, smoking a cigarette and tried to give the appearance he was meeting someone.

It took an interminable amount of time for the journalist and his companion to return to the Via Veneto. The journalist was wheeling one single suitcase, a leather casual messenger bag hung by a strap off his shoulder. It was clear to Lorenzo the relationship between the two was merely cordial, if that. The woman did not have any luggage and Chris DeMarco's could not have accommodated more than a single traveler's necessities. Only now did Lorenzo realize the woman wasn't carrying a purse. No woman Lorenzo had encountered ever ventured out without one. He decided not to mention this unusual duo to Severino. Severino would surely conjure up a scenario requiring Lorenzo's indefinite servitude.

The journalist spoke to one of the bellhops stationed on the street under the hotel's canopy. The bellhop ran to the street to hail a taxi.

Lorenzo caught his own cab and returned to Trastevere in time to witness the journalist and his companion enter the apartment building of Lauretta Jenco.

All day wasted following a man who was only renting a flat. Lorenzo was weary from the stress of it all. He pulled out his phone to make his evening call to Severino.

Chapter Twenty-Nine

It was late evening, the gates of Vatican City would soon be closing, but Cardinal Roselli was still at his desk. Tim Daniels' job required him to remain in his outer office until the cardinal left for the day. Tim had put another call through to Cardinal Roselli from the man with the disconcerting tone of voice. The light on the extension indicated the men were still talking. It had been well over an hour since the call had come through. Tim had grown increasingly suspicious of the cardinal. He intended to uncover whatever was the underlying reason for the phone calls, and the relationship between this man of God and someone who obviously had a different agenda. Tim fingered the empty box of surveillance video software. He'd already installed it in his laptop. Once Cardinal Roselli left for the day, Tim would place the tiny camera in his office. He justified his actions out of a genuine fear for the safety of Pope Joseph. Tim sensed the pope may be in grave danger, and could be harmed at the hands of, or by order of, Cardinal Guilo Roselli, but he needed viable evidence.

Two hours had passed before the cardinal left for the evening. Once Tim secured the tiny camera in a discreet but suitable location, he walked out of the papal offices towards Vatican City. His small apartment paled in comparison to the lavish opulence of the headquarters of the Holy See. It served a purpose for the time being but Tim was growing uneasy. He felt the weight of an unknown entity, some scheme percolating beneath the surface that could potentially be detrimental to the papacy. It was more than just a feeling. Tim knew the cardinal's relationship with Severino Poverelli was untoward to say the least. The man's online profile portrayed him as a self-made gangster who, while not affiliated with any organized crime family, was no less lethal in his methods. Tim was putting himself in danger by dabbling in amateur espionage but it was a risk he was willing to take.

After a sleepless night, Tim found himself back at his desk. Cardinal Roselli's 1 p.m. lunch meeting had been moved up to noon. He was already in his office when Tim arrived at work. Promptly at 11:45, the cardinal walked past Tim with barely a nod in his direction and headed out for his meeting with a Chilean diplomat. Tim knew these luncheons could drag on and he didn't expect the cardinal would return until the next morning. He looked over his shoulder and glanced out the window; the cardinal's driver was opening the door to the black Mercedes Benz designated for Cardinal Roselli's sole use.

Tim used the time to check on the workings of the video surveillance camera he'd set up the evening before. He opened his laptop, stuck in the USB, and clicked the icon. No one was around, he was alone. The discovery that Cardinal Roselli had returned to the papal offices after everyone had left the night before sent chills down Tim's spine. He was accompanied by a gruff man wearing an ill-fitting black suit who stood on the opposite side of the cardinal's desk. Tim adjusted his earphones and raised the volume.

"You have one week to locate and contain the child's mother. After that I'm calling in someone more experienced to handle this. I want the woman dealt with and then we'll make arrangements for the girl. I can't have the woman running around Rome like a loose cannon spilling out some outlandish tale about Pope Joseph fathering her child and attempting to dishonor the Church. As long as she's out there the child has to remain here. First the mother, then the child. You must be discreet. One week, understand?" Cardinal Roselli held up one finger for effect.

"I understand, Cardinal Roselli. Lorenzo and I have been combing the city looking for her. He's been following that journalist. He seems to have checked out of his hotel yesterday, and moved to a VRBO in Trastevere."

The news of the pope's probable involvement left Tim with the sensation that he'd been bitten hard, or that an electric bolt had surged through his body. He felt an unnatural heat rise up his neck, and his heart jackhammered in his chest. While he'd fully expected to uncover evidence of a calculated plot masterminded by Cardinal Roselli, he'd never suspected Pope Joseph. Yet, from the outset, his gut told him it was Cardinal Roselli who held all the power. Tim had been right. The cardinal was in command and did whatever he deemed was necessary in order to keep the papacy at the status quo, and he'd kept his own hands clean by hiring heavy guns.

Now, Tim realized there was more to it. The pope himself was most likely privy to the plans. If the woman's story was contrived, why the need to eliminate her? Tim had been naïve; he'd been indoctrinated since childhood to respect and trust in these religious convictions that were first thrust upon him by his mother, and then cemented in his psyche through years of religious education. Now, free to embrace his own views, he still struggled to dismiss what he now knew about these men: these self-appointed holy men were merely mortal men, nothing holy about them. They'd turned the faith, "the way" set up by a simple carpenter who meant merely to provide guidance for his people to live a sanctified life, into a powerful empire. Their power was limitless, they held sway over multitudes of devotees to the faith, and amassed fortunes to insure the perpetuation of their influence. Tim had inadvertently unlocked the key to a new treasure trove of Church scandals. He'd have to think hard about the repercussions he might incur should he decide to tell what he knew. But the unidentified woman and the child were in danger. Tim didn't have the luxury of time on his hands, he'd have to act. He'd recognized the voice of Severino Poverelli on that video tape; he knew he'd have to find someone other than Pope Joseph to confess all this to and he'd have to do it now.

Chapter Thirty

Pope Joseph walked alone in the Papal Gardens. It was 5 a.m.; lately he hadn't been able to sleep past three, his troubles seemed to be eroding his soul. There was no one to confide in, he had no allies here in Vatican City. Being the first American pope held no cache in Rome; he was a stranger and he was expected to fail. Being torn between his personal problems and Church scandals was taking its toll. He prayed to no one in particular for guidance.

"Your Holiness, I'm sorry to disturb you, may I have a word with you?" It was Cardinal Alfonso. He looked deeply concerned.

"Yes, of course, what is it?"

"I'm worried about the orphan, Nevaeh. I'm aware she has no blood relatives but it may be in her best interest to find someone willing to adopt her. This is no place for a young girl to be living. She's very bright, perhaps a boarding school would be more appropriate for her."

"I'll think about it. It was the wish of her father that she remain here until she turned eighteen."

Pope Joseph wasn't lying, it had been his wish; he'd been advised to keep her within the confines of the Vatican. He heeded that advice but now all he wanted was to be free of her and her mother.

"If she is to remain here at the Vatican, I'd like permission to conduct lessons in the Vatican Archives. She's exceptional, more astute than most children her age. I believe she has the potential to be a scholar, perhaps a theologian. I'd like to broaden our lessons, expose her to ancient texts. I would like to invite several local scholars to meet her and perhaps test her abilities. Would you be amenable to this? I'll arrange it."

The Pontiff raised an eyebrow at the request. "I'll take your request under advisement as well, Alfonso. We'll talk again about potentially moving her, but as far as her education you are the most qualified to make those decisions."

Cardinal Alfonso nodded and left the pope to his wanderings.

Just what I need now, on top of all this, the child needs tending to. Where were the nuns? Couldn't they handle her? Sophia's memory has returned, I know she'll find some way to come for Nevaeh. Perhaps when she's located, she'll accept a bribe. Cardinal Roselli will know how to handle all this. Best to let him deal with it all. The pope mulled over all the burdens he carried.

Tim wavered as he pondered over whether to disturb Pope Joseph whom he'd assumed was deep in prayer. He cleared his throat in an attempt to get the pope's attention.

"I beg your pardon, Your Holiness, I wanted to remind you that it's Wednesday. It's nearly 9:30, people are lining up in the square for your weekly visit with them. The popemobile is ready whenever you are."

"Thank you, Tim. Oh and would you mind calling the journalist, Chris DeMarco? I believe he's staying at the Baglioni Hotel. I'm not up for our lunch interview today, please reschedule it for me."

Tim couldn't reveal what he'd learned about Chris DeMarco's relocation to Trastevere without compromising his clandestine investigation of Cardinal Roselli and his cohorts. He had no choice but to go through the pretense of calling the hotel, asking for the journalist, and then informing the pope that he was no longer a guest of theirs and had left no forwarding information. The growing complexities were becoming overwhelming. Tim struggled to stay one step ahead. To make matters worse, Cardinal Roselli had returned unexpectedly.

"Tim, has Pope Joseph gone to his weekly jaunt in the square?" Cardinal Roselli smirked, it was clear he had nothing but disdain for this promotion of familiarity between members of the Church hierarchy and its people. A once in a while glimpse at the Holy Father would serve to titillate the crowds but this weekly rendezvous would eventually become commonplace and the pope's status as the representative of God on earth would eventually be diminished because of it.

"Yes, he's on his way now."

"What's his afternoon schedule?"

"I think he's unwell, he's asked me to call the Baglioni Hotel and reschedule the interview with Chris DeMarco."

Cardinal Roselli raised an eyebrow before leaving the offices without a word.

Chapter Thirty-One

Chris had barely crossed the threshold to Lauretta's apartment when his female companion, whom he'd learned was an officer by the name of Giovanna Cefaro, employed by the National Center Bureau, a derivative of Interpol, announced, "We were followed."

It had taken Chris and Giovanna two hours to cross town, retrieve his belongings, check out of the hotel and return to Trastevere. Alessandro was still sitting at Sophia's side; the other officer, Vincenzo DeDomenica, stood guard in the hallway. He had a somber, but otherwise expressionless face. His six-foot four stature and sturdy build gave Chris the impression he was under the protection of the descendant of a Roman Centurion.

"What do you mean? I didn't notice anyone."

"There was a man on the street when we left the building, he followed us to the bus, he was the one who hailed the bus at the last minute, he got off when we did, and was loitering outside the hotel smoking a cigarette when we left. He got a taxi after us and followed us back here."

Chris shrugged, "I didn't see him."

"Signore, I'm a trained professional, it's my job to notice such things."

"What did he look like?"

"Black slick hair, combed back, a small gray curl skirting his shirt collar. He was well-dressed in an Italian designer suit."

"Lorenzo Mercuri," Sophia answered.

Alessandro patted her hand. Chris raised an eyebrow before saying, "What do we do now? We can't stay here like hostages indefinitely."

"Lorenzo won't hurt me. I know it, he won't. He probably just wants to talk to me, find out my plans. I don't believe he wants to hurt me."

"I wouldn't be so sure, my dear. If he's working for Severino Poverelli then he's on a mission and I doubt it involves talking."

Maybe Alessandro was right, but Sophia's intuition told her otherwise. No matter what hold this Severino had over Lorenzo, Sophia felt strongly that in the end, Lorenzo would protect her from him.

By 11 p.m., the concert goers had returned to the streets of Trastevere. Energized by the frenetic sound of alternative rock, they filled the bar located across from Lauretta's building in order to extend their evening's entertainment well into the morning. It was Saturday night, most of the crowd consisted of college age students who could spend Sunday sleeping it all off.

"Morettis per favore," an already buzzed young man with a British accent held up all ten fingers in the direction of the bartender. The group moved to the terrazzo and found tables to accommodate them all. Their rowdy conduct had already driven the locals out. The waiter appeared carrying a tray full of beer bottles. Alessandro watched them closely. He'd left his charges for the evening in the capable hands of his two best officers. Alessandro had hoped to find Sophia's Lorenzo Mercuri loitering in one of the cafés. Lorenzo had never been on the Interior's radar before, but he now was a person of interest.

Alessandro walked the streets of Trastevere, pushing his way through the intoxicated crowd hoping to encounter Lorenzo Mercuri. Satisfied that Lorenzo was no longer in the area, he pulled out his phone and called his driver. The driver, while an official employee of the Ministry, sat waiting in Alessandro's personal vehicle along the curb on Lungotevere Farnesina, the drop-off spot for locals and tourists who'd preferred to walk rather than become ensnared in the complex streets of the Trastevere section of Rome. The driver had worked for Alessandro Jenco for over a decade; but this night had been the first time he was hired to partake in an undercover operation.

Chapter Thirty-Two

Sophia stood out on Lauretta's terrace; she held a cup of cappuccino in one hand and with her free hand she pushed aside the fragile branches of a lemon tree that rested against the plastered outer wall overlooking the street, and looked down. The merchants who ran the small shops were already preparing for the day. The sky was brightening but the sun was not fully up. Sophia was antsy, she took a sip of cappuccino, made a face and thought, *I have to get Lauretta's recipe, I've been spoiled for life by her mysterious flavors.*

Everyone was still asleep; she looked around before dumping the remains of the coffee in the sink. Despite being insulated by the nuns in Venice for all those years, Sophia felt freer then than she did now. She had to get out, explore the streets of her old neighborhood, and see what memories could be flamed by familiar surroundings.

Sophia opened the door, tiptoeing into the hallway where the guard was sound asleep on a foldaway bed Lauretta had set up for him. Lauretta, who'd never given birth, had more maternal qualities than most mothers. Sophia smiled when she saw him snuggled under a thick blanket. So much for protection. The two officers had been ordered to take turns on watch.

Once out on the street, Sophia found her way to the café she'd once frequented. She stood at the counter and sipped a cappuccino; it paled next to Lauretta's masterpiece but was far superior to the coffee she'd made. A few people were making their way onto the street. Sophia toyed with the idea of buying herself something; it had been years since she had something new. Returning with a shopping bag would be a sign she'd escaped. She hadn't thought things through and now realized she'd be missed eventually and would incur the wrath of Alessandro who'd been so kind to her. His officers may be fired because of her. But Sophia, enchanted by Trastevere's charm, dismissed the feelings of guilt. She'd never been selfish, but now she needed to live for herself and her daughter. Time was passing and she was no closer to reuniting with her child. Now that she had definitive proof that Nevaeh was alive, she was growing increasingly impatient. Even though Lorenzo was under the spell of Severino Poverelli, Sophia still believed he was a decent man and he would be the one to bring Nevaeh back to her.

Sophia meandered without thinking and found herself in the Piazza Santa Maria Trastevere. She climbed up six steps and sat down at the top of the fountain in order to lean against the façade. The square was filling with camera-carrying tourists. Sophia could spot a tourist even without the telltale camera. Most tourists, she surmised, didn't care how they presented themselves as long as they were comfortable. Uniformed in shorts, tee shirts and sneakers, tourists disrespected ancient churches. Sophia witnessed many of them being turned away because they were improperly attired. The Church had lowered their standards, now allowing women to enter their churches without covering their heads. Shoulders and knees could not be exposed but Sophia knew that rule was short-lived.

Sophia lost track of time, she leaned into the stone wall relishing her freedom.

"Sophia."

Stunned, Sophia inched her way around the perimeter in an attempt to escape without losing her footing.

"I'm not going to hurt you, Sophia, you have to trust me."

"Maybe you won't, but the people you work for will."

Sophia scanned the piazza for signs of a familiar face but she knew that was pointless. Anyone she once knew was long gone, and even if one of her old friends remained, they wouldn't recognize her.

"What do you want, Lorenzo? I trusted you all those years when the whole time you'd been hired to watch me."

"Si, yes that's true, but I grew very fond of you. After so much time had passed, I never dreamed your memory would return. But now, I have to take you with me. I have no choice, too much is at stake."

Sophia nodded. There was nothing she could do. Lorenzo overpowered her, there was no escape. She should have listened to Alessandro. She'd been a fool. Lorenzo pulled Sophia by her arm dragging her down the steps off the fountain. The two were nearing the perimeter of the piazza heading towards the Ponte Sisto Bridge when a loud voice screamed her name, "Oh my God, Sophia, is that you?"

"Look, Zara, it's Sophia. C'mon everyone, it's Sophia."

Zara and Gina were entering the square with a group of seven or eight young friends. Sophia felt relief flood over her but she had no idea how they could help her.

Lorenzo tightened his grip and Sophia winced in pain. Her expression did not go unnoticed.

"Sophia, so nice to see you again," Zara leaned into her kissing her on both sides of her face while whispering, "Is this the man?"

"Si, si, so nice to see you again too. Ciao, Gina."

Zara stayed close to Sophia, she nodded to Lorenzo, while Gina came close and kissed Sophia. She waved the group over; five of them were burly twenty-something young men. Lorenzo was unarmed and no match for them. Severino's insistence that Lorenzo carry a weapon had fallen on deaf ears. Now Lorenzo regretted his choice.

The women's boisterous reunion was drawing attention, people were staring. Lorenzo loosened his grip, giving Zara the opportunity to swoop in, place two hands on Sophia's shoulders and pull her away. Sophia, now free, was absorbed within the inner circle of Zara and Gina's group of friends. The men in the group took her place and stood between her and Lorenzo. Lorenzo had no contingency plan, he hadn't expected Sophia to be rescued. Secretly thanking the heavens he hadn't notified Severino he'd apprehended Sophia, he walked away back into the heart of the Piazza disappearing into the crowds of tourists.

Chapter Thirty-Three

Alessandro opened the door to Lauretta's building with the key she'd slipped into his pocket the day before. He could hear snoring from where he stood on the landing. He approached Officer DeDomenica and pulled the down blanket off of him startling him awake.

"Signore Jenco," the officer stared looking confused.

"Get up, we'll talk about this later. Sophia's missing. My cousin called me a few hours ago. I was in a meeting, I just got the message. Where's Officer Cefaro?"

"Signora Jenco let her sleep in Sophia's flat."

Alessandro pounded on the door. Giovanna opened it a crack, she looked panicked.

"Officer Jenco, what's happened?"

"Get dressed, Sophia's missing."

Vincenzo suffered from severe migraines, he'd kept that fact off his medical record when he'd applied to work at the Ministry of the Interior. Last night's spell left him feeling debilitated, he'd taken too many pills, and had fallen into a deep sleep. His headache was gone but its aftermath left him dazed. He had to pull himself together or he'd lose his job.

Alessandro should have known Sophia would look to confront Lorenzo Mercuri. She'd been desperate to find her daughter, now she may have put them both in jeopardy. Other than sending his two inept officers out to comb the streets, he had no clue where to look for her.

Chapter Thirty-Four

Sophia had expected to be floating in the Tiber by the morning's end; instead she was cocooned within Zara and Gina's group of friends being swept through the streets into a waiting black SUV. Two of the women and one man pushed the middle seat forward and sat in the back, Gina walked around and sat behind the driver. Zara pushed Sophia into the middle and the other two men got in the front. No one spoke as the car sped over the bridge and up towards Aventine Hill.

The car stopped abruptly and pulled up into the driveway of the extravagant three-storied townhouse complex where Oliver had dropped the girls off a week or so before. To Sophia, it seemed like months had passed. Another young man, a near carbon copy of the two who'd come between Sophia and Lorenzo, opened the door and escorted the three women into an elevator. The door opened in the corner of a long hallway where another man nodded to Zara, while gesturing for Sophia to follow the three of them into the penthouse apartment.

The penthouse was sedately opulent, the large open living space overlooked a balcony not unlike that of Lauretta's. *Poor Lauretta,* Sophia thought, *I've put her through so much.*

"Your father's house is beautiful, Zara."

"Actually, this is my house. My father bought it for me when I graduated college. The servants and body guards are his though," Zara laughed. "He's overprotective and insanely possessive of his only child," she said pointing a finger towards her chest. "At least I think I'm his only." Zara laughed again motioning with a backward wave for Sophia to follow her to the terrace.

"There are five guards in residence here, and if you study the landscape around the perimeter of the streets we overlook, he's got at least ten more in surveillance. They all live here in the apartments below."

"If he's so protective, how did you manage to escape all this and end up with Oliver?"

"My father and I have an arrangement. He'd give me a year of freedom as long as I agreed to finish my studies when the year ended. I leave for Oxford next fall."

"I don't want to pry but where's your mother?"

"My mother lives in Milano. Gina and I went to visit her before we took off on our adventure. We were mugged in Verona, had only a few euro left between us when we met up with Oliver, and you know the rest."

"Why didn't you call someone to help you?"

Zara stared at Sophia. "If I did that, the plug would have been pulled on all of this." She waved her hand around the room for effect.

"Tell me about you?" Zara asked.

"I can't involve you in my dilemma, and it's too convoluted to go into. Let me say that there are men more formidable after me than the one you've encountered. They'll stop at nothing to get rid of me."

Zara raised her pierced eyebrow, "This is a fortress, no one will get to you here. Stay as long as you like."

"I hope you don't mind my asking, who's your father?"

"He's a Saudi royal, old enough to be my grandfather, my mother's Italian and twenty years younger than he is. They are still married but live separately. He's set in his ways, but more progressive than most and a big generous teddy bear when it comes to my mother and me. I'm lucky."

"Thank you for helping me, Zara. I'd probably be dead by now if you hadn't come along. It was miracle. Thank God, you were there."

"Allah," Zara said, adding, "Thank Allah." Zara smirked, "You helped me first, Oliver would have left us stranded at that Autogrill if you hadn't come along. We should have something to eat now, we were headed out for breakfast when we found you."

Chapter Thirty-Five

Living out the rest of his life in servitude to Severino Poverelli was not something Lorenzo intended to do no matter what the consequences of it would be. He'd leave his car parked in the alley behind Severino's apartment building and take the train back to Venice. He'd get on with the life he'd begun so many years ago. If Severino and his cohorts came after him, let them. For now, he needed to get home to his beloved Venice and his mask shop.

Lorenzo bought a first-class ticket. The train to Venice would depart in 30 minutes; in four hours, he'd be home.

Tornadic winds and heavy rain greeted Lorenzo when he stepped off the train onto the platform. Sirens sounded the warning of imminent flooding. The polizia posted at the Santa Lucia station assisted shopkeepers in setting up temporary shelters; travelers were being encouraged to stay put for their own safety.

Against his better judgement, Lorenzo settled in for a long night. The whipping wind and pelting rain, fueled by a full moon, drew water off the lagoon and sent it gushing over the low-lying neighborhoods of Venice in a deluge of nearly historical proportions. The next morning the rain was still falling but the wind had subsided. Lorenzo waded in water up to his waist over to the vaporetto station on the Grand Canal. Water taxis had been washed ashore, no one was on the streets, and the vaporetto wasn't in service.

The normal 30 minute walk to Rialto took an hour. Lorenzo struggled to open the door to his shop. When he did, his heart sank. Much of the water had receded, but it was evident by the damage that at least six feet of water had filled the interior. Small bottles of paint floated in the foot of water that remained covering the stone floor. Masks, ravaged by hours spent underwater, puckered up as they dissolved with pained expressions. A large lion mask, the symbol of Venice Lorenzo had refused to sell, remained suspended near the ceiling, it had been spared. Lorenzo took it as a sign that Venice would endure this latest onslaught of Mother Nature's, but it brought him little comfort. He'd never recover from this, he didn't have the strength.

He left the shop without locking it up, and walked over the Rialto Bridge towards San Polo. Tourists, fascinated by the watery phenomenon, were snapping pictures to keep as mementos to show their friends back home. They took no notice of the devastation the locals had suffered; they treated this latest deluge as an event that had been orchestrated for their amusement.

Lorenzo walked on with disgust, his head was pounding and his nerves were frazzled.

The farmacia near his apartment had its light on; it was one of the few establishments that had electricity. Lorenzo paid the woman at the counter for the pills she'd recommended to ease his anxiety. He hadn't been the only one requesting medication, stress levels among the locals were rising at a higher rate than the water off the lagoon. She'd handed tranquilizers out indiscriminately, she doubted there would be any trouble. No one would blame her for providing a bit of relief to the afflicted citizens of her home town.

Lorenzo thanked her and walked off towards home. He seemed unaware of his surroundings, his clothes were soaked through, and his sopping wet shoes were slowing him down. He took them off and walked in the sewage-filled alley that led to his building. No lights were on, he stumbled up to the third floor. No one lived on the first floor anymore for obvious reasons. His landlady occupied the second floor, and his was one of three apartments on the third.

He stripped off his clothes, left them in a pile on the floor, grabbed a bottle of Campari, and laid down on his bed.

Chapter Thirty-Six

Sophia knew it was wrong to wait three days to call Lauretta but she was relishing her time with Zara and Gina. She couldn't remember the last time she'd laughed, really laughed. They were fun and so young. Sophia felt so much older than a woman nearing 40. They'd been kind to her, she felt like part of a group again, and having a servant tending to your every need wasn't too bad either.

"Excuse me, madam, Miss Zara asked me to tell you that breakfast is ready."

Sophia went out onto the terrace where a breakfast buffet was displayed on a large narrow table. Zara and Gina were already seated in front of a wide-screen television that was built into the interior wall. They were watching Sky Italia. The news was on.

"Buongiorno, Sophia. Did you sleep well?"

"Not as good as the two previous nights. I have to leave today. I didn't want to tell you. I can't thank you both enough. I wish I could stay here forever."

"You can come back anytime."

Gina was staring at the television. She pointed to the screen, "Sophia, isn't that him, the guy who had you in the piazza?"

Sophia got up, took the remote and turned up the volume. A young Italian journalist was speaking in English. She lowered her voice as she gave dire news, seemingly directly to Sophia.

"Master mask-maker Lorenzo Mercuri was found dead yesterday of an apparent overdose. His body was discovered by his landlady in his apartment in the San Polo section of Venezia. Maestro Mercuri was the last of his kind, a master of the dying art of mask-making. In other news..."

Sophia's eyes welled up with tears. She wondered if Lorenzo was murdered. Even if he did take his own life, he'd been driven to it.

"Oh, my God, what's next? I don't know what's in store for me. I'm a magnet for trouble all because of one indiscretion. Poor Lorenzo."

"Poor Lorenzo? He was a bad dude. Forget about him, come with us to Dubai, my father's there, he'll love you. We leave tomorrow, he's sending his plane. It's a fun place."

Gina spoke up next, "C'mon, Sophia, don't think, just say yes. It won't cost you a euro. My cousin's father is very rich and very generous. Please come."

Sophia had no time to answer, Alessandro was standing in the doorway accompanied by one of Zara's guards and two uniformed Carabinieri. He was holding *Il Tempo*, the Roman paper.

"Sophia," he called her name with an uncharacteristic harsh tone.

"I know, I'm sorry. I needed time away. I'm so confused, I don't know what I'm doing."

Alessandro placed the paper on the table in front of Sophia. It was opened to an article about Lorenzo. The details of Lorenzo's life and death were laid out in the newspaper for the world to see.

Lorenzo Mercuri, age 63, was found dead yesterday evening in his apartment in Venezia. He'd been dead for at least 24 hours. Police do not suspect foul play. They believe Maestro Mercuri died of an apparent overdose. An empty bottle of pills along with alcohol were found at his side by his landlady who made the gruesome discovery. Maestro Mercuri was found lying naked on his bed, he was wearing a large lion mask. The lion is the symbol of Venezia. Maestro Mercuri was born in Napoli. Having been orphaned at young age, he grew up on the mean streets until his artistic talent was uncovered and fostered by one of his teachers. He was sent to Venezia where he apprenticed with local mask-makers. He was world renowned and loved by many. Locals who knew him, called him a humble man who lived alone; he had no close friends. He was often seen in the company of a young female employee who worked by his side in his small shop near Rialto. She is believed to have died earlier this month. Her clothes were found floating in the Laguna Veneta. Her body has not been recovered.

Maestro Mercuri's mask shop sustained irreparable damage in the latest flood afflicting Venezia.

No next of kin have been located. Funeral arrangements are, pending.

Sophia stood up and put her head on Alessandro's shoulder; she sobbed into his jacket.

"Sophia, you must come with me now. Even though it appears you're safe here in this castle, I need you to be where I can be sure you're out of harm's way. Lorenzo's dead, I'm not certain he wasn't killed, and even if he did take his own life, Severino is most likely still in the employ of someone in the Vatican. We are still investigating but it's probably the Cardinal Roselli you spoke of who hired him. He's a powerful member of the Curia, and seems to be a confidant of Pope Joseph. We cannot take this situation lightly." Alessandro spoke with an official tone.

Zara and Gina sat in stunned silence.

"Zara, I won't be able to join you on your trip, I have a daughter, I have to find her."

Sophia hugged both girls, with promises to see them again. With Alessandro and the police officer by her side, she was escorted out by Zara's guard, handed off to another, and placed in the back seat of an official car. Alessandro sat beside her, "Tell me, Sophia, how does a woman who recently regained her memory, and who'd been isolated in a convent in Venezia for over a decade, meet and befriend Saudi princess, Zara Rashidi?"

Sophia sighed, "Does it matter?"

"No, I'm just curious," he leaned in closer smiling, "very curious."

"I met her and Gina at one of the Autogrills on the Autostrada, actually we met in the ladies room. Lorenzo had stopped for gas, I was asleep but woke up when I heard him on the phone. When he said the name Severino I became alarmed. I knew I needed to get away from him. Zara and Gina helped me; they got me a ride with a guy whom they'd hitched a ride with."

"Why would Zara Rashidi and her cousin Gina need to hitch a ride?"

Sophia shrugged, despite a restful few days, she was suddenly tired and changed the subject, "Where are we going?"

"I'm taking you to my house, Lauretta and Signore DeMarco are already there. You'll be heavily guarded."

"Why? Lorenzo is dead." Sophia's eyes welled up.

"Sophia, with Lorenzo out of the way, Cardinal Roselli will be gearing up. Remember, you're not just a woman looking to find her daughter, you're a serious threat to the Roman Catholic Church. They can't afford any more scandal."

Chapter Thirty-Seven

The official vehicle zigzagged through the streets of Rome with ease, finally stopping near the Piazza di Pietra just beyond the Pantheon and squarely in front of what once was Hadrian's temple. Only the columns withstood the ravages of time. It was eerily quiet for late morning.

Alessandro's small townhouse apartment building rivaled that of Zara's; it was bilevel with glass walls providing a view of a canopied sprawling penthouse garden. The furniture was white, with dark accents. It was stark yet elegant; it didn't look lived in.

"They must pay you well at the Ministry of the Interior," Sophia said, while looking out over the rooftops of Rome.

"This belongs to Lauretta, she inherited a dynasty of real estate from her father. She's loaned it to me 'for-forever,' as she puts it."

"Where is she? Where's Chris? I thought you said they'd be here."

Alessandro opened a swinging door that led to the galley kitchen. Lauretta was aproned and busy cooking lunch. Sophia hesitated before walking in behind Alessandro. The mosaic floor tile was set haphazardly, it had a dizzying effect on Sophia.

"Is the tile getting to you? It affects some people. We'll have to change it eventually. Sophia, you worried me."

"I know, Lauretta; I'm not myself. I'm sorry, please forgive me."

Lauretta nodded, "Lunch will be ready soon."

Sophia found Chris on the landing of the spiral staircase. He'd been sitting in the second floor living room waiting for Alessandro.

"Hello, Sophia. I'm glad you're safe. Alessandro, I'm an American citizen and you are violating my rights by keeping me here against my will. I demand to be allowed to leave. I'm here on assignment and I intend to keep working."

"Signore, it's my job to keep both citizens and tourists, as well as visiting professionals, safe. It was clear that you were the one who led Lorenzo Mercuri to Sophia. He was in the employ of a powerful Vatican entity. I cannot legally hold you here but I must warn you that you're walking into a dangerous situation by continuing your interviews with the Pontiff."

"I assure you, Signore Jenco, I've been in more dangerous places than Vatican City. I will be quite safe."

"Lunch is ready, it's set up outside." Lauretta pointed the way through an opening in the glass wall to the rooftop terrace. A spread of cold and hot antipasto filled the center of a mosaic inlaid table. A heavy silence filled the air.

Alessandro was the first to speak, "There are only three bedrooms here, I'm afraid you ladies will have to share."

"I can return to the hotel or stay at Sophia's apartment if it's okay. I'm a journalist, no one's after me."

"I'm not sure that's true. If Lorenzo told Severino he'd located Sophia in Trastevere then they will use you to get to her. It's best if you stay here."

"I'll think about it, Signore Jenco."

Chapter Thirty-Eight

Tim Daniels had more than enough evidence against Cardinal Roselli to prove him unfit for his position in the Curia. He copied and pasted the video file from one USB stick to another. He wrapped one in bubble wrap, placed it in a small box, and took it to the Vatican post office in St. Peter's Square. The line of tourists waiting to purchase the stamps representing the small country was out the door. Tim sweated through his dress shirt, his nerves were frayed. A half hour later, the package to his mother in New York was on its way along with a note of instruction regarding its distribution should anything happen to Tim. He put the other stick in his pocket, one remained locked in his desk drawer. His lunch break was nearly over, he had to act fast.

Chris DeMarco picked up his phone on the first ring.

"Signore DeMarco?" Tim had been speaking Italian for so many years, he was unused to addressing Americans. "I mean Mr. DeMarco, this is Tim Daniels, I found your number in the cardinal's files. I'm sorry to disturb you, but I must meet with you as soon as possible. I have an urgent matter to discuss with you and it can't wait. We must meet someplace secure."

"Of course, I'm no longer at the Baglioni Hotel."

"I know where you are. You are at the home of Lauretta Jenco in Trastevere. I'll make arrangements to be there in an hour."

Chris grew alarmed, how did Tim Daniels know about Lauretta Jenco? He made excuses to Sophia, and without a word to Alessandro, headed out for Trastevere.

Tim's next call was to the papal offices. He told them he had a family emergency and would not be in for the rest of the day.

It was nearly 5 p.m., when Tim reached Trastevere. Tim found Chris standing outside the door to the Jenco building. He escorted Tim to a local trattoria where they secured a table in a dark corner in the back. Tim was reminded of an old spy movie he used to watch with his grandfather.

Chris ordered an espresso, Tim waved the waiter away. He pulled out his laptop, put the USB in, and pushed the computer across the table towards Chris. There hadn't been much to add to the story Tim had uncovered, the video alone presented the facts. Tim attributed the fact that Chris seemed unfazed by the evidence he'd been shown to his experience as a journalist. Chris remained stone-faced, impartial.

"May I keep this?" was all Chris said in response. Tim shook his head no, he didn't let on that he'd made copies.

"It's the only copy I have," he lied, "I think it's best not to have too many of these floating around."

Tim was nervous and anxious to leave. He'd finished what he came to do and didn't see a need to linger. He shook Chris' hand and they parted company. Tim didn't remember the walk back to Vatican City. He breathed heavily to avoid fainting. He felt the heat of fear rising up inside of him. He hoped confiding in Chris DeMarco had been the right move. He had one more stop to make. Tim flashed his badge at security and entered St. Peter's basilica. The line was short on the side of the confessional of Cardinal Alfonso Aleo. Tim stood behind an elderly woman, he figured she'd be short on sins, and would be in and out in a flash. He was wrong. She was lonely; confession with Cardinal Alfonso was something she looked forward to every week. It eased her sense of isolation to have a once a week captive audience. She didn't have much news, but Cardinal Alfonso was patient and listened to the tales of her neighborhood gossip from one week to the next. Tim was running out of patience, he was thinking of leaving and returning another day, when the woman finally pulled the curtain back and walked over to a pew to say her penance. Tim entered the confessional; he hadn't been in one since his Catholic high school days when he was forced to reconcile his sins with God via the parish priest. His last time was just shy of his graduation thirteen years ago.

"Bless me, Cardinal Aleo, it's been ten years since my last confession. I have no sins to confess, I'm here because I have something urgent to tell you and it's not safe for me to see you outside of this sacred place. Before I reveal this," Tim was on edge and knew he was rambling, he took a deep breath.

"Just tell me, son, I'll try to be of help."

"It's me, Tim from the office of Administration."

"I know, I recognized your voice. What's troubling you?"

For the next hour, Tim relayed the story of his introduction to, suspicions of, and final entrapment of Cardinal Guilo Roselli. He had no proof of Cardinal Roselli's frequent visits to the bar in Rome where Tim first encountered him, but he had damaging video evidence of a potential plot to harm the young girl, Nevaeh, and the woman Tim now believed to be her mother. When he'd finished, Cardinal Alfonso opened the screen between them and Tim slipped the USB stick into the cardinal's shaking hands.

Despite the absence of the true Sacrament of Reconciliation, Cardinal Alfonso gave Tim his blessing, "Bless you, Tim. May God keep you safe."

Cardinal Alfonso sat for a minute, pondering the information he was now privy to. The news he'd heard had not surprised him, he'd long suspected there was something untoward going on in his midst. While he dreaded watching the taped evidence that may implicate the Holy Father, he knew he was obligated to ferret out the truth. He was most afraid for Nevaeh.

A young woman entered the confessional, told him her trivial sins, but the cardinal was distracted and snapped, "Those are not true sins; you are a tourist just wasting my time."

"I'm sorry, father," the woman answered in a tearful voice.

"No, I am, my dear, I just received some distressing news, but it's no excuse. You forgive me. May God bless you."

Cardinal Alfonso left the confessional before the woman had time to finish. He headed towards the sacristy and knelt down to pray in solitude.

Chapter Thirty-Nine

Chris left Alessandro's apartment before anyone else was up. He stopped outside on the street next to one of Jenco's guards; only one was on duty due to the early hour.

"May I have a cigarette? I'm going pazzo in there."

"I left mine in the car, we aren't allowed to have them on our person. We can't smoke while in uniform. Wait here one minute and I'll get you one."

Chris used the alone time, he walked briskly in the direction of the square. He stopped for coffee and a croissant at one of the many cafés in the Piazza di Pietra. Alessandro's warning had fallen on deaf ears. Chris had every intention of keeping his one o'clock appointment with Pope Joseph. He'd been surprised when his meeting had not been cancelled after the invasive questions he'd asked last time; he'd considered the possibility they'd not been able to locate him. He opted out of calling the Baglioni Hotel to see if any messages were left for him, and would take the opportunity to keep his appointment as planned. He finished his coffee, walked into the Pantheon, and latched onto a tour to kill time. The tour guide was telling the disinterested group the history of the Pantheon in a heavy Italian accent. Chris stood on the outer perimeter of the crowd and listened intently to a story he'd heard many times during his days studying Roman art history.

"It's been nearly 2000 years since the Pantheon was built as a temple to all of the gods who were worshipped at that time. It stands today as one of the marvels of early Roman architecture." The guide went on to say, "In the 7th century, the Pantheon became the Church of St. Mary of the Martyrs."

Chris pursed his lips, he wanted to call out but thought better of it. *The Pantheon is a monument to pure pagan genius. It's been buried over time by decree of the Holy Roman Empire. Most Roman Architecture as well as the intricate pomp and circumstance and vestments of purple worn by the clergy in Christian worship ceremonies had pagan origins. The early Church kept some remnants of idolatry and pagan rituals intact while usurping it in order to attract illiterate pagan peasants to emerging Christianity. Chris wondered why pagans and Gnostics had not risen up in protest but had allowed their ancient mysteries to be eradicated. The persecuted early Christians who rose to power under Constantine in turn became the persecutors. Their power still reigns supreme,* Chris thought as he walked the busy streets of Rome.

The Swiss Guard checked the roster, found Chris' name on the list, and granted him access to the papal apartments. But Chris went directly to the Papal Gardens where he'd met Pope Joseph in the past. Vatican City was in a state of flux preparing for Easter. It was arriving late this year; the predicted forecast was for sunny skies with a daytime temperature nearing 70. Pope Joseph would be able to deliver his "Urbi et Orbi" (papal address to Rome and the world) on Easter at noon out on his terrace overlooking the square. Thousands were expected to gather to receive an indulgence for their sins which promised to reduce their punishment after death provided they confessed prior to Easter Sunday. Chris watched the frenzy of activity with a slight interest. It would make for a good story but he wasn't a believer. He felt a slight tinge of envy; he was in awe of the faithful. He wondered if their life was easier or harder than his. He had no fear of death or its aftermath; he didn't angst over the wrath of some spiritual entity who'd single him out for some slight wrongdoing he'd committed in life. He'd walked the straight line anyway, fear or no fear.

As he approached the gardens he saw the child, she was wearing a woman's red sweater. It hung off her shoulders, the sleeves were rolled up, and the color was striking over her white dress. She was barefoot, her feet were dangling in a fountain. Several cats were sitting near her, she had one on her lap. Before Chris had a chance to approach her, he noticed Cardinal Roselli entering the garden from a side door.

"What are you doing out here all alone?" he shouted at Nevaeh, but she seemed deep in thought and didn't respond. Chris remained out of sight on the side of the labyrinth of shrubs.

"Where did you get that sweater, Nevaeh?"

"Shhh! You need to be still, this is a sacred place, Cardinal Roselli."

"Do not disrespect me, young lady. Don't you know who I am? Let me tell you. I'm the next most powerful after Pope Joseph. I'm a member of the hierarchy of the Church," Cardinal Roselli's enraged tone echoed through the trees.

"You act as if you were God, you lack understanding, you're in darkness, you need to be still to find insight. You're not higher or lower, we are all equal."

"What has Cardinal Alfonso been teaching you? Never mind, I don't have time to deal with your nonsensical talk. Don't you know it's Holy Week? You need to prepare for this Sunday when we celebrate the resurrection of Christ."

"Again, you don't understand. The only preparation needed is within yourself. The true meaning of the resurrection is lost in your dogma. Jesus was a shepherd delivering a message, directing His followers towards enlightenment. He is resurrected for the enlightened in spirit not in body."

"Where did you get this rubbish from? It's heresy. You need to stay inside with the sisters where you belong."

"I belong here in this garden." Nevaeh's last remark further incited Cardinal Roselli, he reached over and grabbed her long honey-colored hair. He yanked it until she fell off the fountain's edge, he pulled her by the arm in an attempt to drag her inside. She struggled to free herself. Cardinal Roselli, distracted by the commotion Nevaeh was causing, didn't notice Pope Joseph and Chris DeMarco standing beside him.

"This child's a disgrace," Cardinal Roselli told Pope Joseph when he finally noticed him nearby, "I'm taking her inside where the sisters can watch over her."

"The sisters are busy taking care of the altar linens. They have enough to do. Nevaeh is fine here in the gardens. Leave her alone, Guilo."

"But, she is..."

"Leave her," Pope Joseph spoke sternly to Cardinal Roselli who left without another word. Nevaeh looked up at the pope with her mother's ebony eyes. His heart melted. Chris couldn't help but notice.

Pope Joseph helped the child up off the ground, "Go and get some milk for the cats, I need to talk to Signore DeMarco."

Nevaeh walked off with the cats following her in the direction of the convent kitchen.

"That child is exceptional, I heard her speaking to the cardinal. It was like someone older was talking. It was strange, who is she?"

"She's an orphan, Chris, I told you last time. She's been around adults for most of her life, that's why she sounds old for her age." The pope smiled, trying to lighten the conversation.

"Chris, I'm so sorry but I have to cut this meeting short. My secretary called you to cancel today, but you'd checked out of your hotel and we couldn't locate you."

Chris didn't answer; the pope was uneasy, he looked away as if he was searching for something to say.

"I need to prepare for the papal address and for my trip to South America. I'll be back in three weeks, we can reschedule another interview for when I return. I'll send my secretary out to see you before you leave."

"Your Holiness, my wife is coming for a visit. I was wondering if I could schedule an audience. She's devout, unlike me," Chris laughed. He was nervous, making up untrue stories wasn't his forte.

"Of course, you never mentioned you got married, congratulations."

The pope patted Chris on the shoulder. Chris merely nodded, he didn't want to elaborate on the lie he'd concocted on the fly. Scheduling a sham audience with the pope, he'd decided, was the only opportunity he'd have to get Sophia behind the walls of Vatican City. Once she was face to face with Pope Joseph Morris, the truth would come out, and he'd be cornered and he'd have no choice but to hand over Nevaeh. Chris knew this was a risk but there was no other way.

"Have a safe trip, Holy Father."

"Thank you, Chris. I'll send Tim out to schedule the audience. I look forward to meeting Mrs. DeMarco."

Mrs. DeMarco, I wish, Chris thought as he watched Pope Joseph walk away towards the Papal apartments. A few minutes later, Tim came through the door along with Cardinal Alfonso. Nevaeh was lagging behind with three cats in tow. She was carrying small bowls and a container of milk.

"Tim, this is Chris DeMarco, he's the journalist who's interviewing Pope Joseph. They were friends years ago." Cardinal Alfonso gestured towards Chris.

Tim thought it best not to acknowledge he'd met Chris before. The less explanations given, the better.

"Good to meet you. I'm here to schedule an audience with Pope Joseph for your wife. Will you be joining them?"

"Yes, I'd like that."

"What's her name?"

"It's Sophia." Tim and Cardinal Alfonso looked up at the same time.

"Sophia?"

"Yes, is something wrong?"

"No, it's nothing. I'll need your contact information."

Chris gave Tim his phone number again, but hesitated to give an address. He was interrupted by Cardinal Alfonso before he had time to think up another lie.

"Chris, I was wondering if you would arrange to meet me somewhere while Pope Joseph is away. We are writing the pope's memoirs and you may be of help. We can meet here or anywhere that's convenient."

"I don't mind coming here," Chris told the cardinal.

He suspected something else was on the cardinal's mind. Why meet when the pope was not in residence? It seemed odd. A verbal agreement was made between the two to meet on the day after the pope and Cardinal Roselli were scheduled to leave for South America. Chris noticed Tim didn't register the scheduled meeting in the book of papal office appointments.

Chapter Forty

The noise emanating from Cardinal Roselli's office reminded Tim of the sound a child would make while having a temper tantrum. He could hear books flying off the shelves. As tempting as it was, he couldn't risk looking at the video camera again. He'd have to save that for later. The light on the phone extension lit up indicating Cardinal Roselli had calmed himself long enough to make a phone call. Tim tried to look busy but he was distracted; the air in the papal offices felt heavy, ominous, like something foul was about to happen.

The door to Cardinal Roselli's office flew open and banged hard against the outer wall leaving a gash. The cardinal grumbled incoherently towards Tim and left by a side door. Tim watched out the window as the cardinal's driver opened the door to the black Mercedes. Once it was safely beyond the Swiss Guard's gate, Tim turned on the camera. He'd been right, Cardinal Roselli's office looked like a hurricane swept through it. Tim listened to the phone call.

"It's Antonio Mecelli, it's a go. Pick up Severino, he knows what the woman looks like. The Jenco woman's cousin is an officer in the Ministry of the Interior, they may be staying with him. I'll text you his address when I have it. It belongs to the Jenco woman, shouldn't be hard to find. There may be armed guards. I don't want any screwups. Let Severino drive, he seems tough but he's squeamish. Leave him in the car. No connections back to me, a clean kill. I want them gone." With that he hung up.

Tim was shaking as he punched in the numbers of Chris DeMarco's cell phone.

Chris felt his phone buzz in his pants pocket but he was pushing through the crowd of tourists on the Piazza Navona, and there was no place to stop to retrieve a message. He wouldn't be able to hear it anyway. He walked on; he planned on asking Lauretta if he could return to Trastevere. He would gladly pay the going rate for an apartment of his own. He hadn't been entirely pleased observing the blossoming friendship between Sophia and Alessandro. *What was it about Sophia that attracted her to older men? Didn't she learn her lesson?* Chris thought with disgust.

He was thinking about Sophia, their twisted fates, and reunion. As he walked in the middle of the Piazza Navona, he didn't notice the official-looking car pulling up alongside of him. The windows were tinted; Chris squinted but couldn't see the passengers. The front passenger window opened, Alessandro in a surly tone told Chris, "Get in the back."

Chris opened the door as instructed and was surprised to see Sophia sitting behind the driver.

"Obviously, I can't trust either one of you. Neither of you seem to grasp the gravity of this situation. These are powerful men who will stop at nothing to get what they want and they want you out of the way. Both of you."

Chris wasn't listening; he'd pulled out his cell phone and was listening to his voicemail.

"Alessandro, you need to hear this," Chris played the message Tim had left for him along with the recorded phone call of Cardinal Roselli talking to an unknown potential assailant. Alessandro called the cell phones of the three guards on duty outside his apartment building. When no one answered, he texted Lauretta, "Get Out Now."

The thought of losing Lauretta was too much for Sophia. She began to sob uncontrollably.

"You must get control of yourself, Sophia. This is a crisis. Lauretta's life may be in danger. I can't tend to you. Calm down, and do it now."

Sophia jerked her head back. She was stunned by Alessandro's abruptness. She knew he was right. She took a deep breath, exhaled, and looked up at him.

"I'm sorry. I love her so much. She's the mother I never had, and I can't lose her. It would be my fault and too much to bear. I never should have come back to her."

Alessandro turned away and rolled his eyes. He lost his temper and turned to face Sophia.

"Don't make this about you. My cousin is in danger."

Chapter Forty-One

Lauretta was preparing dinner in Alessandro's kitchen. She was savoring the quiet time when she thought she heard a popping noise emanating from the front of the building, three consecutive pops in fact, each about two minutes apart. She took off her apron and listened carefully at the door; the unmistakable sound of footsteps resonating off the marble entry hall caused her skin to prickle. She grabbed her purse, left the kitchen, and headed for the second floor bedroom she shared with Sophia.

The full-length wall mirror beckoned. Lauretta reached behind it and pulled a small lever downward. The mirror swung forward revealing a large steel doorway set in the wall behind it. Lauretta punched a code into the digital keypad. The door opened as the mirror replaced itself over the wall. Lauretta walked through into a whole different land.

"Thanks, Papa," she said looking skyward.

Lauretta's father had installed safe rooms in each and every one of his buildings in the city of Rome. After the war, he went to great expense to protect *his bloodline from future marauders* as he gently put it. Lauretta continued to talk to her father as if he were there by her side.

"I'm not sure about that bloodline, Papa, I never married as you probably know. There's still hope for Alessandro, he's young, not a direct line I know but he has the name, that's something. Anyway, after all these years, your safe room has proven to be very valuable."

Lauretta walked through the steel hallway towards the living space. The safe room was not just a room, it was a whole house, completely encased in sound proof materials and fully equipped to accommodate a family for as long as they needed to stay, but Lauretta wouldn't be staying. She made her way towards the back room to a long stairway leading to the alley. The wall on the street level was equipped with a two-way mirror; Lauretta's father had thought of everything. The two-way mirror looked out on a muraled façade with cracks and crevices that would appear to all who cared to look to be the effects of the ravages of time; no one would suspect that the fissures in the courtyard wall could open at the push of an interior lever giving way to a hidden sanctuary.

Lauretta looked out, but saw no one. She waited several minutes, exited out through another steel door, locked it with a different code, and watched it disappear behind the mural. She headed towards the piazza. She sat at a café in view of Alessandro's apartment, ordered an espresso, and wondered if she'd remembered to turn off the stove before she left.

On the harrowing ride home, Alessandro made several frantic calls to the Ministry of the Interior. He'd hoped to avoid telling this convoluted story to his boss, but now he feared he had no choice. His car sped through the streets of Rome dodging pedestrians and vehicles en route. He was afraid for Lauretta.

As requested, several cars filled with undercover Carabinieri sat in front of Alessandro's building. The mention of underworld involvement in a potential plot was enough to unleash a small army of military police.

"Wait in the car, I mean it," Alessandro commanded.

Chris and Sophia sat bone still. Alessandro removed a gun from beneath his jacket and walked towards his apartment. The first guard was found face down in the lobby, he'd taken a bullet to the head. The second guard was lying dead on the stairwell, and the third was missing. Alessandro wondered if the missing guard was involved.

Chapter Forty-Two

Alessandro returned to the car and found Sophia still in a state of distress, but now her sobs pulled on his heart and he regretted being harsh with her. Chris was attempting to comfort her but he'd had no effect.

"Get in the front," Alessandro told him while sliding in next to Sophia. He held her hand and put her head on his shoulder. Chris reluctantly did as he was told. This was not the time nor the place to engage in jealous rivalry. It hadn't served him well the last time, and he had the feeling that he'd be on the losing side again this time. There was something magnetic about Sophia, some attraction he couldn't shake free of, but his entanglement with her was overwhelming him. Although he'd asked for it by coming back to Rome and snooping around, he'd let his obsession with her regulate his every move. He realized now if he kept digging into the mysteries the Vatican wanted kept under wraps, he just might end up dead. He'd keep his appointment with Cardinal Alfonso, he'd committed to helping them fill in the gaps in the memoir they were writing about Pope Joseph Morris, but he knew he'd be expected to fictionalize his version of the Joseph Morris he'd known. After he told them what they wanted to hear, he'd return to the US. Writing a candid piece about the first American pope was a lost cause. He saw that now. Honesty was not the policy of the Holy See, they were plagued by immorality and greed. They were masters of deception and had spent thousands of years perfecting their behavior. Perhaps his story lay elsewhere. Alessandro interrupted his thoughts.

"Take us to the Palazzo del Viminale," Alessandro instructed the driver. As the car pulled away from the curb, Lauretta appeared in front of it. Sophia screamed.

Alessandro opened the car door to allow his cousin access, "Where have you been, Lauretta? We thought for sure we'd find you dead."

Sophia continued to sob. Her breathing was rapid.

"You're going to make yourself sick, stop it now," Alessandro ordered.

"It's okay, Sophia, I've lived through worse than this. Look, not a scratch," Lauretta rolled up her sleeves revealing not scratches, but the tattooed numbers she'd never told anyone about.

"Lauretta, what is this?"

"It's what it looks like. I was 16 in 1943 when the Nazis invaded Rome and put us in labor camps. My family survived, that's all you need to know. My father vowed to never let it happen again, and to protect the survivors and the next generation from the horrors we'd endured. He spent a fortune building safe houses within each building he owned to keep us hidden from the world if need be. They are insulated, stocked, secure, and virtually invisible. That's how I escaped this latest onslaught. Now, Alessandro, where are you taking us? Back to Trastevere, I hope."

Lauretta's confession did the trick. With the realization Lauretta had endured unimaginable hardship and loss, and had done so without a whimper, Sophia felt ashamed and quieted down. She wiped her eyes, sat back, and placed her head on Lauretta's arm.

"I have to speak with the minister. You'll be safe waiting for me there," Alessandro informed the group.

The car made its way through the crowded streets. The driver flipped on official lights but the street was too crowded to allow the car, official or not, to pass by.

The Minister of the Interior was waiting in his office; he'd been informed of the day's events. His displeasure was evident. He stared at Alessandro as if willing him to speak.

"I'd hoped to avoid involving you in this convoluted case. I did not expect it to escalate to this point. I underestimated the wide-reaching power that the culprit of this act held." Alessandro's anxiety was showing, he spoke too fast with vague unsteady speech.

"It's time for you to tell me the facts as you know them. I've lost two, possibly three, of my best men."

It took over two hours for Alessandro to brief the minister.

"Where is the woman now?"

"Outside in my car. I'm not sure where to house her."

"This is a sensitive situation involving the Supreme Pontiff and citizens of Vatican City. I don't have to tell you that they do not fall under our jurisdiction. I will have to inform the prime minister. Wait outside."

Another hour passed, Alessandro was called back into his boss' office. He fully expected to be fired. Instead he was informed that he, along with Sophia and Chris DeMarco, would be meeting with the prime minister.

He dreaded returning to his car, it had been parked in the driveway just beyond the gate where armed military security stood vigil. Sophia and Chris were leaning against the car door, Lauretta was laying on a small patch of grass, resting on a makeshift blanket, a pashmina she must have brought with her.

"Took you long enough, what were you doing — solving the Middle East crisis? Did you forget we were out here?" Chris' anger, fueled by pangs of resentment, rose to the surface.

"I'm sorry, I had a lot to report. It was essential that the minister hear Sophia's entire story from the beginning."

"Now what? We can't go back to your house, it's a crime scene."

"Not until tomorrow at the earliest. We can return to Trastevere or find a hotel. You'll be safe, I promise. The minister has promised his own bodyguards to be at your service."

Sophia looked at him with sad, puffy eyes, "Your guards weren't of much help last time. This is all my fault. I need to finish this alone, too many innocent people have suffered because of my indiscretions."

Alessandro reached over and pulled her close. He looked over at Chris, "We have an appointment with the prime minister Monday in the late afternoon."

Chris looked away with disgust, "I'm meeting with Cardinal Alfonso on Monday morning. If I'm back in time, I'll join you, if not I'm heading back to the States as soon as I can."

Sophia gasped, "I thought you were here indefinitely, doing a piece on the pope."

Sophia's feelings for Chris were purely platonic, but still she wanted him close, especially now when she felt vulnerable. She knew he wanted more than a friendship and she hadn't been fair to him, she knew that now.

"I was but it's pointless. He won't reveal any more to me than to any other reporter. He is immune from being charged with involvement in your kidnapping. I doubt he'll tell me any details. Whatever friendship we had is over, past history. There's something else though."

"What is it?"

"I made an appointment for my wife to have an audience with Pope Joseph when he returns from South America so I'll have to wait until after that to return home."

"Your wife?"

"Yes, you. I thought we would catch the pope and his associates in crime off guard. If he sees you, he'd have no choice but to admit that he was involved in the kidnapping of you and Nevaeh, maybe have remorse, and return her out of guilt."

"It's too dangerous. I won't have Sophia acting as bait."

"Excuse me, Alessandro, I'm a grown woman. My goal is to get my daughter out of there and I'll stop at nothing." Sophia burst into tears again, "Please, this has taken so long, I have to find her."

Chapter Forty-Three

Undeterred by the news of shooting victims being found in the posh neighborhood near the Piazza di Pietra or by the headline in the *Leggo* featuring the graphic photo of the dead body of an officer from the Ministry of the Interior floating in the Tiber, a record number of crowds gathered in St. Peter's Square on Easter Morning. It would be several hours before Pope Joseph Morris would appear to give his annual blessing and absolution. Severino Poverelli stood among them, he moved along with a lit cigarette in his mouth. He pressed his weight against the masses of the faithful, knocking rosary beads out of praying hands, until he reached the front of the square just before the flowered loggia below the terrace where the pope would be standing. He stomped his cigarette out with his foot; he didn't want to attract the attention of the Vatican Police, smoking was prohibited. He was visibly shaken. The threatening exterior he'd presented to the world had served him well until now. Cardinal Roselli had connections beyond the penny-ante crooks Severino had been used to dealing with. Last night's job had been more than Severino bargained for. He didn't mind making threats on the cardinal's behalf or battering a woman once in a while but murder was something else. Now he was an accessory to not one, but two, possibly three murders of government officials. If Cardinal Roselli's men didn't kill him, he'd spend the rest of his life in prison. He knew it was too late to make a deal, he was in too deep. At least if he could obtain an indulgence from the pope for his many sins, he'd have a shot at redemption in the next life. He stood patiently up front with the devout Christians who'd been waiting there for days; he'd expected at least a sprinkle of the pope's holy water to fall on his head and hopefully cement a blessing upon him. It was a last act of desperation.

Severino presumed he'd have a closer view of Pope Joseph Morris but he'd stood high above him on a balcony outside the Apostolic Palace surrounded by clergy. The pomp and circumstance surrounding this yearly ceremony included presentations by the Papal guards and Italian Carabinieri. Both Pontifical and Vatican anthems were played before the pope began his speech.

"Buona Pasqua," the pope told the cheering crowd in a poor Italian accent before launching into a lecture on the ills of the world adding a request for prayers for himself.

Severino stood impatiently waiting for the blessing. The plenary indulgence lasted barely a moment. There was no holy water falling from the pope's perch; Severino had been misinformed. Disappointed he pushed through the crowds and headed back to Rome.

He checked his cell phone. *Missed call, Antonio Mecelli.*

Who was Cardinal Roselli fooling with that alias? Severino thought as he looked for a quiet place to return the call. The streets were filled with happy people celebrating the risen Christ. He wasn't one of them. He ducked into an alley, "It's Severino."

"Another botched job, do I have to do this myself? It's imperative that the woman is found and dealt with. I'm leaving for South America in the morning. I'll be back in three weeks. Where are you now?"

Severino hesitated, he didn't want to reveal his whereabouts, he didn't want to let on he'd been in the crowd at St. Peter's. He didn't want to appear weak even though he knew the cardinal had no illusions as to his capabilities.

"I'm walking in the Campo de' Fiori, I'm on my way home," he lied.

"You have three weeks to find the woman. I want her dealt with before I return."

The call shook Severino to the core, he knew his days were numbered. He feared the cardinal was sending an assassin to kill him. He wouldn't be going home anytime soon.

Chapter Forty-Four

Checking the displaced group into a grand deluxe suite at the Hassler Hotel was a brilliant move on Alessandro's part. No one would suspect they would situate themselves in a luxury hotel reserved for visiting celebrities and dignitaries, least of all a cardinal and his henchmen. Sophia and Lauretta took the master bedroom, Alessandro the guest bedroom, and Chris an adjoining double room. Chris showered, toweled himself off, put on the plush designer robe provided by the hotel, and looked out the window at the Piazza di Spagna. The spring-like temperatures normally in the high 60s had been inching up all morning threatening to reach the 80s by noon. Crowds had already gathered on the Spanish Steps. Chris observed tourists sitting on the stairway only to find themselves chastised by the Italian Polizia. Staying in this hotel in this heavily guarded area was a good move, Chris had to admit it.

He checked his watch, his appointment with Cardinal Alfonso had been set for 1:30. The pope and Cardinal Roselli were already inflight and on their way to Peru, their first stop in South America.

Chris opened his door, nodded to the guard in the hall, and retrieved his dry cleaning. The clothes he'd been wearing for nearly 48 hours looked nearly new. He dressed quickly, drank a cup of the cappuccino that the hotel maid left for him, and walked out of his room. The elevator was guarded by two men, one escorted Chris to the lobby. When he followed Chris to the street, Chris turned to face him, "What are you doing? I don't need a babysitter."

"I've been ordered by the prime minister to accompany you, Signore." Chris rolled his eyes, nodded, and attempted to hail one of the cabs that had lined up in the circle outside the Hassler.

"Excuse me, Signore, the minister has sent a car. It's at your disposal," the guard pointed to a black SUV parked in front of the Ristorante Trinitá De'Monte. Chris got in the back seat, the guard slid in beside him, and the car crept downhill in the direction of Vatican City.

Once parked on the Via della Conciliazione, Chris got out and the guard followed.

"I don't think they will allow you access. Why don't you just wait here?"

"I'll wait at the gate in front of the Swiss Guard to the right of the Basilica."

"Seems we'll be joined at the hip for a while so I may as well know your name." Chris looked at the guard raising an eyebrow.

"Officer Gianelli, Signore."

As predicted, Officer Gianelli was not allowed access through the gates to Vatican City. The Swiss Guard on duty directed Chris not towards the papal offices but to the headquarters of the Vatican Gendarmerie.

Chris was handed over to the gendarmerie on duty who gestured for Chris to follow him. He was ushered down a narrow dark hallway to a room labeled, "Directorate of Security and Civil Protection Services." The officer opened the door and Chris went in first; the office turned out to be a series of offices opening onto a waiting area. Chris had been used to the formality of guarded areas surrounding the pope. Both the Swiss Guard and the Noble Guard who surrounded Pope Joseph, and every other pope who came before him, had always been a demonstration of pageantry and nothing more. They were unarmed, but the gendarmerie were a whole different animal. They were armed and seriously so.

"Wait here for one minute, Signore." Chris did as he was told. He was nervous and began to wrack his brain searching for some infraction that he may have committed against the papacy to incur this kind of detainment.

The officer returned, he took Chris through what looked like the inner sanctum. They entered into the offices of the Inspector General towards an interrogation room.

"Excuse me, am I under investigation for something?"

The officer didn't respond; he unlocked the door. Chris looked up, he was in a conference room. Seated at the head of the table was Cardinal Alfonso, another member of the clergy sat to Cardinal Alfonso's right, and a decorated uniformed man was seated at the opposite end. Several other uniformed officers stood at attention around the perimeter of the doorway.

"Come in, Chris, and have a seat please," Cardinal Alfonso instructed, Chris remained standing.

"Am I in some kind of trouble?"

"No, no, I'm sorry for this but it was necessary for us to meet here. This is canon lawyer, Cardinal Giuseppe Giordano, and Inspector General Contini." Everyone nodded towards Chris.

"Now please sit. As you've probably surmised, we're not here to discuss Pope Joseph's memoir." Cardinal Alfonso looked at Chris with a look of expectation.

"No, I guess not. What's this about?"

"Rather than go into a lengthy, convoluted diatribe, I'd like you to look at something."

One of the officers clicked on a computer screen. Once invisible to the naked eye a television screen embedded in the wall came to life. The officer turned up the volume, a familiar voice filled the room. Chris watched as Cardinal Roselli came into view. He was sitting behind a desk facing a sinister-looking man. Chris listened as the Cardinal spewed out instructions to the man he called Severino. They included trailing Chris in the hopes that he would lead them to the woman. He remembered Sophia saying the name of the man who'd physically taken the baby all those years ago, and how he reported via cell phone to a Cardinal Roselli. Despite having seen this before, seeing Sophia's story playing out like a newsreel unnerved him. Chris hung his head, he'd led them directly to her. Chris felt it was unwise to reveal any prior knowledge of this damning information. He noticed Tim was not present at the meeting. He had no intention of betraying his trust. He'd spent many a night in jail for refusing to reveal his sources. He'd feign ignorance and tread lightly with this precarious group.

When all the vile evidence had played itself out, the cardinal was the first to speak, "Can you offer us any insight into this? We have our suspicions but we'd like to know if you can add to this. Tell us what if anything you know about the woman and the child. You don't seem surprised by this revelation."

"Considering the history of the Vatican, why would I be surprised?"

Cardinal Alfonso winced at the remark, "Please, Signore DeMarco, any information you can give us would be appreciated."

"The woman referred to on the tape is a former colleague of mine, she came to Roma to study and remained after finding a job at Sky Italia. She was fluent in Italian, and helped me and the then Monsignor Joseph Morris brush up on the language. She claims she and Joseph had an affair. Sophia became pregnant and gave birth a few months before Joseph Morris was elected pope. She told me she thought he'd been the one who'd tried to send her back to the United States with the baby but now she's unsure if that's the truth. The man in the video, Severino, under the pretense of being a taxi driver, took Sophia and the baby. Apparently, he claimed there was only one seat belt in the back of the cab and he insisted Sophia sit up front. Sophia noticed the picture of the driver was not Severino, they struggled, and she sustained injuries in the process. She woke up weeks later in a convent in Venezia with no recollection of what had occurred. Twelve years later her memory returned. Her first thought was to find her daughter. She sought the help of her employer, Lorenzo Mercuri, the famed mask-maker, who unbeknownst to Sophia had been a childhood friend of Severino's. Lorenzo agreed to drive Sophia to Roma where she intended to confront Pope Joseph. On the way, she learned of Lorenzo's plan to turn her over to Severino. This is moot now since Lorenzo committed suicide. Sophia had taken money from the Reverend Mother, she managed to escape, and found her way here, stopping first at the home of her former landlady in Trastevere who agreed to enlist the help of her cousin, Alessandro Jenco, who works as an officer in the Ministry of the Interior. The prime minister was informed after the officers who were guarding Officer Jenco's home were killed. His guards brought me here, they are waiting outside."

Chris threw in that last bit of information in case he found himself in a precarious situation. He knew very well that the Vatican didn't play by international rules. They were masters of the cover-up.

"Grazie, Chris. We are in a difficult situation."

"What are you going to do? The child was kidnapped, Sophia was intentionally harmed. Her story has been consistent no matter how many times she repeats it," Chris could feel his temper getting the better of him.

"We have every intention of handling this, Signore DeMarco," Inspector General Contini told him.

"Yeah, I've seen how the Vatican handles such matters. Did you honestly believe the child was the orphan of a Swiss Guard?"

"No, Chris," Cardinal Alfonso spoke softly, "I knew that was not the truth but we are bound by Church law. The pope cannot be judged by anyone."

"Unless," Cardinal Giordano said, "it can be proven he's strayed from the faith."

"Cardinal Giordano is a dear friend of mine and an expert in canon law," Cardinal Alfonso interrupted.

Cardinal Giordano continued, "It would require us to have hard facts regarding the parentage of the child. In other words, we would need to have the DNA samples of both Pope Joseph Morris and the child in question. The pope may not agree. If I were to counsel him, I'd advise him against it. As far as Cardinal Roselli is concerned, he's guilty of conspiring to commit murder as well as a myriad of other offenses including orchestrating two kidnappings and the killing of three government officials, all of which, in the outside world, would carry life sentences. We, however, are not the outside world. With regards to a criminal charge against a cardinal, the pope is the one who determines procedure. It's out of our hands."

"The pope and the cardinal are traveling now; can't the Italian police arrest Cardinal Roselli at the airport when he returns to Roma?" Chris asked but he already suspected this would never happen.

"No, Signore, we do not fall under the jurisdiction of the Italian government. We are our own Sovereign Nation. Pope Joseph is essentially the Holy See itself, only the pope has authority over the cardinal. If charges are filed, the pope determines what procedure will be followed to bring justice."

"Justice? It sounds to me like you have no idea how to handle this. As far-fetched as this scenario may appear to you, it's true, and I'm sure the outside world will find it fascinating."

Chris knew he may have gone too far with his last statement. They could keep him here indefinitely if they wanted to. Prodding them to do what's right by hurling the threat of exposure may not have been the wisest move on his part.

"I assure you, Chris, we know the gravity of this and we have no intention of turning a blind eye to any of it. I know that you and your wife have an audience with Pope Joseph when he returns. Am I right to assume, you don't have a wife, and that the wife you refer to is Sophia, the child's mother?"

Chris merely nodded, he didn't trust any of these people.

"I thought so. I will use the time we have left to prepare the child. I promise you that with the help of God we will find a solution and penalties will be paid for the crimes committed."

Chris wasn't so sure. He knew enough about convoluted canonical law, and its lame attempt punishing crimes committed by the clergy, to know they would probably bury this.

"I'd like to leave now," he said while getting up from his chair. "I don't think I have anything else to add. I'll see you again at the Papal Audience. If you have more questions for me before that, Mr. Daniels knows how to reach me."

Chris nodded to the group and left the room; in the hallway he encountered the same guard who'd brought him in earlier and assured him that he'd find his own way out. Chris breathed a sigh of relief once outside in the square. The sun had already set, he must have been inside that office for several hours. It never occurred to him that Officer Gianelli would be waiting for him. But there he stood next to the small Swiss Guard gate to Chris' left.

Once safely guarded inside the official car, Chris stuck his hand in his pocket and clicked off his tape recorder. If these so-called holy men continued to practice what they so vehemently preached against or if the crimes they've committed went unpunished, Chris had all the evidence he'd need to pull back the opaque curtain cloaking Vatican City and expose them all.

Chapter Forty-Five

"Where are you taking me? This isn't the way back to the Hassler."

Chris had enough intrigue for one day, he was exhausted, and wanted nothing more than a hot shower and a night of mindless Italian television.

"Sorry, Signore, Prime Minister Abenante instructed us to take you to his office. He's awaiting you with the Signora and Officer Jenco. Please forgive me for not informing you."

Chris sat back in his seat. Sophia had lit a spark all those years ago and inadvertently dragged him into a conspiracy of epic proportions, and even though he was in the thick of it, Chris knew he'd never be allowed to print a word of it. They'd kill him before they'd let that happen.

Matteo Abenante was younger than Chris expected. He was speaking in Italian to Sophia when Chris entered his office. The language, while clearly Italian, was not Roman, it was Venetian. Sophia, having spent over a decade among the Venetian people, was adept at the dialect.

"Grazie, Signore DeMarco, for coming here at this late hour. I apologize for the inconvenience, but rather than meet you another time, I thought it best if we all gathered at once to review the matter at hand."

"Prego, Prime Minister Abenante, as you know I've just left a meeting with Cardinal Alfonso Aleo. The meeting took place in the headquarters of the Vatican Gendarmerie; there were several men in attendance: Inspector General Contini, Cardinal Giuseppe Giordano, an expert in canon law, and Cardinal Alfonso Aleo, of course. Apparently Tim Daniels, an assistant, had suspicions about Cardinal Guilo Roselli, the confidant to the pope. He set up audio/video equipment in the cardinal's office for leverage should he need it. Cardinal Alfonso is well aware of Cardinal Roselli's involvement in both Sophia and her daughter's kidnappings, and the killing of the officers of the Interior. He has the evidence — Cardinal Roselli admitting to it all on tape to a Severino Poverelli, the man he hired to do his dirty work. In reading between the lines, despite assurances to the contrary, I'm convinced the Church will cover it up. There's no tangible evidence of the pope's involvement. The child remains sequestered in Vatican City. Cardinal Alfonso asked for us to give him time to prepare her to reunite with her mother. He didn't elaborate. We are on schedule for Sophia to meet with Pope Joseph when he returns from South America."

Chris looked up at Prime Minister Abenante. He was unused to all this formal bantering.

"Mi dispiace, I'm sorry to be so bold as to speak first. I felt you should all be aware of what has transpired. We had no idea anyone in the Vatican knew anything about this before now. Apparently, they'd been told that the child was an orphan of a Swiss Guard. I, too, had been told so by Pope Joseph himself. No Swiss Guard has died during Nevaeh's lifetime. Pope Joseph lied."

"Allora, Signore DeMarco, our hands are tied. The Curia holds the cards, they alone will be the ones to pressure Pope Joseph to deal or not deal with Cardinal Roselli. He's a member of the papal household and a citizen of Vatican City. We have no jurisdiction over him unless he is defrocked and leaves the country. Only then can we step in, but only the pope has the power to remove a cardinal. The Holy See is fiercely protective of the sanctity of the sacraments and the Holy Orders in particular. It has been their practice to send the felonious clergy off to remote parts of the world where they are rarely heard from again but free to continue their illicit activities."

Sophia's anxiety was visible, her eyes reflected nights without sleep. No one noticed, men wouldn't, and Lauretta hadn't been included in this meeting. She remained quiet while the prime minister related his past experiences dealing with the archaic, mysterious Church. Her frivolous affair had led to the deaths of three men and possibly Lorenzo as well. Sophia's ability to cope with it all was waning. She felt invisible, the men talked around her.

"I'm a lawyer, and while my former practice was international law, I'm proficient in canon law. Let me put it this way, Mother Church will put pastoral duties aside in order to protect her reputation. There will be no regard for her children she's put at risk, they've been cast aside in the past, and will continue to be in the future," the prime minister shrugged.

Sophia interrupted him in a tearful, shaky voice, "Signore, Abenante, you speak in metaphors while I remain a victim of an unspeakable life-altering injustice. These guilty men of God have all the power, they make laws that suit their purpose and serve to insulate them from prosecution. Let me remind you, three men have been murdered by order of Cardinal Guilo Roselli, and let me ask you this, Signore, where does that leave me, my daughter, and the families of those men who want answers? If I don't have justice, and reunite with my daughter, I will take this story to the masses. I'm sure it will be believed considering the declining reputation of the Roman Catholic Church."

"My dear, I appreciate your situation and I assure you this office will put pressure on the Vatican to comply with your wishes." The prime minister lowered his head, tilting it to the side in a fatherly manner.

"With all due respect, I'm not your dear, I've had enough of the excuses regarding Vatican opacity. I've no intention of giving up, I will pursue this for as long as it takes. I've every intention of keeping the appointment Signore DeMarco has made on my behalf. I will confront the pope directly when he returns."

"That may be unwise of you. I don't have to tell you we're dealing with a formidable adversary here who holds all the cards."

"I don't care, I've wasted enough time. You all are doing a political dance while my daughter may be in danger. If they move her elsewhere, I will lose her forever."

Chapter Forty-Six

Cardinal Alfonso sat on a stone bench in the Vatican gardens. Nevaeh was nearby feeding a flock of sparrows. Cardinal Alfonso checked his watch, he expected the group of theologians from several of the local Pontificia Collegios to arrive at 1 p.m. Nevaeh had demonstrated a vast innate knowledge, an insight he'd not been the one to spark. He had only a few minutes to prepare her. The papal staff was already setting up a few chairs in the garden. Alfonso knew it would be where Nevaeh would be most comfortable. He wondered if she had any idea her life was about to change drastically. He'd have to prepare her for that as well.

"Nevaeh, come here for a moment. I have something to tell you."

Nevaeh looked up, dropped the remaining bird seed on the ground and moved towards Alfonso.

"Si, Papa, is something wrong?"

"No, no, nothing's wrong. In a few minutes, visitors will gather here. I've invited them to meet you."

"Me, why?"

"Because as time has gone by, your knowledge of life matters has surpassed not only my expectations, but you're advanced for your age and experience. I've called in several local scholars to question you so I may better plan for your future education."

Nevaeh nodded unfazed by the news. She looked over at the workers unfolding chairs on the open lawn, "Papa, if I'm going to be questioned, I'd rather walk the gardens with the visitors."

Alfonso waved to the workers. He approached them and told them to remove the chairs just as Tim Daniels appeared with the seven scholars in tow, two monsignors, an Imam, the Bishop of the Pontifical Greek College, a Rabbinical scholar, the Abbot of Rome's Buddhist Temple and a Hindi Swami. Nevaeh curtsied;

the group raised a collective eyebrow at the old-world greeting. Aside from Cardinal Alfonso Aleo, Nevaeh's teachers had been an assortment of European nuns, many of whom had been schooled in the pre-Vatican II era where children bowed and curtsied out of respect for the clergy and their elders. Cardinal Alfonso worried about Nevaeh's ability to fit into today's society where she would soon find herself.

"Shall we get started? This is Nevaeh. I've told you very little about her because I think it best that you remain unbiased as you pose questions to her. She prefers to walk the gardens to talk casually surrounded by nature."

The abbot was the first to speak, "Do you find yourself most comfortable in this garden surrounded by nature?"

"If you look closely at nature it will teach you how to live. I sense the outside world is a troubled place. Even within these walls," Nevaeh waved her hand in the direction of the Apostolic Palace, "there is a lot of arguing and disagreeing going on, lots of anger causing the air to be heavy. In nature, in this garden, the air is light, small trees, chubby, stumpy trees, flowering shrubs, tall trees or thin sticky trees," once again Nevaeh waved her hand over the landscape, "all exist together, one doesn't overpower the other or choke it with its roots. Look at the birds, the dove is a shy creature who rests beneath the tree while the jay drops seed from the feeder to the dove below. Nature takes from nature just enough of what it needs to survive. Nature achieves balance and intuits what is enough. Nature can't be controlled, rain can't be stopped, the heat of the Roman sun can't be lowered at will but nature adapts. I'm never alone out here."

The abbot, and the swami glanced at each other, both nodding in Nevaeh's direction.

"Do you believe in God, Nevaeh?" the rabbi asked.

"What does it matter what I believe? Everyone must follow their own belief, the way of life they learned as children, but life is only known through the living of it. Find yourself and be open to others and then you will know a limitless God. You are more than you think you are. Free yourself and belief will be enabled."

The rabbi breathed heavily, he was awestricken. The monsignors were traditionalists, the elder of the two addressed Cardinal Aleo rather than Nevaeh, "Who has been feeding this child's head with these teachings? You?"

"I have not, I taught her as any other child would be taught. She began to initiate discussions that demonstrated an advanced insight. It was why I called you all. I suggest you address her respectfully."

The monsignor turned towards his colleague, and grumbled something no one else could hear. The other whispered back and then asked Nevaeh, "What is it you believe of Jesus?"

"The concept of Jesus, as he's been presented, has served the Church for centuries. Let's suppose the word of God as handed down was an authentic heavenly declaration and not a narrative manufactured by early religious scholars to keep its people in line. Was not human sacrifice a pagan ritual condemned by God the father? If so, how is it true that he required His son be sacrificed and His children made to worship His death over and over by bowing their heads towards the replica of the cross He died on? That was not the way. A divine being cannot suffer. Jesus was a teacher, His teachings were understood by only a few of His followers, the rest misinterpreted His words. The remnants of those words were further embellished to suit the early patriarchal Church fathers' agendas and continue on today. God created man or did man create God?"

"This is blasphemy," the monsignors cried out at once, "you are a mere girl, a young one at that, what do you know of anything regarding scripture?"

"I know that Jesus was a revealer, we as a people didn't need to be saved, we needed to know ourselves. You are quick believers in Jesus as God, the prophets David and Isaiah, Mohammed, Buddha, the Hindu Deities; they all came to you as revealers of your truth, yet you do not believe there can be another. You are smart but you lack wisdom. Your centuries-old traditional institutions rely on ritual and rote doctrine, all of them burdening the soul. The need for balance is around you but you don't see. I'm merely a girl, but females will restore balance when they are allowed in, only then will you find peace." Nevaeh went on, "You may recognize this from Wisdom 9:34. *For in the beauty of both the man and the woman is God likewise formed, for this mystery I will make known in your hearing, that you are likewise two seeds cast down into the earth, that by your living you might give rise to a nobler form, even Lords many and Gods many.* I will leave you with this: keep in mind, those among you who know, it's the third message from Fatima, *Heaven's wisdom of God will lead you.*"

Nevaeh held two corners of her white dress in her hands, faced her interrogators while glancing at Cardinal Alfonso, curtsied and walked off towards the garden's labyrinth.

Cardinal Alfonso escorted the group towards the papal offices. The monsignors were grumbling to each other, and as Cardinal Alfonso came near, the elder of the two spoke, "Your Eminence, with all due respect, we were wondering if Cardinal Roselli was aware of the child's ramblings?"

"Ramblings? Is that what you think she's doing? You are fools stuck in the muck of old dogma. Cardinal Roselli has no business with the child. Pope Joseph has designated me as her educator without reservation. He is aware of her insight. Last time I checked the Supreme Pontiff had the last and final word on all that goes on within these walls."

The monsignors both nodded, but they knew otherwise. Pope Joseph was merely a figurehead, not only ignorant in all matters pertaining to the political and day to day business of the Holy See, but he had only a feigned interest in any of it. He preferred the limelight and the celebrity aspect of papal rule. He relished the devotion of his followers, eating it up like a teen idol. Cardinal Roselli held the reins. This was common knowledge among the local clergy.

The group thanked the cardinal for the opportunity and said their goodbyes. The abbot was the last to leave.

"Cardinal Alfonso, thank you for including me. The experience for me was awe inspiring. The child is a gift, she's what we call, 'Prajnaparamita,' which means..."

Cardinal Alfonso interrupted the abbot, "The wisdom of seeing nature."

"Yes, in a sense. She has been untouched by outside influences; her high intellect has fueled her desire to search for meaning. She has nearly perfected her abilities. She is what your gospels refer to as 'Ruah.'"

Cardinal Alfonso was impressed with the abbot's knowledge of Judeo-Christianity.

"Yes," he replied, "she has breathed a new way of thinking into this stodgy institution."

"Perhaps she has, but is it the right time for her? I propose this to you: should her teachings, which is what they are, reach the ears of anyone else outside of your realm, she will most certainly be in danger and then you must come to me. The words she speaks will upset the status quo firmly rooted in the minds of the traditionalists who are in power. When it becomes too much for you to handle alone, you may send her to me for safekeeping."

Cardinal Alfonso bowed his head in the direction of the abbot, "Grazie, for your friendship and tolerance. I will call on you if need be."

The abbot nodded, bowed towards Cardinal Alfonso and walked off; his tan robe brushed the marble floor and trailed behind him as he descended the stairs and exited towards St. Peter's Square.

Cardinal Alfonso was left alone with his thoughts. He wondered if he'd done the right thing by inviting scholars in to examine Nevaeh. They hadn't asked many questions yet seemed quick to judge. He wondered if the monsignors would brush her off as a ranting child whose little bit of knowledge fueled a fantasy world of her own making, or they would be threatened. He had a new fear: if they informed Cardinal Roselli, Nevaeh would be endangered. Cardinal Roselli had already ordered the murder of the officers of the Interior. He'd had Nevaeh kidnapped once, he could easily do it again. His power ran beyond the scope of what Cardinal Alfonso had originally thought. There were insidious forces working behind the scenes, the evidence spoke for itself. He had to be careful and he had to work fast to safeguard his prodigy.

Chapter Forty-Seven

Pope Joseph Morris and Cardinal Guilo Roselli were winding down their South American tour in Santiago, Chile. The indigent people were devout and came out in droves to greet the Pontiff. He was in his glory and savored the attention. It was only when he was expected to speak that he had reservations. It was easy when he was young, back then he was in his element, giving homilies to Sunday churchgoers. He kept these speeches vague, he spoke in metaphors, presenting the utopian idea of a world united by love. The masses ate it up and cheered, hanging on his every word.

Cardinal Roselli handled the political entities. He met with both Church and diplomatic leaders; he didn't offer any information regarding these gatherings and Pope Joseph didn't care enough to ask. Cardinal Roselli was in his glory, he spoke fluent Spanish, having grown up in southern Chile. His family had emigrated to Chile from Italy, had profited greatly from the locals' lack of interest in commerce and had instituted a fish farming enterprise in the remote Magallanes Region. Afterwards they'd diversified into other conglomerates, sheep farming and lately oil drilling. They were among the wealthiest families in South America. Guilo had been raised by his paternal grandparents. He was shipped off to boarding school in England and then to seminary in Rome. He hated being away from his beloved Chile, but he'd soon become enamored of the power bestowed on him by the Curia. But Chile was where Guilo Roselli planned to retire.

"Cardinal Roselli, there's a call for you from Roma, it sounds urgent."

Cardinal Roselli was taken aback to receive a call from Monsignor Victor Evans, one of the leading religious scholars on the faculty of the Pontifical College in Rome.

"This is Cardinal Roselli, how may I help you?"

"So sorry to disturb you while you're on your trip but a matter has come up that needs your attention."

For the next 30 minutes, Monsignor Evans recited verbatim the ramblings of the child, Nevaeh. He called her the "gnostic tool" of Cardinal Aleo, and accused the cardinal of heresy.

Cardinal Roselli knew it was time to deal with the child; he'd grown tired of the ineptitude of his hired hands. After Joseph Morris confided in him that he'd feared his former relationship with a young woman in Rome would be a detriment to his reign as Supreme Pontiff should she decide to go public, Cardinal Roselli assured the newly-elected pontiff he would take care of it. To avoid suspicion he'd used his own money to fund first Severino Poverelli, then Lorenzo Mercuri in the orchestration of the plan to eliminate the mother and sequester the child. When Severino and Lorenzo proved themselves inept, he once again authorized the release of personal funds to hire members of an organized crime family to step up his game plan. He was out of patience; the heat was on after officers were killed in the line of fire meant for the child's mother. It was a matter of time before the trail led back to him, someone was bound to talk. In a few days he'd be back in Vatican City where no one could touch him no matter the crime. Pope Joseph Morris was the only one who could authorize the dismissal and potential prosecution of a cardinal, and Pope Joseph was Cardinal Roselli's puppet. But he hadn't counted on this latest development. Now the child Nevaeh had been exposed to clergy outside of the auspices of Vatican City as well as the journalist friend of the pope's. An uncontrolled rage swept over him; he picked up the phone and called his office in the Vatican.

"Tim Daniels, how may I direct your call?"

"Ah, Tim, it's Cardinal Roselli calling from the other side of the world. How are you, my friend?"

"I'm well, Your Eminence, and you?"

"Molto bene, it's wonderful to be back home. Is Cardinal Aleo available? I must speak to him, it's a matter of importance."

Tim had no idea what Cardinal Roselli was referring to when he mentioned being back home. He'd assumed the cardinal was Roman, born and bred. He put the call through to Cardinal Aleo but remained on the line in case a witness was needed.

"Alfonso, Guilo here."

"How's the trip?"

"It's fine, bene, but this is not a social call. I'm calling because I received a distressing call from Monsignor Evans. He's informed me he was called to examine the child, Nevaeh, as you claimed she's exhibiting theological prowess. Is this true?"

"Yes, but I don't see how it's of concern to you, Guilo. I've been given full authority over her education by Pope Joseph himself. I did as I saw fit. She has exceptional insight."

Cardinal Roselli felt his face redden, he was hot with anger. "Alfonso, this child should not be allowed to be exposed to anyone outside of the Apostolic Palace. Is that clear?"

"She's already met with several local religious leaders as well as the journalist, Chris DeMarco. Is she a threat to us?"

Cardinal Alfonso feigned ignorance to test the waters.

"Just keep her sequestered. I demand it." With that he hung up the phone.

Tim entered the inner office and knocked on Cardinal Aleo's door, "Your Eminence, forgive me but I stayed on the line in case there was more trouble brewing."

"As you heard, the child may be in danger. Cardinal Roselli's becoming desperate. Please get Chris DeMarco on the phone for me. I believe you have his number."

Chris answered on the first ring. He was expecting a call from his editor regarding a freelance piece he'd written; he was surprised to hear from Tim Daniels, "Ciao, Tim, what's up?"

"Cardinal Alfonso Aleo wishes to speak to you."

Tim handed the phone to the cardinal and left the room. If Cardinal Aleo wanted Tim to be privy to the call he would have invited him to remain in the room. Tim suspected Cardinal Aleo was protecting him from the wrath of Cardinal Roselli, but Tim had been the one who'd initiated the downfall of the cardinal and it was too late now to pretend otherwise.

"Chris, I'd like Sophia to speak with me prior to her audience with the pope. There are some matters regarding the child I need to discuss with her."

"I'm sure she'd welcome meeting you. She knows you've been close to her daughter."

"Can she meet with me tomorrow morning around 10 a.m.? I can come to the Hassler."

One call was out of the way, the next two would prove to be more painful.

Chapter Forty-Eight

The convent was dark, Alfonso inched his fingers along the kitchen wall feeling for a switch. He cursed himself for not bringing a flashlight. He found the switch, turned the light on, and found it to be dim which suited his purposes. There was no reasonable explanation he could come up with to tell the sisters should he be discovered in Nevaeh's room at this late hour. First he had to find the laundry. Nevaeh had once told him that the sound of machinery often woke her at night. Her room was off the kitchen, the laundry had to be close by.

A night light protruded from the molding near the floor lighting his way; he opened a door only to find a maintenance room where mops and buckets stood in attention. The next room was the laundry. He breathed a sigh of relief and went to work looking for a small white habit that would suit Nevaeh. She couldn't just walk out of Vatican City, she'd have to be disguised. He found what he was looking for. The tiny habit and head covering were labeled, "Sister Floribeth." Alfonso smiled, Sister Floribeth was as sweet as she was tiny. She'd taken the name Floribeth after the Costa Rican lawyer, Floribeth Mora Diaz, who was said to have been cured of a brain aneurysm after praying to the deceased pope, John Paul II. Floribeth Diaz, like her namesake, had been a devotee of John Paul II. It was believed that he'd interceded on her behalf and cured her of an inoperable aneurysm. Her doctors had no explanation as she'd been given merely a month to live. Alfonso knew Sister Floribeth would support his cause if she was made aware of it. He bundled the habit under his arm and went in search of Nevaeh.

Nevaeh's room was stark just as he'd expected; it was devoid of anything resembling what a young girl's room should look like. Alfonso thought back to his young daughter, she would have been nearly 50 now had she lived. Her bedroom had been an explosion of pink. The curtains, bed coverings, walls, and toys had all screamed, "A little girl lives here!" He looked sadly at Nevaeh and wondered what she dreamt about. The walls of her tiny room had been painted a dingy off-white, and with the exception of a crucifix, the walls were bare. Compared to the opulence of the Apostolic Palace, Nevaeh's room was nothing more than a cell.

Alfonso knelt beside her cot, the sheets were cold and coarse, her angelic face radiated innocence; she wasn't aware that her life was anything but normal. Her honey-colored hair brushed the side of her face, its gold highlights sparkled in the dimly-lit room. "Had she been born in an earlier time, she could have posed for Botticelli," Alfonso thought to himself. He'd have to wake her gently so as not to frighten her.

"Nevaeh," he whispered, "it's Papa Alfonso."

Nevaeh was barely awake when Alfonso made his way out of the convent. He hoped she'd been aware of his presence; she appeared to be asleep with her eyes open while he gave her instructions. He'd have to wait and see if she'd show up in the Papal Gardens before sunrise.

He didn't get much sleep worrying about the fate of the child should she remain in Vatican City.

His fears were unfounded; at 4:30 the next morning, Nevaeh arrived as instructed. She looked like a small apparition dressed in the habit of Sister Floribeth. Alfonso linked his arm through hers, anyone who saw them would think one of the nuns was escorting an elderly priest to an early doctor's appointment on the opposite side of the Eternal City, but no one glanced in their direction. It was too early to stop for breakfast, nothing was open. The sky was brightening but the moon was still visible in the Roman sky. The weather was pleasant, unseasonably warm for early morning. Alfonso decided a walk on the empty Roman streets was the perfect way to introduce Nevaeh to her city. In childlike fashion, Nevaeh scraped the bottom of her sandals on the cobblestone streets.

"The street is rough, it's different from the marble floors of the Pope's house."

"Yes, Cara, it is. I must tell you something now. It's important."

Alfonso hesitated. He'd received a call from Abbot Ling late last night.

"Your Eminence," Venerable Ling had begun, "upon further reflection I think it may be unwise to bring the child here." Alfonso's heart sank, this plan had been the only viable option.

Venerable Ling went on, "I propose a better solution. I fear should she be kept here with me, she'll be found. There's a record of my visit to her. All of us who had been present at her examination will be investigated should they care to search for her. I have a plan that may be more suitable. On the outskirts of Trastevere, there's a Zen temple; those who operate the center are a most kind husband and wife. They are Zen monks. They tend their garden which will prove to be a haven for the child as there's a fully equipped small cottage where travelers often stay while visiting Rome. It's a respite from the frenzy of the city. I've called them, the cottage is available, it's secure, and the couple will tend to her. She'll be quite safe and will be kept busy. I assure you I'll oversee her care. No one will think to look for her there."

Alfonso had sighed in relief as he hung up the phone. Now he had the daunting task of informing Nevaeh she would not be returning to Vatican City.

"Nevaeh, the convent is no longer a suitable place for you to be living. I've made a decision for you to continue your studies at a center here in Rome where the practice of Zen Buddhism is conducted in quiet, peaceful surroundings. You'll be able to perfect your ability to commune with nature."

Nevaeh interrupted, "What about my garden?"

"The Papal Gardens were not constructed by nature, they're man-made and were carefully arranged to demonstrate a sense of opulent power. The simple place where you'll be staying, for just a short time, holds a garden that reflects the unpretentious design of the natural world. Your birds will find you. I've been told that there are cats and even dogs in residence. You'll have your own cottage within the garden. You'll be safe. The Zen Monks who live there are waiting for you. They'll care for you with gentleness, it's their way. Abbot Ling will greet us. We'll go there soon."

"Will you visit me?"

"I'll come as soon as I can."

"I think there's something you aren't telling me, Papa. Am I in danger?"

The cardinal didn't answer the question directly. Instead he said, "I'll always keep you safe."

"It's Cardinal Roselli, isn't it? He doesn't like me."

"Why do you think that?"

"He pulled my hair once and yanked my arm. He has a dark heart. I think he would have done something bad to me but the one you call 'His Holiness,' made him leave me alone."

Alfonso marveled at the child's dead on perception of Guilo Roselli. He exuded evil and she'd picked up on it.

"He'll never bother you again, I promise. I'm going to make sure you are safe."

"There's more you want to tell me, isn't there? I feel it. I feel you holding back. You suffer from worry. What is it? I'm strong, you can tell me. I'm nearly thirteen, I'm not a child anymore."

Cardinal Alfonso didn't think the time was right to burden Nevaeh with news of her mother. If they were reunited now they'd both be in danger. Alfonso had no idea who was in the employ of Cardinal Roselli. He feared Sophia would be followed as she'd been in the past. The fewer people who knew of Nevaeh's whereabouts the better. She'd need to adjust to life among the Zen practitioners. It wouldn't be hard for her. Cardinal Alfonso knew their ways and Nevaeh's were one and the same.

"Shall we have some breakfast?"

Cardinal Alfonso knew of a pasticceria that opened at 6 a.m. Walking along the Via Marmorata opened a whole new world to Nevaeh; she watched in awe as the normal routine of Roman citizens presented itself to her for the first time. Everything was alien to her, she'd only read about real life going on around her.

"It's like the books I've read are living here, Papa. It's real."

The spark of excitement Nevaeh was feeling would soon be extinguished, the cardinal thought sadly. She'll have to be kept hidden a bit longer. Her enthusiasm for life was contagious. She both relished the outside world and feared it.

Nevaeh watched as local Romans emerged from their homes on their way to work. A bus stopped and let one passenger off and another one on. The honk of its horn when a taxi sped into the bus lane sent a jolt of fear through Nevaeh, she grabbed the cardinal's arm with both of her hands and held tight.

The pasticceria beckoned with an array of colorful splendor. Its window was dressed with decorative treats looking more like precious jewels than baked goods. Nevaeh's eyes widened.

"Are we going inside?"

"Yes, you may have whatever you'd like."

"Maybe just biscotti, I don't like anything too sweet."

The cardinal gestured for Nevaeh to sit at a corner table, while he went to the counter. He ordered biscotti, due cornetti and due cappuccini. As a toddler, his daughter had savored the taste of cappuccino, she'd often sampled his when he wasn't looking. They'd finally given up forbidding it; she'd become a connoisseur at the age of three.

"For me?" Nevaeh said when the cardinal placed the cup in front of her.

"Si, yes of course, it's a tradition you know, drinking cappuccino in the morning, espresso after noon."

"The sisters never let me have caffé. Most of them are German, sent here to take care of the pope. They didn't know the customs of Italy, but even if they did, they had strict rules and weren't fun. They told me if I drank a caffé at my age, I'd never grow any taller."

Cardinal Alfonso laughed, "Silly old wives' tale. The only thing it will do is keep you awake. You'll be as tall as your ancestors."

"I'll just have to wait and see. I have no way of knowing who my ancestors were."

Nevaeh instinctively dunked the biscotti into the cappuccino like a native. She seemed unfazed by her lack of family, she'd taken it in stride. The cardinal guessed when someone didn't know what they were missing, they simply didn't care to wonder about it.

"May I take off this veil?"

Cardinal Alfonso nodded, they were safely beyond the outskirts of Vatican City and unlikely to be discovered. Nevaeh pulled the head covering off and her hair fell down over her shoulder. The tight covering had caused her hair to curl. Cardinal Alfonso remarked on its beauty.

"You have the hair of the angels."

"Maybe but angels have blue eyes and mine are almost black."

"Paintings don't tell the whole story, Nevaeh. You know that better than anyone."

Nevaeh bit into a cornetto, the cream exploded down her chin. Cardinal Alfonso's eyes teared, despite her insight she was still a child. How much she had missed, he should have looked into her origins before now. He'd always known in his heart that something wasn't right, that the story Pope Joseph and Cardinal Roselli fed him was a fabrication.

"Finish up now, wipe your face, we still have a bit of a walk ahead of us."

Nevaeh lagged behind the cardinal as they crossed the Tiber; she stood in the same spot as her mother had stood weeks before and pointed up the river, "Papa, it looks beautiful from here."

"Indeed, it does," the cardinal answered, looking up towards the majestic Basilica of St. Peter's in the distance. From this vantage point the dome and the Papal Palace shone with a heavenly splendor. The cardinal looked out over the muddy river and up towards the nucleus of the Roman Catholic universe, thinking how rampant corruption within the walls of Vatican City had been cloaked by the charade of archaic religious ritual for as long as he could remember. He was tiring of all the intrigue and cover-ups. He'd sought the quiet life of the priesthood all those years ago, he'd gotten more than he'd bargained for.

"Come, Nevaeh, we're almost there."

Abbot Ling greeted the pair at the entrance to the Zen temple. He reached for the cardinal's hand, placed his palm in the cardinal's upturned palm and repeated the gesture with Nevaeh.

"It's a Zen greeting. Come meet the others."

The temple was home to several Zen monks, students, and tourists anxious to learn the ways of the masters. Some partook of ritual dance and others learned the practice of meditation. A hint of incense filled the air; the sedate atmosphere filled the cardinal with an immediate sense of peace. The décor reflected simplicity, only the minimum of what was deemed essential was provided. It was enough. Everyone moved about respectfully nodding in the direction of the new arrivals. Cardinal Alfonso couldn't help but make the comparison between these austere surroundings and those of the Apostolic Palace. It filled him with shame.

A small woman appeared before them, she bowed her head slightly towards Abbot Ling.

"Lucia is here to escort Nevaeh to the garden cottage. Shall we accompany her?"

"Yes, I would like to see where she'll be staying so I can imagine her here."

The trio followed Lucia out into the garden. They walked a dirt path, it was carved roughly through orange trees and flowering plants. A pond filled with colorful Japanese carp occupied one side. Nevaeh stopped, knelt on the stone façade, and wiggled her fingers in the water. The fish rose to the surface as if to welcome her. Lucia waited patiently for Nevaeh to finish. She radiated kindness putting Cardinal Alfonso at ease.

The cottage stood in the far corner of the garden. Its glass doors were covered with screens reminiscent of a Japanese home. Bamboo plants formed a wall around the cottage. It was a fairy tale come to life. Nevaeh will flourish here, Cardinal Alfonso thought hopefully.

Lucia removed her sandals, Nevaeh did the same, and the two entered the cottage. A bowl of fresh fruit along with a pitcher of water filled with lemon slices rested on a wooden table in the center of the common room. Lucia gestured for the abbot and the cardinal to come inside.

The bedroom held a double bed, the closet was filled with clothes appropriate for someone Nevaeh's size.

Cardinal Alfonso looked over at the abbot and Lucia, "Thank you, in my haste I didn't think to tell her to bring her things."

Lucia bowed again but said nothing. Nevaeh fingered the garments. She removed a white flowing dress; its hem had been slit into ribbons and she held it up against her. There were two white dresses, several pairs of cropped pants and tunics.

Cardinal Alfonso put his hand on Nevaeh's shoulder, "I need to leave now, I'll be back for you as soon as I can."

He knew he didn't have to tell Nevaeh to behave as he would have had to with an ordinary child. Aside from speaking her mind about the ills of stodgy religious doctrine, Nevaeh usually had little to say. Cardinal Alfonso's chronic worrying was burdensome. He wished he could plan a future retreat at this temple, it would do him good and calm his soul. The thought of it made him smile; how the traditionalists would grumble and rage over that if they could hear his thoughts.

Nevaeh hugged the cardinal in a tearful goodbye, "Don't forget me, Papa."

Cardinal Alfonso knelt before her, "Mai e poi mai — never ever, Nevaeh."

Abbot Ling escorted Cardinal Alfonso through the garden and out towards the street.

"I'll stay the night to be sure she's settled. I'll be in touch, try not to worry."

Cardinal Alfonso nodded, he'd only recalled one other time in his life when he'd been so burdened by grief.

The nearest taxi stand was a block away, Cardinal Alfonso found it easily, and got in a waiting cab. "Hassler Hotel," he instructed the driver. The car circled and sped over the bridge back towards the Spanish Steps.

Chapter Forty-Nine

It was exactly 10 a.m. when Cardinal Alfonso pushed his way through the lobby filled with both arriving and departing tourists. His status as cardinal still afforded him a bit of respect in the secular world. The hotel receptionist waved him ahead of the crowd.

"I have an appointment with Sophia Travato, would you ring her room, per favore?"

"I'm sorry, Your Eminence, we don't have this person as a guest here."

"Perhaps, she's with Mr. Chris DeMarco?"

The receptionist typed the name into the hotel computer to no avail, "No, no guest with that name either."

Cardinal Alfonso panicked, he'd forgotten to ask Tim for Chris DeMarco's number. He should have been better prepared. He should have known Sophia and her companions would not register under their legal names. He walked through the lobby, dodging the tourists and their luggage, and was about to return to the street when he heard a woman call his name. He turned around and came face to face with an older version of Nevaeh. Sophia possessed the same angelic honey-colored hair and penetrating deep ebony eyes as her daughter. The resemblance left no doubt they were mother and daughter.

"Are you Cardinal Alfonso Aleo?"

"Si, yes I am." The cardinal stared, gaping at the nervous young woman.

"I'm Sophia. I'm Nevaeh's mother."

"There's no doubting that. She resembles you a great deal."

"She does?" Sophia's eyes welled up with tears.

"Shall we have a caffé in the bar?"

"Allora, yes." The cardinal followed Sophia through the lobby. They found two seats at a table in the corner. It was far from quiet but it would do.

"Thank you, Cardinal Alfonso, for caring for my daughter. I've been told you've been her teacher but it seems you've been more than that."

"I love her very much. She's very special. We are very close. I think of her as a daughter. I lost a child too. I was married, my wife and daughter were killed. I entered the priesthood shortly after their death. Nevaeh is a gift. It's what I want to talk to you about."

"I'm sorry for your loss. I know how it feels, believe me. I never knew if my daughter was dead or alive all these years. I don't know what kind of child I will get back. I imagine her life has been odd, growing up as she did."

"This is true, but Sophia, she has an insight, an innate knowledge, a perception of life that runs deeper than most who've devoted their lives to quiet reflection. This past week I invited theologians and scholars of diverse faiths to question her. Her responses were astounding for someone so young and inexperienced. I believe many of them found her to be nearing an enlightened state rarely encountered in modern times."

Sophia knew her baby would not be returned to her unscathed should she ever be back in her arms. But she didn't know what to make of what the cardinal was saying.

"What does this mean?"

"I know what I ask of you is difficult and that you're anxious to reunite with Nevaeh, but it may be best to have patience. We're not only dealing with powerful men who have demonstrated that they will kill if necessary to keep the Church free of implication in this scandal, but we're faced with a child who's gifted and potentially could transform the faith. With fostering, through proper education, she'll be a beacon for us all. We can discuss this in detail at another time. It may not be wise to thrust her into a world she may not be able to adjust to. She's extraordinary and she needs to be nurtured. But right now, she's in danger and needs protection."

Sophia grew more and more alarmed. She looked beyond the cardinal and spied Chris and Alessandro sitting at the bar. She should have known they would not leave her unattended.

"Your Eminence, my child was kidnapped, ripped brutally from my arms. Just as your powerful leaders will do anything to protect the Church's reputation, I, too, will stop at nothing to find my daughter and bring her home to me where she belongs."

Cardinal Alfonso's age was getting the better of him. His patience was wearing thin. He was shouldering the burden of this woman's suffering, the potential ramifications of the pope's downfall, and the possibility of Cardinal Roselli inflicting further harm. The weight of it all was overwhelming. He snapped.

"I'm sorry to say this, my dear, because I know a mother needs to be with her child, but she may not belong with you anymore."

Sophia's rage got the best of her, her screeches seemed to echo off the marble walls and into the crowded lobby, people were staring, "How dare you come here and tell me this? How dare you tell me that my own child doesn't belong with me?"

"All I'm saying is her uniqueness will cause her pain in the real world. She will be misunderstood." Cardinal Alfonso's words wafted through the air unheard.

Sophia's anxiety had been escalating since she witnessed the murders of Alessandro's men, and felt the terror of possibly losing both her child and her beloved Lauretta. Cardinal Alfonso dealt the final blow by dangling the return of Nevaeh in front of her. Now he'd left her with the impression that Nevaeh would remain sequestered to suit an ecclesiastical agenda where she would be groomed by the Church to become a female modern-day Messiah.

Sophia sobbed, speaking with incoherent speech. Chris and Alessandro jumped simultaneously off their bar stools and ran to her side just as she collapsed. Chris carried her through the lobby, towards the elevator. Alessandro followed, thinking it may be time to leave the Hassler. A spat between a cardinal and a woman was an unusual occurrence, and sure to arouse suspicion.

Cardinal Alfonso hung his head. He'd handled this badly. His agenda with regard to Nevaeh had been self-serving. She was his protégé and he wanted to see her reap the benefits of her gifts. He realized now it wasn't up to him. He'd keep her hidden until Cardinal Roselli was dealt with and Pope Joseph could be reasoned with, then he'd turn her over to her mother and hope for the best.

Chapter Fifty

Cardinal Alfonso tilted his head in greeting to the young Sister of Charity who held the door for him at the entrance to Casa Santa Marta where he'd lived for well over a decade. It was far from the lavish apartment Cardinal Roselli occupied in the heart of Vatican City. Many in the Curia, Cardinal Alfonso Aleo among them, had raised an eyebrow at the extravagant lifestyle Cardinal Roselli enjoyed, but Pope Joseph seemed unfazed by the implications of such grandeur.

In retrospect, Alfonso felt certain that Guilo Roselli kept himself isolated from the other members of the clergy who resided in the Vatican, in order to conduct his unseemly business activities free from scrutiny. It was a well-known fact that Guilo Roselli came from wealth, but the vows of poverty he'd taken during his ordination had failed to stick. He'd employed the services of a personal chauffeur and owned a current model black Mercedes sedan equipped with tinted windows.

Cardinal Alfonso opened the door to his single room. It suited him; it held a desk, a private bathroom, and a twin bed. He needed little else, he thought, recalling the mantra of the Zen Buddhists. He pulled the spread off the bed, folded it down at the bottom and laid down on the blanket. A clean sheet was turned down over it. The cardinal smiled, recalling how the sisters had changed his linens on schedule, like clockwork, on the same day every week for years now. In thinking further on it, Cardinal Alfonso supposed this simple task was one more example of the ritualistic performances conducted at every level of this organization. On the surface it was a well-oiled machine, but wave away the spiritual smokescreen and you'd find a Church riddled with scandal fueled by hypocrisy and a thirst for power.

Bringing the current situation to light would disgrace the Holy See but Cardinal Alfonso had no choice. This scandal sparked by the pope's indiscretion all those years ago, had triggered a web of conspiracy implicating the highest member of the Church Curia, Cardinal Guilo Roselli.

Cardinal Alfonso lay on his bed, he was desperately tired but unable to rest. In an hour, he'd return to the Headquarters of the Gendarmerie. Canon lawyer Cardinal Giordano, the Inspector General of the Gendarmerie, several members of the Conclave of Cardinals, and members of two Vatican Tribunals were meeting to discuss the repercussions should Pope Joseph refuse to allow Cardinal Roselli to be prosecuted. The collective hope that Pope Joseph would also find it in his best interest to resign was what Cardinal Alfonso was aiming for. He knew the decision to step down had to be made freely by the pope alone. But pressure could be applied. Vatican law had not been designed with this scenario in mind. It was beyond the scope of rational theological thought.

Despite the possibility of further damaging the Church's reputation, Cardinal Roselli needed to be held accountable; he was guilty of two counts of kidnapping, conspiracy to commit murder and orchestrating the slaughter of two, possibly three government officials. A cover-up would not serve the Church well in the future should word of this blatant corruption reach the ears of the public.

Cardinal Alfonso got up and walked into the bathroom; when his bare feet hit the stone floor a shiver of cold surged through him. The mirror over the sink reflected his disillusioned spirit. He'd been naïve with regards to his Church; he'd dismissed the reports of molestations inflicted on children by his fellow clergymen as the embellishment of a prejudiced media. He deemed the stories, if any were true, to be a result of the lenient disregard most of the Catholic world had for the articles of faith. He splashed water on his face and picked up his phone.

"Papal offices, Tim Daniels, how may I direct your call?"

"Tim, it's Cardinal Alfonso, I was wondering if you are free in an hour? I'd like you to accompany me to a meeting with an emergency counsel I've set up in order to discuss our options with regards to the matter you've brought to my attention."

Tim felt his throat tighten, a wave of nausea swept over him. He'd heard the news of the shooting at the home of Alessandro Jenco. He hadn't slept since, he had no knowledge of who in the Vatican had an allegiance to Cardinal Roselli. Tim was paralyzed by fear and paranoia knowing he'd been the one to expose Cardinal Roselli's criminal enterprise, but it was futile for him to have regrets. He'd had no choice at the time, lives had been in danger; now he worried about his own safety, and he wanted out.

"Grazie, Your Eminence, I appreciate you including me but I'd prefer if I was kept out of it. I wish to be an anonymous source from now on, nothing else. Please respect my wishes."

"Of course, I won't mention your name."

Tim turned on the answering machine, took the USB out of his desk drawer, and walked out of the office. St. Peter's Square was packed with visitors, tour guides and their charges. He pushed his way through and hurried in the direction of the river. A light rain was falling, wind was kicking up, the muddy Tiber looked angry. Waves splashed against the concrete shoreline. Waitstaff at the riverside restaurants were pulling down umbrellas while attempting to catch the blowing tablecloths before they were lost in the sudden squall. Tim leaned his arms on the wet stone and looked down at the river. He rolled his copy of the USB around in his fingers for a few minutes before tossing it into the raging river. It flew through the air and landed with a slight splash before disappearing forever into ochre water.

Chapter Fifty-One

Cardinal Alfonso was escorted to the Inspector General's office. Everyone he'd called was already seated in the room. Aside from Inspector Contini and Cardinal Giordano, the others had no idea why they'd been summoned.

"Thank you all for coming on such short notice. What I'm about to tell you is of an urgent nature and I'm asking you to keep it in the strictest of confidence."

As if on cue, each member of the group turned their head towards their seat mate with a perplexed look on their face. They nodded in agreement towards Cardinal Alfonso in a silent gesture of fidelity as he began to disclose the sordid tale of Pope Joseph Morris' past indiscretion. He'd allow the visual evidence to speak for itself with regards to Cardinal Roselli's involvement.

"I beg your indulgence. Before we begin to discuss how this is going to be handled, I have more news to report. But let me first show you the evidence we have."

Cardinal Alfonso handed the USB stick to the uniformed officer. The lights were lowered and once more Cardinal Roselli's office appeared on the screen. When the screen went black, an eerie silence hung in the heavy air. Everyone was collectively drained.

Cardinal Giordano was the first to speak, "I've known about this for over a week. As difficult as it is, we must put aside our personal feelings of shame and look to canonical law to guide us. Initially I considered an accusation of heresy in order to depose of Pope Joseph since his transgression constituted a direct abandonment of the faith as well as his vows of celibacy. However, despite overwhelming evidence, we have no tangible proof and he can simply deny the allegations. He is within his right to refuse DNA testing which would confirm or deny parentage. He's the Supreme Pontiff, he holds the power. Should we find a loophole that would enable us to depose him, his removal would reflect poorly on the conclave who elected him. Another possible scenario is the pope could overrule a tribunal decision and interfere with due process. Former popes have respected the rule of canon law but it was within their right as sovereign leaders to dismiss the findings of the Vatican court." Cardinal Giordano cleared his throat, took a sip of water and continued, "My friends, we are faced with a monumental dilemma which could potentially cause irreparable damage to the Holy See. We must protect our interests and those of the Church."

"What about Cardinal Roselli? He's the orchestrator of violent crimes. He can't be allowed to walk freely," Monsignor Santori, a visiting canon lawyer from Turin, said.

"With regards to Cardinal Roselli, our hands are tied. Pope Joseph has full jurisdiction over the cardinals. Only he can discipline a cardinal, and it's my understanding Cardinal Roselli is the confidant and advisor to Pope Joseph Morris. Perhaps there's more to that than appears on the surface considering the facts of this case. I propose Cardinal Alfonso, myself, and Inspector Contini approach the pope and inform him of our findings. I've been told that the mother of the child is due to have a Papal Audience when the pope returns next week. He is unaware it is she who will be visiting. I think we should be nearby onsite at that time. If anyone has anything to offer, now is the time to speak."

Cardinal Alfonso addressed the group, "I would like to convene again after we've confronted the pope. Then we'll have a better handle on if he will step down and how he intends to deal with Cardinal Roselli. Thank you for your time, I realize this was burdensome news. After you've had time to reflect, feel free to contact me should you have any questions or suggestions. God bless you all."

Cardinal Alfonso had been holding the edge of the table the whole time he'd spoke. His fingers were numb. He stood up, and the others followed suit. They walked around the room towards the exit, shaking their heads, bidding each other goodnight before leaving the building.

Cardinal Alfonso was alone in the conference room. He'd expected to feel relieved now that he'd lightened his burden by sharing it with other members of the Church hierarchy, but he felt the same heavy load on his shoulders. He readied himself to leave; he hesitated, he didn't want to engage in conversation with anyone once outside on the piazza. He pulled the computer towards him to retrieve the USB. It was gone.

Chapter Fifty-Two

Lauretta's concern for Sophia was escalating by the day. The group collectively had been more or less asked to vacate the Hassler after Sophia's outburst in the lobby. Dealing with temperamental celebrities was a commonplace chore for the management but there were no rules regarding blatant disrespect for the clergy. Sophia's shouting match with Cardinal Alfonso Aleo had invoked the ire of many a well-heeled hotel guest. The hotel could not afford to alienate regulars. Alessandro, Lauretta, Sophia, and Chris now found themselves back in Trastevere.

Sophia had been kept mildly sedated courtesy of the Hassler's doctor on call. She lazed around Lauretta's apartment, and except to ask for another tranquilizer she'd barely said a word.

"Where are my pills, Lauretta?"

"Pills are not the answer here, Sophia. It's another week or so before your audience with Pope Joseph, I suggest you start pulling yourself together."

"Meeting him is a waste of time, they aren't going to return her to me."

"You don't know that," Lauretta took Sophia's hands in hers. "Let's look for the positive; a few short weeks ago, you didn't know if Nevaeh was alive. You didn't know if she'd been sent away where you'd never be able to track her down. I can imagine how hard it is to be patient after so much has been taken from you. I know about this, I've lost much in my life. But as my father used to say, where there's life there's hope."

Sophia looked up without emotion, "I'm so afraid, Lauretta."

"I know what it's like to be afraid. How about we distract ourselves for a few days? How about we go to Venice, we can return the money you borrowed, drink some Venetian wine, have some fresh seafood, breathe the sea air. I'll make the arrangements."

Lauretta didn't wait for a response, she picked up the phone and began to rattle off instructions to whom Sophia assumed was a travel agent.

"Lauretta, excuse me a minute please."

Lauretta placed her hand over the mouthpiece, "Si, Sophia, what is it?"

"I don't want to fly can we take the train?"

Lauretta nodded and returned to her call.

"All set, we leave in the morning. We'll be in Venezia by lunchtime tomorrow."

Sophia didn't respond. She'd use the nearly four-hour train ride to reflect on her life, and attempt to make plans for her future with or without her daughter.

With the exception of a few businessmen who got off in Florence, the high speed train was unusually empty. Lauretta fell asleep as soon as the train departed Rome. Sophia smiled thinking about how Lauretta often complained about being a light sleeper.

Sophia used the alone time to watch life in the Italian countryside unfold. Farmland gave way to mountainous terrain to fields of sunflowers. It was all reminiscent of her trip to Rome, first with Lorenzo, and then with Zara and Gina. She wondered, for a moment, if they'd returned from Dubai. She was grateful to all the people who'd been placed in her path to help her find her daughter, but now she realized that once again she'd lost control over her own life. No matter what was in store for her, she had to regain control.

Lauretta stirred and then opened her eyes.

"Sorry, Sophia, all the intrigue and drama has finally caught up with me. Where are we?"

"Just outside of Bologna, a little more than an hour to go. Would you like a caffé?"

"No, I'm okay. I can wait. How are you doing?"

"Allora, I've been thinking while you were sleeping, I need to regain control of my life. I can't have Alessandro, or Chris, or anyone else lead me around. Whether or not I reunite with Nevaeh, I must take care of myself. When we return to Rome, I'm going to ask for my old job back."

"This is good, bene, molto bene, Sophia. You need to recover from all this trauma. I don't want to control your decisions but remember you always have a home in Trastevere with me."

"Grazie, Lauretta," Sophia rested her head on Lauretta's fragile but capable shoulder.

Chapter Fifty-Three

"Attenzione, Venezia, Mestre," the conductor announced first in Italian and then in English to accommodate the tourists, "Mestre Station next stop."

The few tourists who were sitting in Lauretta and Sophia's car left their seats to retrieve their massive amounts of luggage from the rack. Mestre was located one train stop away on the mainland and provided cheaper lodgings.

Lauretta looked out the train window and observed the tourists struggling with their bags.

"So many get off here."

"It's cheaper to stay here but not the same."

Sophia grew anxious as the train crossed over the lagoon towards Venice. She wasn't sure if it was excitement to return to the place she'd called home for so many years or if it was fear of the unknown. She was returning now with all her faculties intact. How would she react seeing the Reverend Mother now knowing the truth? Were the sisters, whom she'd shared a home with for all those years, complicit in the cover-up enacted by Cardinal Roselli? They must have known something otherwise why were they chosen to be her caretakers or wardens as it turned out?

Sophia flushed, her rising anxiety didn't go unnoticed by the ever-observant Lauretta.

"Are you alright? I imagine you are both excited and fearful to be returning to Venezia, my dear. Be strong, don't be afraid to ask the questions you want the answers to. No one can hurt you here."

Sophia took a deep breath and nodded but she wasn't so sure.

The train eased its way into Santa Lucia Stazione before coming to a full stop. Sophia grabbed her and Lauretta's small overnight bags and slid through the aisle towards the exit. Sophia tossed the bags down the metal steps, then she turned to help Lauretta maneuver the stairs.

The two walked arm in arm down the platform towards the crowded station. The shops were filled with tourists buying last minute souvenirs.

The pair made their way through the hoards. Sophia stood on the landing of the station's steps marveling at the view. The impressive sight of this medieval water city never ceased to take her breath away despite the memories it evoked. Lauretta was equally impressed.

"Bellissimo, I haven't been here since I was a child. I'm so happy you agreed to come back."

"I think there is a ramp somewhere if you can't manage the stairs."

"Si, that would be better."

Sophia took Lauretta's arm; the two bags were looped over her shoulder weighing her down. They walked to the back of the station and found a ramp leading down to the canal.

A man with a luggage cart approached them but Lauretta turned him away. Sophia rolled her eyes. Lauretta was wealthy beyond words, but remained frugal.

The hotel Lauretta had chosen was located on the outskirts of the Jewish Ghetto. It was a modest B&B, clean and nondescript. It would be fine for a night.

Lauretta checked in, handed the host their passports and received the key to one room.

It would be hard for Sophia to come and go with Lauretta underfoot, and she wondered if Lauretta could manage the bridges and cobblestone streets. Sophia was antsy, she wanted to have a quick bite and head over to the convent, return the money, get the reunion over with, and put this part of her life behind her.

Lauretta, despite being a prudent spender, had readily offered to pay the Reverend Mother what Sophia owed her.

After a light lunch of Caprese salad for two and the two glasses of vino rosso Sophia drank to calm herself, they made their way by vaporetto towards Dorsoduro. The still ravaged waterfront held saturated wreckage as a blaring reminder of the devastating flood that had plagued Venice weeks before. Small motor boats remained landlocked, wedged in canals now suffering from low tides.

"You're lucky not to have been here for all this," Lauretta remarked as they left the vaporetto.

Sophia's chest started to hurt, she knew she'd have to remain calm. She didn't want to appear foolish or accusatory without ferreting out the facts first. The Reverend Mother had always been kind to her but now Sophia doubted her sincerity.

Sophia should have known the ancient structure of Santa Maria della Visitazione could not have withstood Mother Nature's latest onslaught. Sophia walked through the alley as she'd always done. She was greeted with, "Pericolo! Vietato l'accesso!" She didn't need to read Italian to know it meant, "Danger, keep out." The wood was rotting, and stones were eroding and covered with a moldy residue; there was no sign of life except for the scratching sound made by rats, the only beneficiaries of Aqua Alta.

"Are you looking for the sisters?" an old man, Sophia thought she'd recognized, asked.

"Si, do you know where they've gone?"

"The younger ones scattered. I only know that the older nun is teaching here in Dorsoduro at the Ca' Foscari. You will find her there."

"Grazie, Signore."

"Lauretta, maybe it's best if you go back to the hotel and wait for me. It's a bit of a walk to Ca' Foscari."

"I could use a rest, if you're sure you'll be okay on your own."

"Yes, of course. Sister Rosa, the Reverend Mother, isn't a threat. I'll be fine. I'll take you back then take a vaporetto to Ferrovia. I won't be long."

Once Lauretta was settled, Sophia made her way to Ca' Foscari. She decided a long walk would be best. She needed time to think, she needed time to figure out how confrontational she'd need to be with the Reverend Mother.

Stepping through the gate into the compo Palazzo Foscari which now housed the university, Sophia found herself in the midst of a crowd of young students. They'd gathered in groups; a small one formed in front of an older woman, clearly a professor who was giving an impromptu lecture. The woman's back was turned and from Sophia's vantage point it was only her voice that was familiar; it reverberated off the stone walls in the secure courtyard. Her hair was gray and closely cropped. Sophia had grown used to the unexpected showing up on her horizon so the shock of seeing the Reverend Mother dressed as a laywoman had little effect on her. Her many near death evasions over the past few months had left her with an excess of bravado, and a sense that there was nothing left to lose. Without hesitation she intruded on the group of admiring students and interrupted the Reverend Mother or whomever she was now.

"Sister Rosa, Reverend Mother?"

"Oh, that's not me anymore," Maria Jilani said turning around to face her questioner.

"It's me, Sophia."

Maria excused herself from the group, "We'll continue this discussion in class tomorrow. Please forgive me, I must leave now." She was visibly shaken at the sight of Sophia risen from the dead.

"I always knew in my heart you were alive. Come let's go somewhere where we can talk."

Maria took Sophia's arm, held it tight, rubbing her fingers lightly over the flesh as if to make sure it wasn't an apparition she was seeing.

"You don't wear a habit anymore? You look so different. I almost didn't recognize you. If I hadn't heard your voice I would have not known you at all."

Maria led Sophia to a back alley where a lone trattoria rested alongside a small shuttered apartment building whose balcony was bursting with bougainvillea blossoms rivaling those of Lauretta's. The sight and flowery smell gave Sophia an immediate sense of peace. She took a seat on a wobbly chair over the cobblestone patio and stared into the weary eyes of Sister Rosa.

"Sophia, what happened to you?"

"Before I tell you anything, I want to return the euro I took from your desk."

"There's no need, it wasn't my money."

Sophia didn't know where to start, she didn't think she was the one who should be offering explanations. There were still gaps to be filled in. Before she had a chance to begin a litany of questions, Maria spoke.

"Sophia, first I have to tell you that the convent flooded badly after the last episode of Aqua Alta. We had over seven feet of water rush in off the lagoon. It left the structure beyond repair. The city condemned it and we were left homeless. The younger sisters were relocated throughout Italy but I couldn't endure it any longer."

"I saw, I went there looking for you. But I don't understand, endure what?"

"The hypocrisy, the lying, the bribery I had to live with all those years. When you came to us that night, we were instructed not to ask questions, we were merely given your name and nothing else. In return, we were supported by a Church official as our meager salaries could not sustain us. I was responsible for the welfare of the young nuns and you of course. I felt I had no choice but to keep silent when I knew in my soul there were holes in the 'Sophia story' we had been given. When Lorenzo Mercuri hired you as his assistant I knew it was to keep you close to the culprit but still I said nothing. I thought it best at the time since you had no memory. What was the harm? But I tried to find out where you came from. I checked missing persons Internet sites and newspapers for information. No one was looking for a lost woman. I had to be careful, not to attract attention from Cardinal Roselli's cohorts. His reach spanned far beyond the Vatican. When you disappeared, we were no longer useful to him and the funding dried up. I spoke of this to no one but my faith was fractured. I left the Church. I use my given name now, Maria Jilani. I'm Professor Maria Jilani."

"Cardinal Roselli," was all Sophia said in response.

"Yes, he was behind it but I never knew the reason for any of this. I promise you, Sophia. I know it's no excuse. I should have gone to the authorities but these are powerful men. I'm guessing you know this."

"I have no family that I know of. I was raised by Catholic charities in the United States. Someone left me in a church when I was five years old, I think it was a man but it could have been a woman. I have only vague memories. The only possession I have from my childhood is this ring, it was hanging on a necklace that held a medal with the same inscription. My daughter has the medal."

Sophia pulled the necklace containing the ring out from under her blouse. She held it up for Maria to view.

Being a linguist, Maria recognized the markings. "It's wise of you to keep this hidden, it's gnostic and very old. While there's been a resurgence of Gnosticism in parts of the world it's still considered an ancient pagan rite by the Vatican hierarchy and not a root of early Christianity as is currently claimed elsewhere."

Maria quickly changed the subject, "You have a daughter?"

"I had an affair with a powerful man of God, I got pregnant, and became a threat. I had to be silenced and she had to be sequestered to avoid more scandal. It's as simple as that but laws that govern the rest of us don't apply to the Vatican."

"The Vatican, you had an affair with a cardinal in the Curia?"

"Yes, and now he's pope; Cardinal Roselli orchestrated not only the kidnapping of my child and my near demise, but also the killing of government officials in order to protect the reputation of the Church."

"How did you manage to get away, Sophia?"

"I trusted Lorenzo, loved him like a father. He agreed to help me when I confided in him after my memory returned. He drove me to Rome, but on the road I heard him talking to a man whose name was familiar. It was the man who'd kidnapped my daughter. I managed to escape. I have help now. I hope to reunite with my child who has been missing for thirteen years. I'm not sure who can be trusted. I was once a journalist for Sky Italia. If they refuse to relinquish my daughter to my custody, I will tell this story, expose the Church for its covert, illicit activities, and hope for retribution. But I'm a realist, I know there are risks. I've lost more than years. I've lost a lifetime."

"Anything I can do to help you, I will, I owe you that much. I can testify on your behalf, verify your story."

"Grazie, thank you, Reverend, I mean Maria. I doubt a court proceeding will be forthcoming. We're dealing with another country. It's complicated. I meet with Pope Joseph next week. He's unaware that it's me he's meeting. I have to go now, someone's waiting for me. I return to Roma domani, in the morning. Are you sure you don't want this euro?"

Maria put her head on the table, she inhaled hard letting out a pitiful sob. Sophia placed a hand on her shoulder, "It's okay, you did what you thought was best. I don't blame you."

Maria looked up, "Thank you, child. Bless you, I hope you find your daughter."

Sophia left a few euro on the table and walked off without glancing back. She didn't know what to feel, she wasn't entirely sure Maria Jilani was the protectress she'd thought she'd been. It had been all about money as usual. People, Sophia determined, would sell their souls to the highest bidder in order to provide creature comforts for themselves and those in their care.

It was nearly five o'clock. Once outside the isolated alley, Sophia encountered a swarm of Venetians cramming the streets, many were returning home from work, most were carrying grocery bags filled with ingredients for one night's supper. Sophia pushed her way through the crowds. She didn't have the strength to shove her way onto the waiting vaporetto. She preferred to walk as she'd done in the past. Walking freed her from the constraints of time and place, gave her time to think and clear the clutter from her overloaded brain.

Sophia was surprised to find Lauretta sound asleep when she opened the door to the hotel room. She wondered if Lauretta was ill, but shrugged off the thought, attributing it to travel fatigue. She took a shower, taking care to make a bit of noise, hoping to wake Lauretta. Sophia had no intention of spending her only night in Venice trapped inside. The night held promise; the Venetian sky spun its evening web shaded in purple and gold. Its natural beauty provided the backdrop for many an Italian painter. Sophia dried off, dressed quickly, wrote Lauretta a note, and left the room.

It wasn't her intention to stroll towards Rialto, her feet seemed to go on without her. The small mask shop too had been plundered by the latest storm, but the damage to it was worse than Mother Nature could have inflicted. The store had been pillaged and razed as if the door had been left open to the world. Sophia stood for a moment, put her hand over the stone doorway and peered in at the now hollow space. It looked like an empty grotto had been carved into a stone wall; there was no evidence left of anything that came before. It had all been wiped out, erased with no hope of returning. She felt a fleeting sense of relief that she had her memory back, and could return to some semblance of normalcy; they hadn't succeeded in entirely obliterating her. Not yet anyway.

On the other side of the Rialto Bridge, a familiar looking mask hung on a hook near the doorway of a shop. Sophia removed it, turned it over, and saw the initials, "LM."

"Quanto costa?"

The merchant began to tell Sophia the story of the famous mask-maker who'd been found dead under mysterious circumstances weeks before. Sophia's eyes glazed over as he relayed a tale only a Venetian could weave.

"Si, Signora, Lorenzo Mercuri and I were childhood friends. We grew up playing in the compos just over the bridge."

"Allora, bravo, bene. He was lucky to have your friendship, Signore."

Sophia handed 40 euro to the merchant and muttered, "Highway robbery," under her breath. She'd spent every day for twelve-plus years of her life with Lorenzo, and never once did she see or hear mention of this man. He'd bought stolen goods or had stolen them himself. He was just another person profiting from the misfortune of another. She couldn't help herself, she flushed with anger, "Mi scusi, Signore, I'm the niece of Lorenzo Mercuri," she lied, "My uncle grew up on the streets of Napoli." She tucked the mask into her bag and walked back up and over the bridge.

Sophia returned to find Lauretta sitting in a chair by the window looking out at the courtyard.

"It's nice here, bellissima Venezia, but I prefer Trastevere."

"Everyone prefers their own place, if they have one. Shall we go out for dinner?"

"Si, where shall we go?"

"Anywhere you'd like, we have 800 euro to spend."

Living in Venice with the Benedictines did not allow for outside dining. Sophia had only frequented a local café but she'd heard the locals rave about different restaurants and she was versed in Venetian cuisine.

"I rarely left the convent for meals but I know where the good places are. I suggest seafood of course."

Sophia took Lauretta through the alleys towards the Cannaregio. She had a particular restaurant in mind. She'd overheard many a tourist and local alike rave about the place.

It was 6:00 p.m., a bit early for a Venetian dinner, but they were warmly welcomed, and offered a table of their choice.

"Let's sit outside and watch the crowds, Lauretta."

"There'll be smokers out here, you don't mind it?"

"It's too early for smokers," Sophia laughed, her troubles elsewhere for the moment.

The Hosteria Al Vecio Bragosso, with its authentic Venetian ambience, attentive service, and delicious cuisine, was just what Sophia and Lauretta needed after all they'd endured.

They shared a large bowl of risotto al nero di seppia, laughing like school girls when their teeth turned black, stained by the ink of the squid. Two glasses of Prosecco and an order of scampi alla Veneziana sealed their fate with the waitstaff. Despite speaking Italian fluently, the women were determined to be tourists. Sophia didn't want the night to end. She dreaded returning to Rome, but she wouldn't think about it now.

She paid the bill and left a hefty tip with the euro meant for Sister Rosa. The funds actually belonged to Lauretta. It gave her a warm feeling watching Sophia's moment of happiness.

"Let's stay out a little longer. We can get a drink at a compo I know, it's nearby. I used to stop there when I didn't want to go home to the convent. It was dreary compared to the life out here."

They found two empty seats; once again Sophia took a wobbly chair and offered the stable one to Lauretta.

"Due Aperol Spritzi, per favore," Sophia told the server before adding, "Avette gelato?"

The server nodded and put a menu down on the table before going off to retrieve their drinks.

"Would you like gelato, Lauretta?"

"Due pistacchio gelati, per favore."

"Allora, grande porca," Lauretta said patting her stomach, "I ate so much, but gelato, who can resist?"

"Oh, Lauretta, thank you for bringing me back here. I almost feel normal again. No matter what happens, maybe I'll be alright."

"You must have hope, life doesn't always work out as we planned or hoped for but somehow destiny finds us. Of course, you'll be alright. What happened to you was unspeakable. You may never fully recover but karma finds its way around. You are a good person, try to be patient. You'll see in time."

Sophia had no idea what Lauretta was talking about. Must be the Prosecco/spritz combo talking. Her words reminded Sophia of something she'd heard before in another life perhaps. It was the karma reference. She'd once worked on a story of Zen Buddhists who were hoping to relocate themselves to Rome. If her job ever rematerialized she'd have to resurrect the story.

Chapter Fifty-Four

For Sophia, the Termini Train Stazione in Rome did not evoke the same breathtaking response as Venice's Santa Lucia Stazione. Overcast skies met the pair as they exited the nondescript station. They stood in a long, but fast-moving line, and waited their turn for a cab ride back home to Trastevere. A displeased Alessandro met them on the landing outside Lauretta's apartment after he heard them unlock the heavy outer door. Sophia looked up and saw him raise his hands over his head before shaking his fists in a typical Italian gesture.

"Please, Alessandro, I know you were worried, but it did me a world of good and we're safe." She slammed the door to her apartment leaving him in the hall. She could hear him chastising Lauretta. She thought for a moment of going to her rescue, but Lauretta was tough and could handle her cousin. Sophia had more important things to worry about. Pope Joseph would be returning from his South American trip tonight and her audience was scheduled for 10 a.m. the day after tomorrow. She wished she'd stayed in Venice another day to distract her from the pain of waiting. There were a few pills left of the ones the Hassler's doctor had prescribed. Sophia fingered the bottle, sleeping through the next few hours would help alleviate the torment of waiting, and anticipating the unfavorable outcome she dreaded. She took the bottle to the bathroom, dumped the remaining pills into the toilet, and went in search of Lauretta.

Lauretta was in her kitchen preparing an espresso for herself. Alessandro was still on a rant about the dangers that lurked out on the streets. Lauretta was oblivious. She looked up when she saw Sophia, "Caffé?"

"Si, Lauretta. Calm down, Alessandro, I know how frustrated you are but you can't hold me hostage here. In fact, I want you to take us out tonight. I need to get my mind off my upcoming meeting. Please."

Alessandro took Sophia by the hand and led her out of the kitchen away from Lauretta.

He pulled her from behind out into the hallway and into her unlocked apartment. He turned to face her, "An unlocked door too, Mama Mia! Were you not present when my apartment was raided and my men killed by orders of that cardinal?"

"Yes. Si, I know but I notice you aren't holding Signore DeMarco here. He's free to wander Roma without restraint," Sophia raised her voice without meaning to.

"Sophia, Chris is being tailed by one of my men. He's unaware of it. But Chris isn't the target, you are, and I'm not in love with Signore DeMarco. I love you, Sophia. It took me a lifetime to find you, and I can't bear the thought of losing you. Don't you understand that?" Alessandro pulled her close and kissed her hard. She pushed him away.

"I can't do this, please. I'm sorry. I have so much to deal with right now. You've been so kind to me. I know how you feel, I saw this coming but I'm unsure of my own feelings. So much has happened over the past few months, it's left me frazzled. I'm hanging on by a thread. I don't have a response to you, Alessandro. I think you're an amazing man, more so than I deserve but now is not the right time. I'm not ready, I may never be. I'm damaged goods."

"I understand," Alessandro answered before walking out the door. Now guilt was added to the pile on Sophia's overloaded plate.

Sophia opened the door to Lauretta's apartment. She stood in the hallway and listened as Lauretta turned the tables on Alessandro. He must have gone to Lauretta looking for sympathy after Sophia had rebuked his advances.

"E pazzo? Are you crazy?" Lauretta shrieked. "Sophia is in a fragile state, she has no idea what's coming, her whole future is in a state of flux. She can't make plans, she has nothing to count on for sure. Her flesh and blood has been missing for thirteen years; the child's been in the hands of religious zealots who've most likely molded her since infancy to be beholden to them and their way of thinking. Neither you, nor I, can possibly fully understand the impact that the thought of one's child being in harm's way can do to a mother. She can never be free of any of this until she knows for sure or until she has answers, or is reunited with her daughter and finds out for herself. And what do you do? You who've not found a suitable mate all these years couldn't wait a bit longer. You had to dump this on her now. Dio Mio! Alessandro, what did you expect? Did you think this fragile creature would fall into your arms and ask you to take her away from all this? Now if I know her as well as I think I do, she's riddled with guilt over this on top of everything else she has to deal with. And just when she was coming to terms with how to get on with her life with or without her child. Did you know she's planning to return to Sky Italia if they'll have her? Do you know anything other than what's in front of your face? Do you ever actually talk to Sophia? Pff! No, you don't."

Lauretta picked up her espresso and a pitcher of water, "The plants need watering," she told Alessandro before leaving the kitchen.

Chapter Fifty-Five

Sophia stood on the terrace to her apartment, she looked down at the street below in time to see Alessandro and Chris exchange a few words before parting company. A few minutes later, she heard a light knock on her door before Chris appeared. Once again, she'd neglected to lock the door.

"Everything okay?" Chris asked. "Alessandro was a bit abrupt when I met him on the street."

Sophia sighed and looked away, "He told me he loved me."

Chris suppressed a laugh. Sophia was barely back to normal and already a man was falling at her feet.

"I'm guessing by his demeanor your response wasn't to his liking."

Chris hated his role as Sophia's confidant. A best friend status had never been his intention and now it was growing old. He'd been burdened by her drama ever since they'd reunited, and now he felt like screaming the words his mother used to say when she'd been saddled with other people's troubles, *Not my pig, not my farm.* But it wasn't Chris' style to be so abrupt.

"I barely know him. I'm overloaded right now. I'm not ready for a relationship with him or anyone else. I have to think about what's going to happen to me whether Nevaeh returns or not. I'm thinking of asking for my old job back, maybe do some freelance to start."

"It's good you aren't rushing into anything, I'm glad you didn't fall into his arms. I'm sure it was tempting." Chris realized he was sounding sarcastic, he tempered his tone. "I mean, the last time it didn't serve you well. But you were so young back then. Maybe a little impulsive."

Sophia furrowed her brow.

"Sorry, your love life is none of my business. What do you plan to tell Sky Italia regarding your long absence? You'll have to tell them something."

"I don't know. I guess it depends on the outcome. Chris, would you do something for me?"

"If I can, sure. What is it?"

"Will you write my story? Write it and put it away for safekeeping, you know, as leverage should I need it."

"Shouldn't you be the one to tell it?"

"No, I'm too close. You're more credible."

Chris nodded, "I'll do it now, I'll send it off to New York to a trusted colleague. He'll keep it confidential until, if, or when it needs to be made public."

Chapter Fifty-Six

"Excuse me, Holy Father, we will be landing soon, would you care for anything else?" the flight attendant asked. She was young, and seemed unsure of herself despite her flawless English and impeccable skills.

"No, thank you." The pope smiled trying to put the woman at ease.

The Alitalia Charter, turned Shepherd One for papal use, was posh. The food had been plentiful over the fourteen-hour flight from Santiago to Rome, and was far superior to standard airline food. Pope Joseph had his fill early on. He reflected on the trip. He wished he could travel around the globe and back again, enjoying his celebrity status to avoid the administrative part of being the representative of God on earth. But the South American trip had left Pope Joseph in a state of complete exhaustion. It had been too much of a trip in too short of a time. He felt depleted; all he wanted to do was get back to his apartment and sleep but this was not likely to happen. He'd received an email from Cardinal Alfonso requesting an emergency meeting when he returned to the Papal Palace. He wasn't sure what to expect, but he had his suspicions.

Overall the trip had been a success, record numbers turned out to greet the American pope. Even Cardinal Roselli had been delighted to accompany the pope on the journey; he was returning to his homeland. His school boy excitement, while out of character, had been infectious. He was more than cordial to the press corps as he regaled them with stories of his childhood in Chile. But in the last few days, the old Guilo Roselli had returned. He was on edge, sullen, and quick-tempered as if he'd received some off-putting news.

Whatever it was that had set Cardinal Roselli off was of no interest to the pope. He'd always held Cardinal Roselli in low esteem. Cardinal Roselli was an overbearing, pedantic old-world clergyman who wielded his power like the megalomaniac he was while claiming to be dutiful solely to the Church and her people. Everyone noticed, but had turned a blind eye to the comings and goings of the shady-looking characters who frequented the offices of Cardinal Roselli. The pope cringed at the thought. He knew he should be more authoritative and address the situation with Cardinal Roselli, but after twelve years, he still felt like a newbie. And the fact was he had his own problems. In a few days, Chris DeMarco would be back pestering him with intrusive questions and he was bringing his wife. Joseph had forgotten to ask if she was a journalist. He'd be surprised if she wasn't since Chris was entrenched in his work and had little time for non-journalistic ventures. He'd find out soon enough. He closed his eyes as the plane entered Italian airspace. They'd be landing soon.

The pope mobile was idling on the tarmac. The plane landed with a thud and sped across the airstrip before coming to a jerky stop. Cardinal Roselli stood up and was the first one at the door. Before deplaning, Pope Joseph walked to the back of the plane to say goodbye to the press.

"Anyone who wants a blessing, please stop me."

Cardinal Roselli grew impatient, "Your Holiness, I have some pressing matters to attend to."

The pope ignored him and continued greeting the passengers. It was within his right as Supreme Pontiff to ask Cardinal Roselli just what those pressing matters were, but he didn't want to know, he was afraid of the cardinal, and he suspected he knew it.

It was nearing 1 a.m. by the time they reached the Vatican. Cardinal Alfonso was seated outside the papal offices. He stood when he saw Pope Joseph. Due to the hour, there was no staff present to act as a liaison so Pope Joseph, himself, escorted the cardinal to the inner sanctum.

Cardinal Roselli sat at his desk studying the surrounding office. His eyes narrowed as he spied a small black metal object in the corner of the molding on the ceiling nearest the door. Outside in the hall, he found the utility closet; he took out a stepladder and a broom. With the broom handle, he reached the object and batted it to the floor. The small camera was barely detectable unless one was looking for it, now it was smashed beyond repair.

The cardinal was irate. He picked up the phone.

"Monsignor, it's Guilo Roselli, yes, si, I'm back. Thank you for contacting me. Do you have the item? Okay, I'll send my driver for it. I'll be in touch."

The cardinal had to act fast, he didn't know what the pope would do when he learned of his untoward activities. He assumed Pope Joseph would do nothing about it but he couldn't take a chance.

A half an hour later, his phone buzzed. His driver was back, he'd retrieved the item as requested.

Cardinal Roselli gathered up his papers, picked up his suitcase, stepped over the smashed camera, and walked out the door. He opened an inconspicuous door on the side of one of the many marble hallways and entered a tunnel. He followed it to the end and opened the obsolete green door which now served as merely decoration to the outer wall of Vatican City.

The streets were desolate. He walked along the clay colored wall and looked up at the majestic city behind it for the last time before getting in the waiting car.

"Your Eminence," Severino turned to face the cardinal. "Here's your new passport."

Cardinal Roselli jerked his head back in a gesture of surprise, "I almost didn't recognize you with that beard. Gray hair becomes you. You better lose the holy titles and start calling me Antonio."

"And I'm now Ernesto Ciacci."

Cardinal Roselli didn't care what name Severino used from now on.

The chauffeur stopped, bid his farewell to both men, as Cardinal Roselli handed him an envelope filled with euro before he and Severino exited curbside at the airport. Cardinal Roselli handed Severino, now Ernesto Ciacci, a one-way ticket to Thailand.

Severino glanced at the ticket, "I thought we were traveling together."

"It's best this way. I'll contact you in a week or so with further instructions," Cardinal Roselli lied handing Severino another envelope of euro.

"Signore Bultamante, would you care for something to drink before we take off?"

"Si, I'll have scotch on the rocks with a splash of water." Cardinal Roselli sat back in his seat. The fatigue he'd felt earlier after arriving in Rome had now been replaced by exhilaration. He was going back home to his beloved Chile. He'd been notified months ago that his great uncle, his grandmother's youngest brother, had died leaving his estate to him, the only remaining heir. His uncle's business had been thriving for decades. The Magallanes property was expansive. It ruggedly hugged the southernmost coast of Chile, but the townhouse in the city of Punta Arenas had presented a luxurious respite for the hard working family. Sadly, Guilo was the sole beneficiary of all their labor. After spending one night in Santiago, he'd take a four-hour flight on any available Chilean airline to Punta Arenas. Once there he'd be a short drive to his uncle's residence. The sheep farm was remote and difficult to reach. It would serve his purposes. With the exception of a few neighboring farms it was isolated; he looked forward to the solitude. No one would find him in his family home, should they care to look. He removed his collar, tossed it in his carry on, slouched down in his seat, brought the glass of scotch up to his mouth and as the ice brushed his lips he thought smiling, *I'll have to readjust to the cold Chilean climate, but I did my job protecting the reputation of the Church and I got away with murder doing it. May God forgive me.*

Chapter Fifty-Seven

"It would be easier to bring this matter to the attention of the Vatican court if you still had tangible evidence. Are you sure Tim doesn't have another copy of the USB?"

"Holy Father, I don't know, we can ask him in the morning. But there were many witnesses at the meeting who saw the tape, including the Inspector General, several gendarmerie, Cardinal Giordano, and others. Someone took the USB, someone who was working for Cardinal Roselli." Cardinal Alfonso was visibly shaken. It seemed obvious to the pope Cardinal Alfonso was also afraid of Cardinal Roselli.

"None of this is your fault, Cardinal Alfonso, it's mine. I'm responsible for all of this. I will handle it. Cardinal Roselli will be dealt with. You need to rest now."

Cardinal Alfonso bent to kiss the pope's ring before returning to his modest room in the Casa Santa Marta. His bed had been turned down, the sisters were kind to him and they cared for him like they would a hotel guest. He took off his cassock, walked over to the bureau where he kept his whiskey. The top to the glass decanter was ajar. *The sisters had themselves a little nightcap,* Alfonso thought before pouring himself a shot. The pope was right, he needed a rest, a long one.

Chapter Fifty-Eight

Despite exhaustion compounded by jet lag, the Holy Father had a sleepless night. The burden of Cardinal Roselli's criminal activities rested on his shoulders alone. He had sole jurisdiction over all cardinals worldwide. Their behavior was a reflection on him. He was responsible and he alone had to deal with the repercussions and ramifications. Cardinal Roselli had gone to the extreme to keep the pope's secret from being made public. He'd orchestrated the murders of several people, had ordered the kidnapping of both Sophia and Nevaeh, and may very well still be at it, all due to a misguided sense of duty to the Church. Cardinal Roselli wasn't the first to kill in the name of God and he wouldn't be the last. How to handle the cardinal weighed heavily on the Holy Father's mind. Without concrete evidence, the charges against Cardinal Roselli were based on hearsay and innuendo. If he could be brought up on criminal charges before the Apostolic tribunal, laicized, and possibly sentenced to live out his life in an Italian jail, the pope himself would be implicated. After all he'd been the spark that set this fire.

The sun was up, a walk in the Papal Gardens might do him some good. He hoped to see his daughter roaming about with her menagerie of creatures but she was nowhere to be found. He thought it odd but dismissed it. Perhaps she was having a lesson or the stern German sisters had given her a task. He pitied the child having to grow up here behind these walls. It had never been his intent. It was too late for regrets, but he never should have confessed his indiscretion to Cardinal Roselli all those years ago. He'd merely intended to ease his conscience and cleanse his soul before embarking on his new life as Supreme Pontiff.

Pope Joseph walked through the labyrinth of greenery and came out near a stone fountain. On the ledge around the bubbling water he found a scrap of paper and a woman's compact. The paper had been crumbled, the scribbled words were smeared but recognizable. A force of nature prompted him to hold the paper up to the mirrored compact. The name Nevaeh spelled out in reverse read "heaven."

There was something about this child of his that put him off balance. It was a subliminal perception, perhaps innate, that riled him up whenever he'd been in her presence. Even as a very young child she'd aroused perplexing feelings in him. He'd attributed it all to guilt, but now stepping back, he wasn't so sure. He'd heard enough about her abilities to decipher the spoken words of Jesus to realize she was no ordinary child. He suspected she'd been exposed to taboo writings. All of this was one more drain on his weary soul. One day at a time and one thing at a time. He had no choice but to seek counsel regarding Cardinal Roselli; he'd deal with the problem of Nevaeh afterwards. Maybe return her to her mother with a caveat. His name needed to be kept out of both affairs.

Perhaps the tale Cardinal Alfonso weaved had been the ranting of a confused old man. Pope Joseph needed to go to the source to ferret out the truth behind the missing USB.

After a breakfast of assorted pastries and a cappuccino, the Holy Father found Tim Daniels at his desk. He stood when the pope entered the room. His face was flushed and he appeared frazzled.

"Good Morning, Holy Father, can I help you?"

The pope pulled a chair up close to Tim's desk, "I need to ask you a few questions."

"Okay," Tim was nervous, he wasn't sure how much the pope knew about Tim's involvement in entrapping Cardinal Roselli. He wasn't entirely sure that the pope didn't condone the cardinal's actions considering he was the one being protected. Tim had to be careful especially now.

Tim had arrived at the office earlier than usual. He knew Cardinal Roselli would be back from his trip and he wanted to make sure the camera was still in working order. It wasn't, the screen appeared blank. He'd knocked lightly on the door to the cardinal's office, had opened it slightly, and found the smashed device on the floor in front of him. There was no doubt, judging by the condition of the office, that Cardinal Roselli had uncovered Tim's amateur setup. Tim had put himself at risk knowing full well that Cardinal Roselli had proven himself to be a dangerous force to be reckoned with. Tim could be his next target.

"Are you alright, Tim, is something wrong?" Tim thought it best not to reveal what he'd found earlier. He had to weigh his options.

"No, I'm fine. How was your trip, Your Eminence?"

"It went well, thank you. Let's get started, shall we? Cardinal Alfonso has told me that you became suspicious of Cardinal Roselli after witnessing him in the company of an unsavory-looking character, and that you took it upon yourself to set up a video camera in order to spy on him, is this true?"

"Yes."

"And when you had sufficient evidence you confided in the confessional to Cardinal Alfonso and gave him a USB stick containing taped conversations between Cardinal Roselli and a thug by the name of Severino Poverelli. Is this true?"

Tim was alarmed, he'd always thought the confessional to be a sacred place where the priest, or in this case cardinal, was the vehicle for a confessor to speak directly to God. He grew up being told what was revealed in the confessional never left the holy space. He mustered up bravado and said, "Let me pose a question, please. What happened to the confessional being a consecrated place? I'd always been told whatever was revealed could never be told. So much for that. You know what I think? You're hypocrites, all of you. I knew the cardinal would have to reveal what I discovered but I specifically asked him to keep my name out of it." Tim couldn't let his anger get the better of him. He stared at the pope, waiting for a response.

"Cardinal Alfonso's betrayal of his confessional duties is a burden on his shoulders. I'm certain his intent wasn't to cause harm to you but to protect the honor of the Church and to put an end to Cardinal Roselli's reign of terror."

"Yes, poor Cardinal Alfonso. It seems to me you collectively hide behind the cloak of service to the Church to do your dirty work, covering up for each other's improprieties. It's all been catching up with you, hasn't it?"

The pope had not expected nor had he been prepared for Tim's hostile behavior.

"Tim, it appears that someone has stolen the USB stick. Cardinal Alfonso had a meeting with members of the Curia, canonical lawyers, monsignors, and the Inspector General of the Gendarmerie. He showed the video implicating Cardinal Roselli; someone who was present at the meeting took the USB stick. There is no other evidence other than that of witnesses to prove or disprove Cardinal Roselli's involvement in any of the crimes he's accused of. Do you have another copy?"

"No," Tim lied, "I gave the only copy to Cardinal Alfonso. I'd hoped to be done with the nasty business of it by turning it over to him."

"I see," the pope answered before rising and leaving the room.

Tim took a deep breath. He'd wait a few days to see how things played out but he knew he'd have to leave Vatican City as soon as possible. Leaving out a few details had been smart, he'd be the one who held the key to the demise of all this.

For the first time in his life, he felt empowered. The regret at having planted the camera in the cardinal's office he'd felt earlier had faded. He held the cards, cards they'd pay a hefty price for. He pulled his cell phone out of the desk drawer and called his mother.

Chapter Fifty-Nine

Cardinal Roselli slept for ten of the fourteen hours on the flight to Santiago courtesy of the generous offerings of scotch and wine available in the first-class cabin. He'd decided to stay at the airport terminal Holiday Inn in Santiago. His flight home left mid-morning. He'd had enough traveling in the past two days to last a lifetime. He opted out of renting a car or hiring transport just to be able to stay at a higher-end hotel in the city. Besides, Santiago, Chile ranked as one of the top ten worst cities for traffic jams. Bangkok, Thailand was number one if he remembered correctly, he laughed to himself thinking of poor Severino. He wondered how he was faring. Severino had never traveled outside of his native Italy before. But he could live like a king in Thailand on the money Guilo had given him for services rendered. Severino was capable, it wouldn't take him long to find his way into some Southeast Asian criminal enterprise or to establish one of his own.

"Passport please, Senor Bultamonte." Cardinal Roselli had ditched the Antonio Mecelli in favor of Guilo Bultamonte. He took the surname of his deceased uncle but had kept his given name in order to avoid confusing the housekeeper who may remember him as a child.

The room he'd occupy for less than 24 hours was comfortable and provided enough amenities to keep him entertained. He looked out the window, the area had an industrial unappealing vibe.

The four-hour flight to Punta Arenas took only three due to a strong tailwind. The driver he'd hired to take him to his uncle's estate stood at the baggage claim holding a sign that read, "Senor Guilo Bultamonte."

Guilo only had a carry-on. He'd decided he'd shop for clothes once he was settled, or he'd wear some things of his uncles to tide him over.

His uncle's Punta Arenas estate was located on the outskirts of the city overlooking the Strait of Magellan. Guilo surveyed his newly inherited property, shivering in the arctic air. He went in search of the head housekeeper who'd kept everything in working order since his uncle had passed.

"Pleasure to meet you finally, Senor," the elderly woman greeted Guilo in English.

"You speak English very well. Nice to meet you too, gracias for caring for the estate in my absence. It's quite large, I didn't expect so many rooms. He lived here alone? No?"

"Oh no, Senor, it's a resort hotel. Senor Bultamonte renovated it and created a luxury resort to accommodate tourists from all over the world who required posh surroundings. He was a good businessman, your uncle, he diversified and everything he touched was a success. The sheep farm in Magallanes turned out to have soil rich in oil. Drilling began soon before he died. You're the heir to a fortune, Senor, and now with the onset of biological expeditions and tours to Antarctica, this resort is in the perfect spot to house the explorers before they venture out to sea."

The initial distaste Guilo had for the concept of resort hosting gave way to a sense of gratification. His mind was racing with ideas on how to fuel the already thriving businesses his uncle had established. To start, he'd keep the current staff, if worthy, give them a generous raise to keep them happy and loyal, move into his uncle's quarters, and hire a marketer to lure international travelers to this remote but enchanting corner of the world. Maybe even form his own expedition company. The prospects were boundless.

Guilo found his uncle's office in a sorry state of disarray. Papers were strewn all over in no particular order. The will was laying out on the desk for all the world to see. He was clearly listed as next of kin and sole beneficiary; when he died or should he be found to be incompetent the entire estate would be divided evenly among Senor Bultamonte's loyal employees. The attorney apparently held an addendum to the will which spelled out specific details.

He opened the file cabinet next. It appeared that the sheep farm which spread over the vast property was overseen by a manager. In the last few years, his uncle had been an absentee landlord. First order of business, after recovering from his whirlwind trip, Guilo would hire a sea plane to check on the Magallanes property.

As much as Guilo hated to fly in small planes, looking out at the rough seas below him, he knew he would not have fared well boating over to Magallanes. The pilot seemed young and inexperienced at first glance, but he'd proven to be adept at navigating the winds in the arctic skies. The plane landed without incident on the cusp of the property nearest to the coast.

The temperature was a balmy 60 degrees, a bit of an anomaly for this time of year. Guilo chose to walk the land despite having been greeted by a jeep driven erratically by the nervous farm manager. Guilo was sure he feared his job was in jeopardy. It just might be, Guilo thought as he walked on and observed the spartan patches of grass. Even he knew that this grass was not suitable to produce healthy sheep for market.

Guilo stood on a cliff and looked out to the sea. He'd need some time to make a proper assessment of all of his uncle's holdings in order to determine which ones were most profitable and which could be sold off to aid in the sustenance of the more successful businesses. It was a daunting responsibility and not what he'd planned to do in retirement but it would afford him security, and a steady flow of income, and he had no other choice.

His phone buzzed in his pocket, it both startled and amazed him. How it managed to find a signal here at the bottom of the world was astounding. It was Severino calling from the other end of the earth. Guilo shook his head. He stuck his hand in his pocket, raised his arm up over his head, and tossed the phone along with the USB stick, and his collar, out into the angry sea.

The wind kicked up; Guilo, used to the intense Roman sun, struggled to remain standing.

He'd decided to stay a few days in order to get a handle on how things were run or not run, which seemed to be the current status. The manager, Vincente Perez, stood idly watching as three farmhands along with a mangy dog herded the sheep into a dilapidated barn. Guilo figured this was business as usual, or the manager was usually absent and the farm was run solely by the laborers. In a few days, he'd have a better idea of finances and maybe have the time to survey the neighboring farms, maybe lure a more capable manager with a wad of cash.

He folded his arms across his chest, thrust himself shoulder first against the wind, and moved in the direction of his uncle's rarely used cabin. The provisions were spartan, consisting of a cot, a ragged chair, and a table with one chair. The kitchen held some canned foods, and a few pots and pans. There was running water, several flannel blankets, and barely worn work clothes hung in the closet.

Guilo heard a slight knock on the door before the manager presented himself, "Is there anything you need to see before you leave, Senor?"

"I'm not leaving today, I'm staying a few days. I can handle the farmhands if you'd like some time off."

Vincente Perez looked alarmed. He'd never been offered time off. He suspected his days as manager were limited now that the nephew was in charge.

"Whatever you wish, Senor. I'll catch the boat to Punta Arenas. I'll come back tomorrow to check on you if I can. The weather is turning. It's our cold, wet season with little hope of a reprieve until September. There's firewood, if the power goes out it's all you'll have. Are you sure you want to stay here alone?"

Guilo waved Vincente off, escorted him to the door and said, "I'll be in touch."

Guilo regretted having thrown his phone into the sea, but he'd been lucky so far and didn't expect his luck to change now.

Vincente caught the last boat to Punta Arenas. The farmhands remained, they were among the few inhabitants of the punishing Magallanes region. The weather near the edge of Antarctica was unpredictable. When it rained it was torrential, the cold was biting, and a snow squall could fly in off the sea and blow for hours.

Vincente startled his mother, Isa, when he walked into the kitchen of the house in Punta Arenas. She hadn't seen him since Senor Bultamonte died.

"What are you doing here?"

"I was told to take time off. I think I'm about to be fired. Maybe we all are."

"Something is strange about the nephew. I'd always heard he'd become a priest and had been made a cardinal. And that he was a high up one in the Vatican. Why would he want to be all the way down here if he was a powerful cardinal?"

"I don't know, Mama. He insisted on staying in that old cabin. He thinks he can oversee the laborers. How's he going to fare if the weather turns as predicted?"

"I wouldn't risk your life going to rescue him, especially if you think he's going to let you go. Let him see firsthand how hard life is here."

Chapter Sixty

Sophia was frantic. She'd been up since sunrise, rifling through her closet full of dated clothes looking for something to wear to her audience with Pope Joseph. Her bed was piled high with dresses she'd deemed unsuitable. Lauretta knocked lightly before opening the still unlocked door to Sophia's apartment. There was no sign of life coming from the apartment next door now occupied by Chris. He didn't have the same wardrobe woes and could sleep another hour or so.

Lauretta had two black dresses and a lace veil draped over one arm; she held a cup of cappuccino in the other.

"I'm thinking of wearing this white dress, what do you think, Lauretta?"

"You do know I'm Jewish, Sophia, but one thing I know about Papal Audiences is only royal women have the privilege of wearing white. Black dress is what's required for all other visitors. I took the liberty of bringing these two dresses for you to consider."

Sophia took the dresses from Lauretta. One was a black lace Armani dress with long sleeves; it was fitted, had a high collar, and fell just below Sophia's knees. A matching mantilla completed the outfit. The other dress was a simple black shift with a jacket. Sophia chose the Armani. She'd wear the plain black pumps she'd bought just before she'd been taken. They were still in the box.

"You look stunning, Sophia," Chris said when he saw her, "Pope Joseph will get more than he bargained for with this audience."

Chris knew he was staring at Sophia, he knew he was making her uncomfortable. He knew, too, if he didn't break free of her spell, his breaking heart would never mend. He'd gotten Sophia this far, she'd confront the pope face to face in an hour, thanks to him, regain custody of her daughter, probably marry Alessandro, and live forever after here in Rome. He'd have to adjust to life without her as he'd done before. How strange fate was. Why did she come back into his life only to be snatched away again?

Chris left the room to make a call. He'd promised to notify Cardinal Alfonso when they were on their way. He wasn't answering. Chris left a brief message and hung up. The next call was to the Inspector General of the Gendarmerie who'd agreed to provide protective services to Sophia while she visited Vatican City. The Vatican Police intended to be on guard and would arrest Cardinal Roselli should the pope condone it.

"We'd better get going, Sophia, the traffic in Rome can be fierce at this hour."

Sophia hugged Lauretta, "Thank you for the dress, I'll see you later, hopefully with Nevaeh. She'll be needing a nonna. Will you be her nonna?"

Lauretta's eyes filled, "Si, si. Sophia, be safe. Don't worry, whatever happens, you are stronger than you know."

The prime minister's car was waiting on the outskirts of Trastevere. Chris held the door to the back seat open for Sophia. She slid into the car and found herself seated next to Alessandro. Chris grunted in his direction before placing himself in the front passenger seat. The car drove off towards Vatican City.

"Alessandro, what are you doing here?"

"I wasn't about to let you go alone, Sophia."

"She's hardly alone, Alessandro," Chris told him.

"Boys, please. I can't referee, not now."

Tim Daniels escorted Chris and Sophia into the inner offices of the Apostolic Palace.

"His Holiness will be here shortly to greet you."

Tim placed two wooden chairs in front of the Pope's elaborate chair designed for occasions such as this. Tim left the room and the couple remained standing in wait.

"His Holiness, that's rich," Sophia said under her breath.

Alessandro stood guard at one of the exits, the Inspector General joined him and instructed his army of gendarmerie to scatter around the perimeter and wait for further instructions should Cardinal Roselli need to be contained.

Sophia was on edge. Her skin was clammy and she struggled to maintain her composure. It wasn't her intent to make a scene, she wanted what was rightfully hers, she wanted back what had been stolen from her. She'd never be able to make up for all the time she'd lost. She'd have to attempt to form a bond with her thirteen-year-old daughter for the first time. A fear of unknown possible scenarios that could follow this meeting filled Sophia with a dread she'd not experienced before. It felt like she was at the edge of a new horizon which could transform or devastate her. It was hard for her to breathe.

She stood in the corner of the room with her back to the door. As instructed, she veiled her head with the black mantilla Lauretta had provided. Chris waited near the door; he'd protect Sophia, running interference if need be.

Tim opened the door, "Holy Father, may I present Chris DeMarco and his wife."

Chris was the first to greet Pope Joseph, "I apologize in advance for what is about to happen."

Sophia remained facing the back wall. She turned around once Chris finished with his impromptu apology which she found unnecessary and inappropriate considering the circumstances.

Sophia adjusted her veil. She turned to face the pope just as he thrust his hand towards her in order for her to kiss his ring as was customary at Papal Audiences.

"I don't think I'll partake," Sophia told him narrowing her eyes while trying to remain calm.

"Sophia, my God!" The pope was visibly shaken. Sophia was exquisite. The last time he'd seen her she was a young girl, now despite all she appeared before him a sophisticated woman, a vision of loveliness.

"Chris, please leave us."

"I don't think that's wise," Chris told him.

"I'll be quite safe; the palace is surrounded by gendarmerie and the prime minister has sent his own protective guards to watch over the border."

"Sophia, what do you mean?"

"Seriously, Joe, I don't care how powerful you are. You know as well as I do what has been done to me. I know you're the supreme ruler of this tiny nation and you hold the cards but I want my daughter returned to me. Many people have been apprised of this tragic situation that you sparked somehow by allowing the corrupt Cardinal Roselli and his band of thugs to arrange for the vile assault on me and the kidnapping of my baby. I'm sure you're aware of the murders he ordered, all to protect the Church and you from potential scandal. How could you? How do you sleep at night? How do you let yourself be called 'His Holiness'? I demand to see my daughter and I demand Cardinal Roselli be held accountable."

Sophia was beginning to unravel, she felt her eyes well up. She willed herself not to cry.

Pope Joseph stiffened in his seat, he scrambled to think of how to respond.

"Sophia, I will order the return of Nevaeh to you but first I need some assurances. It isn't a simple matter to hold Cardinal Roselli accountable for his actions. I'll need tangible proof that he had direct involvement. It's a complicated process and not one I devised. These procedures have been in place long before I became pope. I heard that you had an injury and lost your memory. It was in Nevaeh's best interest that she remain here. If I return her you'll have to assure me that you will keep the origins of her birth between us. I have an obligation to protect the Church from suffering irreparable damage due to our past indiscretion."

"Spare me. I have no interest in your insane excuses. I wouldn't have had an injury if you'd let us be. If I could kill you with my bare hands I would. You are beneath contempt. You are a hypocrite of epic proportions. Now send for Nevaeh or I will release this story to the press. Given the current climate in the Church, I'm sure it will be readily believed. After all, stealing children from their mothers is imbedded in its history."

Pope Joseph was astounded; Sophia had done her homework. He picked up the phone, "Tim, please tell Cardinal Alfonso to bring the girl to me."

Chris paced the hallway outside of Tim Daniels' office, "What is going on, Tim?"

"His Holiness asked me to call Cardinal Alfonso, he wants him to bring the child."

Chris sighed with relief. "But," Tim continued, "the cardinal isn't answering his phone. I've asked one of the sisters to go to his room."

Sophia took a seat, she stared hard at the pope. It was taking an interminable amount of time for Nevaeh to materialize.

Sister Anna, a young nun barely out of the novitiate, knocked on the door to the humble room Cardinal Alfonso occupied. She knocked again; when he failed to answer she took the household keys out of her apron pocket and unlocked the door. She opened the door slightly at first so as not to startle the cardinal. She called out his name. Still hearing no response, she walked into the narrow vestibule and turned the corner to the side of the room towards the unadorned bed with the simple wooden cross above it. She covered her nose as she took in a whiff of vomit.

"Oh no," Sister Anna gasped.

Cardinal Alfonso lay face down on the bed, his body was sprawled half on and half off with his arm dangling along the side. Sister Anna made the sign of the cross first over the cardinal and then over herself before leaving the room. She ran through the marble hallway, screaming for the other sisters.

"I think Cardinal Alfonso has died. Call someone!"

Sister Dorothea, an imposing German nun who'd been in the service of the Papal Palace for twenty years, had witnessed many a death. Her bulky body pressed itself through the narrow hallway. Sister Anna followed. Sister Dorothea stepped over the puddle of vomit undeterred, she placed her fingertips on the cardinal's neck.

"He's not dead, his pulse is faint, go call an ambulance, ambulanza, now Sister Anna, then call the papal offices."

Sister Dorothea had known Alfonso Aleo for many years. Aside from quiet grief, he had no afflictions. His yearly physical had recently taken place, he'd returned home afterwards, and had jokingly reported he had the heart of a teenager. Sister Dorothea had a sixth sense, she'd been in the Vatican a long time. While she knew her place in the pecking order, Sister Dorothea was no fool, she'd doubted the sincerity of the American pope. Something was amiss. Why was a young girl living in the Vatican? Cardinal Alfonso had sole charge of her but Cardinal Roselli was always lurking about them. She was wary of the company Cardinal Roselli kept. She kept her distance, but whenever she was in his presence, she sensed his malevolence.

She looked around the room for signs of foul play. An opened crystal carafe sat on the cardinal's desk. A matching glass was filled a third of the way with whiskey. Sister Dorothea bent down to smell the contents. She touched nothing.

Sister Anna returned with the emergency squad.

"Any history of stroke, heart problems, or any other relevant medical issues we need to know about?"

Sister Dorothea shook her head, "No, he just had an exam. He's perfect."

"Is he on any medications?"

"No, but it seems he had some whiskey?"

"Do you suspect something, Sister?"

Sister Dorothea knew she was crossing the line, but the old teachings she'd been indoctrinated in, whereby she was obligated to respect and obey her superiors, had dissipated in light of the unholy activities she'd silently witnessed.

"Yes, I do. I'd rather not elaborate but I have sincere doubts that this episode is a natural occurrence."

The medical team worked to stabilize the cardinal before moving him onto the stretcher. Sister Dorothea followed them to the waiting ambulance where the Vatican Police were already standing guard. They abandoned their post and were escorted to the cardinal's room.

"Seal this room off. I'll need to speak to Pope Joseph. Take samples of the vomit and seal the whiskey bottle, the glass, and anything else you find," the Inspector General told his men.

Tim Daniels' skin grew hot with anxiety, he had a heaviness in his chest making it difficult to breathe normally, "Chris, Cardinal Alfonso was found unconscious in his room, he was barely breathing. He just got a clean bill of health; how could this happen?"

"It happens sometimes, Tim, but considering all that has gone on I'd be suspicious of foul play."

"The Inspector General is combing the cardinal's room. He needs the pope's permission to call in a Roman CSI team."

"Where's Cardinal Roselli?" Chris asked.

Chapter Sixty-One

"Please excuse me for a moment, I have to tend to an emergency," Pope Joseph informed Sophia, leaving her no time to respond before he left the room, closing the door behind him.

Sophia had the feeling she was being stonewalled. Something was wrong, she felt it. Maybe she was being paranoid. It had been foolish of her to think she could walk into the Vatican, demand the return of her long-lost daughter, and they would comply without incident.

Sophia was running out of patience; she reached for the doorknob just as the door swung open. She was a breath away from the pope. He looked at her with the same soft affectionate eyes that had once mesmerized her. The spell he'd cast no longer had an effect, her heart had hardened.

"Where is my daughter?"

"Sophia, Cardinal Alfonso has taken ill, he's unconscious, he was transported to a hospital in Rome."

"Is it foul play?"

"Why would you say that?"

"Seriously? What do you call what was done to me, our daughter, the policemen who were killed, and who knows what else all to safeguard your reputation?"

Pope Joseph maintained his composure, "Sophia, I've sent someone to the convent to retrieve Nevaeh. I'm asking you to please refrain from referring to her as 'our daughter.'"

Sophia shook her head in disgust wondering how she could ever have let herself fall in love with this man. All she wanted to do now was to get him out of her sight.

The butterflies in Sophia's stomach had become a permanent affliction, but now after hearing a slight knock on the door, she felt them rise up into her throat. She thought she'd pass out with anticipation as she fully expected her daughter to appear, but it was Tim Daniels summoning the pope. The two went into the hallway, leaving the door ajar. Sophia pushed the door fully open and barged in between the two men, "No more secrets, what's going on? Where's my child?"

Tim looked at the pope for guidance.

"Tell her," Pope Joseph instructed.

Tim was stunned. The pope whom he'd respected, even admired, now appeared weak. All this, compounded by the fact that the pope had revealed he was aware of Tim's confession, was beginning to take a scandalous turn in Tim's mind. Pope Joseph must have innocently confided in Cardinal Roselli. Perhaps he'd been unaware of the power Cardinal Roselli held, unaware the cardinal would exert his power, and resort to whatever it took to maintain the status quo. Or, Tim thought, maybe the pope knew all along what the cardinal would do upon hearing the pope's confession and he'd turned a blind eye to it.

"She's gone," Tim told the anxious mother. "The sisters haven't seen her for at least a week, they'd assumed Cardinal Alfonso took her away. She lived with them, but she'd spent most of the time with him. The Inspector General sent his men to search for Cardinal Roselli. They've notified the Roman police."

Tim left something out, he didn't want to further alarm Sophia. There were no pictures of Nevaeh to provide to the authorities. There was nothing for them to show the public to aid in the search for a child missing in Rome.

"She could be anywhere by now," Sophia screeched. "Look at all the guards here, checking people in. No one has access without being scrutinized yet a child can be taken out of here unnoticed. You stole her from me only to let her be lost possibly forever. You put her in danger, into the hands of a dangerous criminal parading around as a man of God. Who are you? How could I ever have been with you? I must have been insane."

Tim's eyes widened upon hearing Sophia's rant, the plot was unraveling in an unexpected direction. The pope was the child's father, Tim knew it, he wondered why he hadn't figured it out before. It all fit.

Chris had been assisting the gendarmerie, filling them in on details they may have overlooked regarding Cardinal Alfonso's involvement with Cardinal Roselli. He'd heard Sophia's cries and burst into the room.

"What's going on?"

"Find Alessandro for me, please, Chris." Chris frowned but left the papal offices and went in search of the new man in Sophia's life. He'd see this to its conclusion, no matter the outcome, and then he'd be done. He had to be. Every rejection took a piece of him, he felt wounded.

Chapter Sixty-Two

Inspector General Contini sat at Tim Daniels' desk waiting for him to return to his office. He knew he'd need the pope's permission to interrogate the cardinal if he was found, but Tim Daniels was a civilian, and even though he was on the Vatican payroll, he was free game.

Tim stiffened in his tracks when he saw an armed gendarmerie officer standing outside his office door. He feared he'd be implicated somehow, be accused of aiding and abetting Cardinal Roselli. He nodded at the officer, entered his office, and came face to face with Inspector General Contini.

"Have a seat, Tim."

Tim did as he was told. He sat at his desk, rubbing his perspiring hands on his shaking knees in an effort to calm himself.

"Tell me everything you know about Cardinal Guilo Roselli. Start with how you, a layperson, came to acquire this position."

Tim relayed the story of his casual meeting with Antonio Mecelli, he told the inspector of his suspicions, and about the setting up of a hidden camera which the inspector already knew. He omitted the part where he'd sent a copy of the video to his mother in New York. It was his safety net. He ended the rendition with his discovery of the smashed hidden camera in Cardinal Roselli's ransacked office. Tim assured the inspector that he had seen Cardinal Roselli only in passing just after he'd returned from his South American trip.

Inspector Contini rose from his seat; without a word, he pulled out his cell phone and called the office of the prime minister. Italian Interpol National Central Bureau (NCB) in Rome had the jurisdiction to check passenger lists on International flights. Inspector Contini awaited their call. He had no authority to detain or to extradite Cardinal Roselli. The pope held all the authority. He'd have to sanction all investigations regarding the cardinal, but the child was another matter.

The call from the NCB officer came through faster than expected. Inspector Contini learned that a Guilo Bultamonte had landed in Santiago, Chile a fortnight ago, he traveled alone, and there was no evidence of his having left the city. The inspector mulled over the possibilities. If the child had been seen with the cardinal, an extradition could have been instituted immediately. The child's whereabouts were anyone's guess. Cardinal Roselli may not even be involved in her disappearance. Inspector Contini headed out the door. The official car he used to travel outside Vatican City was waiting outside in the square.

"Ospedale, Salvator Mundi," Inspector Contini told the officer who was his designated driver. The official car sped through the streets of Rome with its siren screeching. It stopped abruptly at the emergency entrance to the private hospital on the outskirts of Trastevere where Cardinal Alfonso was fighting for his life.

Chapter Sixty-Three

Ever the optimist, Lauretta set the table out on the terrace for five. It promised to be a lovely evening. The skies were clear and a light breeze blew the fragrant lemongrass scent up and over the patio. Hours had passed, and while she knew Sophia, Alessandro, and Chris wouldn't return for lunch, the sun was setting and she was starting to worry.

The slam of the outside door startled her and she rushed to the hallway in time to see Alessandro ushering the clearly distressed Sophia up the stairs. They were alone, there was no child.

No one had sought the counsel of the older and wiser Lauretta when the plan to blindside the pope by masquerading Sophia as Chris DeMarco's wife was enacted. She'd have told them the old cliché "honesty is the best policy" which held as true today as it did when whomever first said it was quoted.

Lauretta held Sophia's other arm, she placed her head on Lauretta's shoulder. Sophia was suffering, probably wishing she'd never regained her memory. Lauretta sent Alessandro to the kitchen for some wine and took Sophia into the bedroom. Sophia could not be left alone; whatever had transpired today in the Vatican had inflamed the already volatile situation. This pope had nothing to gain and everything to lose by relinquishing custody of Nevaeh to Sophia.

Sophia lifted her arms mechanically for Lauretta to remove her dress; Lauretta replaced the black lace dress with a white hand-embroidered cotton nightgown she'd bought on the island of Burano years before. Sophia was emotionless, drained, almost as if she'd been anesthetized. She sat childlike in front of the mirrored vanity while Lauretta brushed her long honey-colored hair. Sophia was soothed by the motherly gesture.

"No one ever brushed my hair before," she said in barely a whisper.

"Well I'm doing it and I'll do it forever if it helps you."

"I don't deserve you, Lauretta."

"You deserve me and so much more. Don't talk, don't think, don't fill your mind with what ifs, just be in the moment, be calm."

Lauretta recalled her days in the concentration camp. With her mother long gone, her father had said those words over and over to her the few times she'd been in his presence. They'd helped her live in the moment then, as she hoped they'd help Sophia live in the moment now. Worrying and anticipating never did anyone any good. No one can predict the future; one can only guess. Best to let nature take its course. It was easy for her to say. She was old looking back; the young looked forward and tried to manipulate the outcome. She knew better.

Alessandro came in with a carafe of wine and a panino. Sophia hadn't eaten all day.

"Take this, eat," he told her.

She looked up at him with vacant eyes, "What now? Maybe she's dead, maybe she's been sold into one of those sex rings, maybe she's been adopted by a family far away. I have no way to find her. I have no hope, after all this, no hope."

Alessandro felt helpless, "I will do everything in my power to help you find her."

He said the words but he knew they were meaningless; he didn't know what the child looked like. It was like searching for an Italiana child with brown eyes in Roma. There were no distinguishing marks that would set her apart, make her stand out among the rest, and cause someone to cry out, "Here she is!" Their fate was in the hands of the universe, it was the only hope.

Alessandro heard the buzzer to Lauretta's apartment building ring out. Who on earth was it, he wondered. Lauretta looked at him with pleading eyes. She held the hairbrush in her hand. Sophia's locks were free of knots, but she leaned into the brush and relished the comfort it gave her.

"Pronto," Alessandro said, holding the button to the intercom down.

"Pronto, Signore Jenco, it's Inspector Contini, may I have a word?"

"Si," Alessandro buzzed the inspector in and led him to the terrace to have that word in private.

"Any news I need to know about?" As an official in the office of the Roman Prime Minister, Alessandro Jenco would have outranked Inspector Contini under normal circumstances, but the Vatican world was a convoluted web of covert policies meant to bamboozle the outside world.

"As a matter of fact, I've been to the hospital. Cardinal Alfonso Aleo is in the Intensive Care Unit at Salvator Mundi outside of Trastevere. The doctors were cryptic, but informed me that the poor cardinal has been poisoned. I'm awaiting the toxicology report from our team. They took samples of the vomitus found in the room as well as from the carafe and the glass of whiskey."

"Anything else?" Alessandro asked.

"Si, apparently, Cardinal Roselli had an alias. Long story short, he traveled to Santiago, Chile three days ago under the name of Guilo Bultamonte. He was alone."

"So, the child wasn't with him. Where is she? What about Severino Poverelli, Cardinal Roselli's henchman?"

"He's vanished without a trace. We're looking for the cardinal's chauffeur. Italy has an extradition treaty with Chile but we can't put any action in place without the pope's approval."

"He just may get away with murder, it's unbelievable." Alessandro looked up at the inspector. Despite his high-powered rank, he felt vulnerable. The woman he loved was being battered emotionally and there was little he could do about it.

"Did the woman, Sophia, learn anything new during the audience she'd had with Pope Joseph?"

"I wasn't present. She's distraught so I assume no, and the child is now missing. How do we find her?"

"If there's a God, and I have my doubts after all I've been privy to, fate will lend a hand. We have nothing to go on. Perhaps Cardinal Alfonso placed her somewhere for safekeeping. It's been made clear that he loved her. He may have realized the danger she was in. He had to have known walls were closing in on Cardinal Roselli and he'd be desperate enough to do something rash. Let's have hope she's secure and unharmed."

"Si, yes, let's hope. Grazie, thank you, Inspector Contini, for keeping me apprised. Here's my mobile phone number. Please call me if anything develops."

The men shook hands. The inspector left and Alessandro remained on the terrace looking out at the nightlife on the streets of Trastevere. How carefree they all looked, tourists and locals alike, enjoying the ambience, taking in the sights, sounds, and flavor of this slice of Roman life. Part of him longed to be unencumbered but the better part of him knew he'd found someone special. He'd waited a long time to find her and he was willing to wait as long as it took to make her a permanent part of his life.

Lauretta joined Alessandro on the terrace. She picked a bougainvillea blossom and placed it behind her ear. She wasn't sure why, perhaps she was searching for a bit of frivolous normalcy in this state of turmoil.

"She's asleep, I confess I crushed one of my sleeping pills into her wine. She fell asleep mid-sentence, poor thing. She was .mostly rambling on about her life in Venice. Oh, Alessandro, what a tragedy this is."

"Laura, what life was more tragic than yours?"

"Si, but I'm a survivor and she's so fragile, our Sophia."

Chapter Sixty-Four

The sun had set, the sky was cloudless and dark, but the moon provided enough light for Pope Joseph to find his way through the Papal Gardens. It soothed him to be outside. He felt trapped inside a world he knew deep down he wasn't meant to be a part of. Perhaps he'd always been afraid of growing up, of adult responsibility; the priesthood had been the perfect vocation to avoid all the things he'd feared. He'd have guidance, have little responsibility, be free of financial burdens, and the woes of family ties. Becoming pope had not been on his radar but when he'd shot up the ranks, was made cardinal, and had secured the admiration of his colleagues, his ego soared. He'd known he was ill-equipped for the role as Supreme Pontiff. He was young compared to popes in the past but it wasn't youth making him a poor fit, it was the fact that he'd never been in charge of anything or anyone. He'd been frivolous, hiding behind the collar, using it to insinuate himself, using it as a manipulative tool. Once he'd ascended to the throne of St. Peter, he'd expected to follow the rote set of rules the Church had exercised for centuries to maintain the status quo. When the "holier than thou" hypocrisy emerged into the limelight, the hierarchy had been exposed, and now he would be as well. It was a matter of time. Too many people knew about his affair with Sophia, and soon they'd put the pieces of Nevaeh's parentage together.

Pope Joseph sat on a stone ledge and rested for a few moments, the trickling sound of a nearby fountain installed decades ago to provide a place of solace to those seeking it did little to comfort him. Self-reflection had not done him any good. He had to step up and be a leader. He mulled over a few differing scenarios. He could wait for Sophia or Chris to bring the story out in the open or he could do it himself. He could appeal to the people, be contrite, ask their forgiveness in a public forum;

be the first pope in history to humble himself in such a way. It could serve to humanize the Church. The world already knew of the scandals, why not be candid about all of it; it would be a novel approach. There was the risk of the Curia forcing his resignation. He'd broken his vows; if he openly admitted to it all, there'd be no denying it later on. With Nevaeh missing, there was no way to prove he was her father. Suddenly, he had another thought.

The lights in the convent were on despite the early morning hour. The sisters rose early, first to pray and then to ready the pope's linens for the upcoming week. Pope Joseph entered through the kitchen door startling the young novice who was preparing breakfast. She dropped to her knees when she recognized the visitor.

"Please get up, I need you to do something for me and I want it kept between us. Will you do that?"

"Of course, Your Holiness."

"The child, Nevaeh, won't be returning, she has found a home, praise God. Please see to it that her belongings are packed up, and her room cleaned and readied for the next guest. Have her things delivered to my offices. Thank you, Sister."

Pope Joseph extended his hand and blessed the young nun. The shame he felt had to be put aside. As far as anyone who'd been involved in Nevaeh's care knew, she was an orphan of a Swiss Guard. Anyone who'd suspected otherwise had no proof. Now he was out from under the heavy hand of Cardinal Roselli, and could execute the authority that was his God-given right.

The sky was brightening by the time he'd walked back towards the papal offices. Chris DeMarco was sitting in the outer lobby.

"Chris, what are you doing here so early?"

"I never left, I spent the night attempting to aid the gendarmerie in their investigation. It's odd that Cardinal Alfonso took ill, and Cardinal Roselli has vanished along with the girl all within a day, don't you think?"

Chris had not been privy to any findings of value the police may have uncovered. He wondered if the pope was hiding something. He pressed on.

"Have you heard any news of Cardinal Alfonso?"

"No, it seems the police suspect foul play. I'll have Tim call the hospital when he comes in."

"Any idea where Cardinal Roselli has gone?"

"No. Is this an interrogation, Chris?"

"No, but you do seem unconcerned. The child is missing too. No one has seen her in a few days. Didn't you know?"

"I've just been made aware."

"Aren't you alarmed? She's your daughter, she could be in danger."

"There's no evidence of either of those things."

"What do you mean?"

"I mean it's Sophia's word, she has no proof I fathered her child."

"Did you have something to do with Nevaeh's disappearance?"

"No, I most certainly did not."

Chris knew the pope would have the most to lose if Nevaeh is found. He noticed a strand of loose hair on the pope's collar and he changed his approach.

"Well, I just came by to tell you that I'm leaving. I've been reassigned. I wish you all the best, I really do. It won't be easy trying to unite this institution with all the renegades swimming against the tide. I'll be in touch."

As much as Chris wanted to be free of Sophia and the scandalous mess she'd created, he knew he had to find evidence to prove her story to be true. He couldn't just walk away. Chris moved towards the pope and put a hand on his shoulder as a gesture of feigned friendship. He removed his hand and the strand of hair in the process. It may not hold up as a DNA sample but it was the best he could do. He'd bring it to Alessandro to have it secured in case Nevaeh turned up. He couldn't entrust it to the Inspector General; for the most part, the gendarmerie were under the pope's jurisdiction.

Alessandro made arrangements to meet Chris at the office of the Minister of the Interior. As much as he hated to admit it, Alessandro knew Chris and he were on the same side. Both of them had affection for Sophia and would do whatever it took to help her.

Alessandro arrived first. He was escorted to the minister's office.

"The weather has been exceptional, don't you think, Officer Jenco?"

Alessandro hated small talk. He merely nodded. A knock on the door saved him from more of the mundane conversation the minister was famous for when he'd needed to kill time.

The minister stood when Chris entered the room.

"Pleasure to meet you, Signore DeMarco, your reputation precedes you."

"Thank you, sir."

Alessandro pursed his lips and prepared for the minister's speech on the accomplishments of journalist Chris DeMarco. It didn't matter that Alessandro's life had been on the line. No one handed out Pulitzers to Officers of the Ministry of the Interior.

"Signore DeMarco is an award-winning journalist, his bravado as a war correspondent is something to be admired."

"Again, I thank you."

Alessandro wished his first impression of Chris DeMarco had been correct. He'd labeled him a young rogue news guy who had more brawn than brains. He researched Chris and he knew he'd been driven by jealousy; Chris was younger than him, he was Sophia's contemporary while Alessandro was older by nearly a decade. But he'd softened after Sophia had sent Chris to bring him to console her after her meeting with the pope. He felt secure now; he'd won her heart, he'd give her all the time she needed.

"I would like your permission to pursue this story, Signore."

"To what end, Signore DeMarco. Will it ever be told?"

"Maybe, maybe not, but it's worth finding the truth."

"Spoken like a true journalist."

For the next hour, Alessandro and the minister filled Chris in on their findings. He handed over the lock of Pope Joseph's hair to the technician the minister had summoned to retrieve it.

"We intend to authorize two Interpol officers to search for Cardinal Roselli in Chile. This investigation needs to be kept confidential. We will not share any news with the Vatican unless he's found. It is our belief the pope will not defrock him, but will protect him from prosecution to avoid implicating the Holy See in this plot."

The minister hung his head and continued, "This is a tragedy not just for the inner sanctum of the Church but for all believers. Faith will be shaken to its core should this scandal be allowed to surface. It will rock the very foundation of our society should the pope be incriminated. I urge you to consider the consequences should you decide to reveal what you know to the world."

Chris nodded, "I'd like to accompany the officers on this trip. I have some time, I'll go off the record. What I decide to write, if anything about this, remains to be seen. Sophia's suffering a great deal. She isn't going to give up without a fight. But she's up against a powerful entity. It may be a fight she can't possibly win."

Chapter Sixty-Five

An epic ice storm swept across the southern coast of Chile leaving the landscape a frozen tundra. The wind had blown in from the sea first, providing a warning for those with experience, giving the shepherds time to herd the sheep into the heated barn. They, too, hunkered down in the attached fully-equipped living quarters Signor Bultamonte had built for his workers. He'd respected their laboring on his behalf and had rewarded them with comfortable surroundings. One of the laborers, a robust man, about twenty years old, was the last one to enter the dwelling.

"I asked the Senor to join us. I told him he'd be more comfortable here but he frowned and shook his head."

The group exchanged collective knowing glances and shrugged with the gesture of "what can you do?"

Guilo had little knowledge of the ways of nature. There'd been no up-to-the minute newscast foretelling of an imminent storm. He had no worries; soon he'd be rich beyond his dreams, maybe he already was. He couldn't very well lower himself to sleep among the laborers. That would send the wrong message.

The shed abutting his meager shelter held enough wood to keep him warm for several weeks. When he reached into the stack of wood to gather enough for the night a random spider, then another, sheltered under the logs ran up his arm. He brushed them off wondering how they could possibly survive in such a harsh environment.

There hadn't been much in the way of appetizing food in the cupboard. Guilo thought nothing of it, he relished the thought of shedding a few pounds. He started a fire, poured himself a glass of his uncle's whiskey, and laid down in the rickety bed.

It rained ice for six days straight before clearing. Roads were impassible; heavy winds blew across the Bultamonte

Magallanes property leaving the inhabitants isolated from the outside world. The shepherds tended to the sheep as best they could. They were used to living in the punishing climate but the current weather system had blindsided them. July 4th, the coldest day of the Chilean year, was approaching. Temperatures usually hovered around 30 degrees in the Magallanes Region; this pattern had been an anomaly catching everyone off guard.

"Vincente, it's clearing, it's time you went to Magallanes to check on the Senor."

"Mama, the wind is too strong and the drive is long with many impassible roads. I'll wait another day or so but my time might be better spent looking for another job."

"Don't be a pessimist. Senor Bultamonte is new to this, he just needs an experienced hand to show him the way. Give it time."

"He's arrogant. Hard to believe he shared the same blood as his uncle."

Two days passed before Isa could convince her son to travel to the sheep farm. The drilling had stopped for the winter so the only men on the property were the laborers tending to the sheep. They were experienced natives used to the climate fluctuations at the bottom of the world. Vincente trusted their judgement, he knew they'd fare well. He wasn't worried about the farm, it survived worse. Truth was he wasn't worried about Guilo Bultamonte either; worrying meant you cared and he didn't care. The only reason he'd agreed to venture out to the farm on the coldest day of the year was to appease his mother.

The small plane he'd used for this purpose shook violently as it hit a pocket of rough air over the sea. Landing was difficult and the plane swayed from side to side before touching down.

Vincente instructed the pilot to wait for him; he didn't expect to be long. Vincente went first to check on the laborers. They were huddled in their bunker, drinking coffee, and enjoying their free time. They looked content and unscathed.

"Anyone see the Senor?"

"No, he refused to stay here, preferred to be alone in that hut. We offered, he declined, end of story," the youngest in the group told Vincente.

"I'm here to check on him, Isa insisted."

"Ooh, Mama said so," the group of men yelled out teasing Vincente.

He was used to it. He waved a hand at them, before braving the cold on the pretense of possibly rescuing a man he'd quickly come to despise.

"One of you need to come with me in case I need help."

The youngest of the group raised his hand, "I'll come with you."

The wooden door to the cabin was frozen shut. Vincente pounded on the door loosening some of the ice. Signor Bultamonte did not respond. Vincente grabbed a shovel half buried in the ice near the shed. It took the two men over an hour to clear enough ice to be able to open the door just enough for them to squeeze through.

Guilo Bultamonte was laying on his back in the rickety bed. Small crystals adhered to the wooden ceiling, icicles were beginning to take shape.

"Senor, it's Vincente Perez, wake up. I've come to escort you back to Punta Arenas."

When there was no response, Vincente pulled the heavy plaid blanket back. Guilo had been dead for several days. The fire had long been extinguished.

"He must have frozen to death," the young laborer said. He drew closer to the body and saw the unmistakable bites of the reclusive brown spider. The venom usually wasn't fatal, but if left unattended to it could be. Apparently, it had been.

"Spider bite, several of them." The laborer stepped aside to allow Vincente a look.

Guilo's arm was necrotic up to the shoulder. Vincente carefully pulled the blanket up and over Guilo's head as a sign of respect but mostly to avoid encountering the vicious spiders.

Miraculously, Vincente's cell phone worked despite the strong winds. He called his mother first. She was adept at dealing with death.

He resented having to deal with this vile man in any fashion. He'd shown Vincente no respect and now Vincente was expected to sit vigil with his body until the authorities arrived.

Despite his guilt or innocence of the charges against him, had Guilo Roselli, now Bultamonte, died while in the Vatican, he would have had a funeral with all the pomp and circumstance befitting the elevated status he'd enjoyed as cardinal and advisor to the pope. Fate intervened and Guilo Bultamonte was buried in a small family plot on a bluff overlooking the sea alongside his uncle whom he'd barely known in life. Isa Perez and a local parish priest were the only mourners. The priest said a few generic words and the pair left the graveside. The Bultamonte attorney scheduled a meeting with Isa and Vincente for later in the afternoon.

Chapter Sixty-Six

Bundled up in a Sherpa and down parka in the month of July was counterintuitive to Chris' body and his mind. Twenty-four hours earlier, he'd stood sweating in the heat of the Roman sun saying his goodbyes to Sophia on Lauretta's terrace. Silent tears had fallen from her eyes as if someone had turned them on with a switch. She'd been without emotion otherwise. She'd become used to loss. He'd simply told her he'd been reassigned, that he'd gotten nowhere with Pope Joseph, that he may not be allowed to write her story, and he was going to be doing investigative journalism in South America for a while. It wasn't entirely the truth but it wasn't an outright lie either. Neither he nor Alessandro thought it pertinent to inform Sophia of Cardinal Roselli's whereabouts, or that he'd traveled alone. They knew she'd be furious when she learned of their deception but for now she was in a fragile state. Who knew for sure what she was thinking. Who knew if it was better if she believed Cardinal Roselli had the girl or if he'd left her off somewhere. Nevaeh had vanished without a trace. The gendarmerie had finally gotten around to searching Nevaeh's scantily appointed room for signs of foul play after scouring Cardinal Alfonso's quarters, now deemed a crime scene; Nevaeh's room had been stripped bare.

Chris' traveling companions were already known to him, his old compatriots from the first round of dangerous escapades in this Sophia saga. NCB officers Giovanna Cefaro and Vincenzo DeDomenica stood next to him at the baggage claim in the Santiago, Chile airport. They didn't look happy either, they attributed this assignment to be a punishment for the botched Trastevere job. Chris' Italian wasn't perfect but he'd deciphered that much from their conversation in flight.

"It's late, let's check into the airport hotel, get some rest, and start fresh in the morning."

The pair nodded, too tired to argue. They were on an expense account and within reason could have afforded more upscale accommodations. The three took the airport shuttle to the hotel and checked in just as Cardinal Roselli had done a few weeks prior.

Chris pulled the shabby draperies back and looked out at the same industrial landscape the cardinal had viewed. He fell asleep to the sound of a dripping faucet and woke before sunrise, disoriented from jet lag. He took himself to the lobby and poured a cup of stale coffee courtesy of the airport hotel. On a lark, he pulled out the picture of Cardinal Roselli the Interior Minister's office had on file, and had given to each of the three on this assignment.

"Have you seen this man in the past few weeks?"

The young reception hostess took the picture from Chris scrutinizing it before handing it off to her colleague, "Oh yeah, he flew in from Roma. Senor Guilo Bultamonte. Yes, that's him."

"Any idea where he went?"

"No, Senor DeMarco, sorry."

Chris wasn't authorized to check airline or any other transport's list of passengers. He'd have to wake the NCB officers.

"Look the sooner we locate him the sooner we can put this assignment to bed."

"I'd like to go to bed, Chris," Giovanna said with a hint of annoyance.

Chris raised an eyebrow. "Not what I meant, go get Vincenzo. He may as well join this party." Giovanna called the local police precinct, told them who she was, but they didn't seem to care, "We can't see your credentials over the phone, Senora, you'll have to come in."

The traffic in Santiago lived up to its reputation. It took three hours to arrive at the police precinct. Giovanna's frazzled nerves got the better of her; she screamed in broken Spanish to the officer on duty, flashing her papers in the process.

"Take me to the superior officer now," she instructed.

The Chief of the Santiago district police sat behind a messy desk, his portly body spilled off the sides of his chair. He wiped crumbs from his mouth and stood when Giovanna, Vincenzo, and Chris walked in.

He spoke English and enough Italian to pass an inappropriate remark about Giovanna to Vincenzo. Giovanna let loose with a litany of Spanish curses causing the employees in the outer offices to erupt with laughter.

They got what they came for in a matter of minutes. The local Interpol office had been expecting their arrival. They complied with their request. A Guilo Bultamonte had taken a flight from Santiago, Chile to Punta Arenas two weeks prior. He shouldn't be hard to track down.

Isa Perez was a gracious host, she led Chris and the two officers through the entryway and into the kitchen where she was preparing lunch for the staff.

"Please sit and tell me how I can help you."

"Can you tell us where we can find Senor Bultamonte, Senora?"

Vincente could be heard stomping the ice off of his boots in the front hallway.

"This is my son, Vincente Perez."

After the introductions were complete, Giovanna continued, "Have you seen Senor Bultamonte?"

"Si, but not recently, I'll explain."

Isa poured three cups of coffee and placed several small sandwiches in the middle of the table. The three looked famished and to prove it took the food readily.

"Senor Bultamonte, our dear employer, died a few months ago. His nephew Guilo was the sole heir, he arrived here about a week ago. He insisted on visiting the sheep farm in Magallanes.

The region is rugged with unpredictable weather. An ice storm left him stranded in an old cabin that had been basically abandoned. Vincente went to him as soon as it was safe to travel and found him dead."

"From exposure?" Chris asked.

"No, Senor, he had several spider bites on his body. It's odd to find the reclusive brown spiders in Magallanes. They must have hitched a ride on a shipment of wood. The Senor may have been bitten after disturbing the insects in the pile of logs. Usually the venom isn't fatal but the Senor had no treatment and may have had an underlying medical condition. His arm was nearly fully gangrenous. He'd been dead for many hours when Vincente found him. He's buried next to his uncle and grandparents in the family plot. You are welcome to visit the gravesite but it's in Magallanes on the sheep farm. It's not an easy trip. The coroner examined the body and the parish priest said a few words over the grave. If you want to speak to them, you'll have to wait until morning. You are welcome to stay here at our resort."

It felt liberating calling the resort "ours." Isa and her son had worked for decades maintaining the property for Senor Bultamonte, the elder. He'd rewarded them handsomely but his nephew in a few short days had promised to be an adversary. No one was saddened by his passing. The Perezes and the faithful laborers who'd toiled the land would share in the bounty of what Senor Bultamonte had left behind.

When the journalist and the NCB officers left for the day, Vincente retired to his cabin behind the resort stopping first to clean up the ant colony gathering around the oat cereal that had spilled on the outer sidewalk. One of the housemaids must have dropped it on her morning rounds. Vincente scooped them up carefully and placed them in a container. They'd be perfect. He carried the ants to the rarely used garage on the outskirts of the resort. The collection of aquariums where he'd kept the tropical fish he'd had as a kid before moving to this unsuitable climate now held a colony of recluse spiders.

"Eat up, my friends, your buddies did their job. I'll be leaving you soon," Vincente said in a satisfied tone.

Chris related the story Isa had told of Cardinal Roselli's final days to Alessandro on the phone later that night. They'd opted out of staying the night and had no desire to pay respects to the cardinal. They trusted Isa Perez was telling the truth; they'd ask for the medical examiner's official report to be sent to Rome.

"How's Cardinal Alfonso doing?" Chris asked.

"His recovery is slow, he's not regained consciousness yet; the doctors are cautiously optimistic."

"Any findings you'd care to share?"

"Seems it was some kind of insecticide. One that dissolves in alcohol, it's tasteless."

"Huh, isn't that ironic? Cardinal Roselli tries to poison Cardinal Alfonso with insecticide and in turn Cardinal Roselli is killed by spiders. Fate lent a hand in this case, don't you think?"

"Si, seems so, I just wish Sophia would have some happy news of her daughter."

"How is she?"

"She's refusing all sedatives, prefers to feel as she puts it. Lauretta is sick with worry. Sophia's insisting that Cardinal Alfonso holds the key to finding Nevaeh. I'm not so sure. Cardinal Roselli was heartless and unscrupulous, he could have disposed of the child in an unseemly manner I shudder to even think about."

"I don't think so, Nevaeh was afraid of him. I saw her, remember? If he tried to take her out of the Vatican, she would have made a fuss. Someone would have noticed. It's something else. I'm leaving Chile tomorrow, headed to New York. I'll be in touch. Give my best to the ladies."

Chapter Sixty-Seven

Prime Minister Abenante and Inspector General Contini sat side by side in the outer room of the papal offices, each waiting for the emergency audience with Pope Joseph they'd requested. Neither spoke nor revealed to the other just what occurred that necessitated the emergency appointments.

"Holy Father, Prime Minister Abenante and Inspector General Contini are here, they both claim it's urgent but neither have stated a reason," a seminarian who'd been called at the last minute to man the offices told the pope.

"Where's Tim Daniels?"

"I don't know, Your Holiness, he hasn't come in yet."

"Show the men in, please, and call Tim Daniels and see what's keeping him."

Inspector General Contini held the door for Prime Minister Abenante and gestured for him to go first.

"Please sit," Pope Joseph told the men, "now tell me what the urgency is."

Inspector General Contini was the first to speak, "Holy Father, I regret to have to be the one to tell you this, Tim Daniels was found dead in his apartment this morning. The cleaning staff discovered his body when they arrived there at 9 a.m."

"Oh my God, Tim? What happened? He was so young."

"He was strangled. There's more but this information must be kept confidential. It's an ongoing investigation."

"Of course," Pope Joseph responded, and Minister Abenante nodded in agreement.

"The Swiss Guard on duty last night reported seeing Cardinal Roselli's black Mercedes exiting the gates of Vatican City around 10 p.m. We are searching for the car."

"It wasn't Cardinal Roselli, if that's what you're thinking."

"Why is that, Minister Abenante?"

"Because he's dead. I ordered Interpol to dispatch two men to search for the cardinal after it was discovered he used an alias to leave the country. He was tracked to Chile where he had family ties. According to the housekeeper on the family estate, the cardinal adopted the name of his uncle and presented himself as Guilo Bultamonte. He was the sole heir of his uncle's vast estate, and at the time of his death was exploring the family sheep farm in Magallanes, Chile. The climate there is erratic; a storm blew in suddenly, stranding the cardinal. He was held up in his uncle's rustic cabin where he succumbed to several bites from the indigenous brown recluse spider. The laborers on the farm buried him in the family plot. But it is within your right as Supreme Pontiff to have his body exhumed and brought to the Vatican for proper burial if you see fit to do so. The death of Cardinal Roselli is somewhat ironic; it seems Cardinal Alfonso ingested an insecticide. Traces of it were found in his whiskey glass. Strange that an insect killed the alleged murderer."

The Prime Minister continued, "The child has not been found as of yet. Cardinal Roselli traveled to Chile alone, she was not with him. She could be anywhere. We have not located Severino Poverelli, and Cardinal Alfonso has not regained consciousness. The doctors are optimistic but he isn't young and complications can arise."

Pope Joseph was stunned. He had no words except to say, "You know, Cardinal Roselli once told me he was raised by his father's family. His parents never married, his mother never wanted a child, thought her life was ruined when she became pregnant. She named him, 'Guilo,' not Guilio like most people assume, but Guilo, which means 'treacherous' in Spanish. I guess he lived up to his name."

The two men finished depositing their collective dreadful news in the pope's lap and left him to ponder it all. Guilt flooded over him in waves. He vacillated between feeling culpable for having confessed his indiscretion to Cardinal Roselli all those years ago, inciting an already disturbed man to commit crimes on behalf of the Holy See, and being relieved he was free of the cardinal and all evidence of his having fathered Nevaeh. He had no idea where she was or who had taken her but he hoped she'd never be found. Should she be found there would still be no proof he was her father. They'd have to obtain a DNA sample from him and he'd refuse. Nevaeh resurfacing was the least of his concerns at the moment. Cardinal Roselli was dead, Tim Daniels too, along with several officers of the Ministry of the Interior, and Cardinal Alfonso Aleo was fighting for his life in a Roman hospital; it wouldn't be long before people would start asking questions. If the news of the deaths and suspected poisoning of Vatican citizens seeped through the walls of Vatican City and out into the world, another scandal would befall the Church from which she may not recover unscathed. He'd need to be proactive. He sat at his desk, picked up the phone, and dialed Cardinal Giuseppe Giordano.

Chapter Sixty-Eight

Canon lawyer Giuseppe Giordano was sitting vigil at the bedside of his longtime friend and colleague, Alfonso Aleo, when his cell phone buzzed. He was taken aback to hear Pope Joseph's voice on the other end and not his secretary who'd usually made the pope's preliminary calls.

"I apologize for disturbing you, Cardinal Giordano, I need to meet with you as soon as possible. It's a matter of utmost importance."

"Of course, Your Holiness, I'm sitting with Cardinal Alfonso. I'll leave immediately."

Cardinal Giordano was privy to most of the story Pope Joseph was telling him. He knew of Cardinal Roselli's alleged involvement in the kidnapping of the child, Nevaeh, and the murders carried out on his order, while his men were out pursuing the girl's mother.

"The administrative assistant, Tim Daniels, was found dead this morning. Foul play is suspected."

"Do they suspect Guilo?"

"No, Cardinal, he'd already traveled to his family home in Chile where he apparently succumbed to an insect bite. They buried him in the family plot. But his car was spotted leaving Vatican City earlier in the evening. This is beginning to unravel like an Agatha Christie novel. I never meant for all this to happen. I confessed to Guilo in order to obtain absolution before I became pope."

Pope Joseph hung his head, the cardinal had little sympathy. As Supreme Pontiff, Pope Joseph held sway over Cardinal Roselli but instead he'd looked the other way while he'd put the Church's reputation deeper into harm's way.

"Questions are going to be asked. How do we handle Cardinal Roselli's death so as to not plunge us further into scandal? He should have a funeral fit for a cardinal but under the circumstances it's hard to swallow doing that. However, few of us are aware of his criminality. I need your counsel."

Cardinal Giordano thought for a moment; he detested the idea of sending that vile Cardinal Roselli off into eternity in a hail of glory but as always appearances must be kept up.

"I can draw up a will and fake his signature. It could state his desire to retire in Chile, and be buried there when the time came. Something along those lines. It will keep the status quo for now. If another USB is found implicating the cardinal, and the child is found and it's proven that you are her father, then you may be encouraged to resign. This is all worst case scenario, of course."

"Can't I refuse to give a DNA sample?"

"Yes, I would advise you along those lines. It would be beneath you to provide your DNA, but it wouldn't stop the tongues from wagging. We'll bear that cross if it falls on our shoulders, not before."

"Yes, but better to be armed just in case. How's Cardinal Alfonso, I should have asked earlier?"

"The doctors are optimistic but he's not regained consciousness. His symptoms mimic that of a stroke but his brain function appears to be normal. It's odd."

"I'll remember him in my prayers. I think it's best if you draw up the will. I'll announce the death, and we can plan for a Vatican funeral."

The first to be notified was the Dean of the College of Cardinals, Cardinal Georgio Bianchi. He was small in stature with a gruff manner and had stemmed from a small town in Calabria. He took his job much too seriously; he'd be the perfect person to preside over the funeral of Cardinal Roselli, lavishing it with the usual pomp and circumstance the funeral attendees would expect. It didn't take long for Cardinal Giordano to script the deceptive will. It looked authentic to the untrained eye and if anyone was surprised the seemingly devoted Cardinal Roselli chose to be buried in a remote area of Chile instead of the Vatican, no one said a word.

Since there was no physical body to bless, Pope Joseph skipped the funeral, raising some eyebrows. He made his apologies through Cardinal Giordano, stating his grief over the loss of Tim Daniels was overwhelming. He wasn't exaggerating. Tim had been the only other American working in Vatican City, and Pope Joseph had taken comfort in having him around.

Pope Joseph was despondent and on the verge of plunging into a deep depression. He'd considered the ramifications of resigning the papacy. Where would he go? He'd have to remain at the Vatican for safety sake but what would he do? He was still young but lacked the skills for scholarly pursuits. He wasn't much of a writer and producing a memoir would require fictional talents beyond his scope. The truth would not set him free. So far there was no evidence to prove any of the allegations made against Cardinal Roselli. Those who viewed the USB Tim Daniels had produced were under papal jurisdiction; they'd be subject to prosecution according to canon law if they revealed what they had witnessed.

He'd given little thought to the child, he had no paternal feelings for her. In all the years she'd lived in the Vatican, he'd only seen her in passing. He'd had no interest in her, in truth he feared her. Her presence had been a constant reminder of his transgression, of his breaking his vows. He'd been weak, probably still was. Probably was never cut out for the priesthood, never mind the papacy. He'd been pushed since early childhood, groomed for a future as a clergyman, but in retrospect he'd been ungroomed for the secular life. His mother saw in him her ticket to redemption, from what he'd had no clue. She'd been devout and expected him to follow her example. He'd craved her approval but longed to be a regular person living an ordinary life.

The seminary had been his gateway to power. The attention he'd sought from his mother was lavished upon him by the faithful who flocked to hear his sermons. He'd enjoyed the celebrity. He spent hours and hours formatting homilies, practicing inflections, when and where to pause, raise his voice perhaps in order to provoke a reaction that would resonate with the congregation, seep into their souls, and make him memorable. It worked, he'd been good at that part of religious life; he relished it but it was short-lived. He was transferred to Rome, and found himself without the words to properly convey his scripted message. His words fell flat onto the ears of the Italian churchgoers in Lazio, where he was first assigned. It had been a blow to his once soaring ego. He distracted himself by venturing out into the secular world with an old acquaintance, journalist Chris DeMarco, who in turn offered the services of Sophia Travato, a fellow journalist fluent in everything Italian both language and culture. She, he was told, would transform him, she could make him as charismatic to the Italians as he'd been to his American parishioners. He'd gotten more than he'd bargained for. She was all Chris said she was and more. He'd perfected the language in a few months, and with Sophia at his side, he'd experienced the flavor of Italy. In addition to learning all things Italian, he'd studied Sophia. She'd unwittingly mesmerized him. He'd made outlandish excuses to his superiors in order to spend time with her. He'd lied, said she'd needed his counsel, and she in turn introduced him to other young people in need of his services. He'd spent countless evenings at Sophia's apartment. One fateful night, she washed and he'd dried the dinner dishes, accidently brushing her hand as she'd placed a wet wine glass on the toweled counter. The light touch sent a spark of electrified emotion surging through him. Everything he'd missed, hadn't experienced before was there in front of him for the taking. He'd not considered the fallout. He hadn't loved her beyond all reason, it had been lust. He'd expected to walk away and continue pursuing his lofty ambition as an orator of note. But then she'd come to him, stunning him with her news. He'd avoided thinking about it then, as he had even with the evidence living within his realm. He'd been wrong but what could he have done? He'd have been shunned, should he have confessed earlier. He'd only told Cardinal Roselli because his conscience was overloaded with guilt at having broken his vows. He'd given little thought to Sophia and what she'd be facing. She would be okay, she'd find help, and raise the baby as a single mother in a time where it was acceptable. He'd go on as if nothing happened. It was a mere blip or so he'd thought.

He knew that there would be some chatter regarding the two deaths that occurred in such a short time frame. Cardinal Roselli had died of a tragic accident but Tim Daniels had been murdered and Cardinal Alfonso poisoned; there would be an investigation and it would be out of his control. Implicating him in any of the sordid occurrences of late would be unlikely unless the child was found. She now posed the biggest threat to his papacy. It was in God's hands as the religious zealots were fond of saying. For now, he would tend to Church matters. Too much time had been spent dwelling on the matter of Sophia. There was nothing more to be done.

Chapter Sixty-Nine

The newly built Buddhist Temple in Rome attracted more visitors than Abbot Ling or his superiors expected. He was inundated with requests for lectures and tours. He'd not only neglected the child, Nevaeh, he'd forgotten about her entirely. It wasn't until Lucia delivered a message expressing the concern the monks had regarding the child and asking him to visit, did he finally remember. He felt great remorse and intended to right this wrong immediately.

He escorted Lucia to the temple on the outskirts of Trastevere. As they walked, she told him about Nevaeh.

"At first, she adjusted well. She could be found in the garden, feeding the birds, talking to the cats. She learned our ways quickly. She is a born healer, she cultivated an herb garden for healing purposes in a matter of weeks. She speaks with an uncanny wisdom, as if the voices of the ages speak through her. She intuits the nature of things. One of the monks thinks she's the Buddha, but a female Buddha? We are not so enlightened, Abbot Ling."

The abbot raised his eyebrow at the remark, "What of the cardinal? He has not come for her?"

"No, Your Reverence, he has not called either."

"For weeks, Nevaeh kept busy, learned meditation and ritual dance, she mingled with the tourists showing them her herbs and offering them tea. She tended to the candles. It was a vacation for her, perhaps. Lately, she's become solemn, introspective to a distressing degree. While it's our way to self-reflect, she has not engaged in conversation, she barely eats or drinks. It is not our way to retreat from life. We find the truth in it. She has withdrawn from it. We believe she feels abandoned. We're afraid for her. There was no one else to reach out to. She is underage, we are her caretakers but not her guardians."

Abbot Ling found Nevaeh sitting on the edge of the garden's pond. A small gray cat with exceptional blue eyes sat on her lap. She held the cat with her left hand petting its fur, while her right hand dangled in the koi pond. The fish swam without fear to the water's surface, brushing their scales across her palm. Her hair was striking, it hung over her shoulder shielding her face. It was a thing of beauty. Locks of such lushness stood out in the midst of the shaved heads of the residents.

"Nevaeh," Abbot Ling called out, she seemed not to hear.

Abbot Ling put his hand lightly on the cat's fur, he pushed Nevaeh's hair to the side. Nevaeh looked up at him. Her eyes were sunken and red. It was obvious she'd been crying.

"Do you remember me, Nevaeh?"

"Yes," she answered softly.

"How are you faring here?"

"It's nice."

"Lucia tells me you are not well."

"I'm okay. How are you?"

"Good, I'm okay too."

"Abbot Ling? Do you know why Papa Alfonso hasn't returned to take me home?"

"I don't but I'll find out. I'm sure there's a good reason."

Lucia entered the garden carrying a pitcher of lemon water. Abbot Ling went to the inner offices to make a call.

The news of Cardinal Alfonso's illness saddened Abbot Ling. He didn't know if Nevaeh should be told. He knew he didn't want to be the one to break the news especially if it was dire. He didn't think the child's psyche could handle it. She'd need balance, harmony, and strength if she was to face the possible death of the only person who'd cared for her. Abbot Ling turned the music playing in the inner rooms of the temple up so the chants would penetrate the walls and be heard in the garden. He hoped it would soothe the child.

Cardinal Alfonso was sitting in a wheelchair on the side of his bed; he had the same faraway look that Nevaeh had. His appearance alarmed Abbot Ling. The cardinal seemed to have shrunken into himself. He was awake but looked like he was sleeping with his eyes open. He was looking out over the abbot at something unseen. Abbot Ling had seen the look before on the faces of the dying and the souls who had just given up on life. He would prepare Nevaeh but for what he wasn't sure. If Cardinal Alfonso didn't survive he didn't know what would happen to Nevaeh. She was underage and incapable of making an informed decision to join the Buddhist sect. He'd shelter her as long as he could to keep her safe, as promised, but he'd put the whole organization at risk doing so. He reflected on the possibilities. It would work out as the universe intended. He would follow the path.

Chapter Seventy

The news of Cardinal Roselli's death did nothing to allay Sophia's fears. Nevaeh was still missing.

"Where is Cardinal Alfonso? Does he have any idea if Nevaeh left with Cardinal Roselli? Or with anyone else?"

Alessandro didn't want to fuel Sophia's anxiety, but he had to tell her the truth.

"Sophia, sit down."

"I don't want to sit down."

"Sophia, please, sit down. I want to talk to you and I need you to remain calm."

"She's dead, isn't she? Please tell me, I have to know."

Alessandro sighed, "Sophia, I don't know where Nevaeh is. I have no news of her. We are still searching for her. Chris went to Chile with two of our officers."

"Chile, why?"

"Cardinal Roselli had an alias. He used it to travel to his family home in Chile. He traveled alone. Nevaeh wasn't with him. He died of an apparent insect bite while stranded in the Magallanes during a storm. He was buried in a family plot by the farmhands. Chris returned to New York."

"Is that all?" Sophia looked up at Alessandro.

"No, Sophia. Cardinal Alfonso was poisoned. He survived and is in the hospital. He regained consciousness but is not speaking. He may have suffered a stroke. Do you remember Tim Daniels, the administrative assistant in the papal offices?"

"Yes, of course. What about him?"

"He was found dead in his apartment. He'd apparently been strangled."

Sophia slumped down into the chair, "I should have stayed in Venice. All this suffering and death because of me. If Cardinal Roselli is dead in Chile, who did this?"

"We suspect Cardinal Roselli is responsible for the poisoning but not Tim Daniels' death directly. His car was spotted leaving Vatican City the evening before Tim's murder. We suspect Cardinal Roselli's chauffeur was acting on his behalf or it may have been Severino Poverelli. We've yet to find him."

"It's getting late, Alessandro, I want to go to sleep now."

It disturbed Alessandro when Sophia didn't comment on all he'd told her. He worried about her mental state. She kissed him lightly on the cheek and left the room.

Lauretta was in Sophia's apartment turning down her bed as she'd done since Sophia returned that day without her daughter. Sophia sat at the vanity while Lauretta brushed her hair. It calmed Sophia and had become a nightly ritual.

"Lauretta, what is going to happen to me? I don't know how to feel."

"Maybe you should visit Cardinal Alfonso in the hospital. I know he upset you when you met with him that day at the Hassler, but imagine how he felt. He'd been the one to care for Nevaeh in your absence. He's a good man I'm sure, who only wanted to protect the child. Maybe seeing you again will help him to recover. Maybe he knows something. It's worth a try."

Chapter Seventy-One

Abbot Ling found Nevaeh in her room the next morning. He'd need to gain her confidence before he saddled her with bad news. His calendar had been cleared, his assistant was capable of handling tourists. Their numbers had dwindled now that the Buddhist Temple in Rome was no longer a novelty. He would spend the day with Nevaeh.

He tapped lightly on the Shoji screen door to her little garden house to get her attention.

"You can come in, Abbot Ling, but first take off your sandals," Nevaeh said laughing. "I guess you know the rules."

"Good morning, Nevaeh, did you sleep well?"

"I don't sleep much, I like the night. Here's tea, I make it myself out of the herbs I grow. It's medicine, nature's medicine."

Abbot Ling sat at the small dining table and sipped the tea.

"Licorice?"

"Si, yes, there's a bit in there."

By lunchtime, Nevaeh had shown the abbot her garden, described each herb's curative properties, and how they could be used on humans. He was in awe of her innate abilities and knowledge. She was so young, barely approaching her teenage years, and had been kept cloistered behind the walls of the Vatican her entire life. Perhaps that was the key. Her isolation had kept her from outside influences therefore enabling her to see the world around her with a clarity few people in modern times had.

"Nevaeh, how do you intuit nature so well?"

Nevaeh shrugged, and as if she'd read his thoughts answered, "It's all I have."

"Abbot Ling, do you know why Papa Alfonso forgot me?"

The abbot intended to wait a few days before discussing the cardinal with the child, but now she'd pulled at his heart with her question.

"He didn't forget you. He's ill. He's in the hospital here in Roma."

Nevaeh looked up at the abbot without emotion and said, "You have to take me to him, I can heal him. I'll make some tea and then we'll go, right?"

Cardinal Alfonso's nurse was moving him into a wheelchair when Nevaeh arrived.

"I'm here now, Papa."

Nevaeh held the tea she'd prepared up to the cardinal's lips. He sipped it; his once vacant eyes indicated a flicker of life was returning. Nevaeh took the cup, placed it on the bedside stand, and put her head in his lap. Her hair fell over him. The cardinal stroked her hair in a wordless gesture of love. She removed her necklace and placed it in the cardinal's hand. She'd researched its origins, she knew it was forbidden. It was a Gnostic blessing, a healing amulet. Its ancient origins held mysteries long buried but the metal was of the earth, and the earth, Nevaeh knew, held the key to healing. Cardinal Alfonso closed his fist over the amulet, nodding at Nevaeh. They held themselves in the moment like a snapshot in time. Abbot Ling stood in the corner, marveling at the wonderous child.

Chapter Seventy-Two

Alessandro proved no match for Sophia and Lauretta when they approached him with the idea of visiting the ailing Cardinal Alfonso.

"I don't understand the point of visiting the man? What do you hope to gain? He's barely conscious from what I hear. You're risking your health, Sophia, reopening old wounds, over and over again. I don't like it."

"Too bad, if you don't like it," Sophia softened her tone adding, "Alessandro, I appreciate your concern for me, I do, but you aren't a parent. Even though nearly all of Nevaeh's life has been spent without me, a mother's bond is strong. I can't shake free of it, I can't forget about her, I can't let go. I have to try."

Lauretta nodded in agreement. Alessandro shot her a disapproving look before giving in and ordering the car be sent around to pick them up. The three would visit the cardinal together. Alessandro would be there to pick up the pieces, yet again, should this meeting prove as unproductive as the others. His greatest fear was that one of Cardinal Roselli's men had gone rogue and was hovering waiting to finish Cardinal Alfonso off. Considering all that had transpired in the safeguarding of the Church, nothing was out of the realm of possibility.

Sophia hadn't been inside of a hospital since Nevaeh was born. The sight of the drab colored walls and the smell of illness filled her not with dread but with an overwhelming sensation that something was about to happen. The intuitive skills she'd had as a young person had resurfaced along with her memory leaving her now with the sense of some impending occurrence, either menacing or uplifting, on her horizon. Her face flushed, her heart raced, and her breathing was noticeably rapid. She stopped in her tracks to catch her breath.

"Sophia, what is it? Let's go home, this is a mistake."

"Alessandro, no, I'm just anxious, that's all."

It wasn't all, there was something else going on inside of her, something she couldn't quite figure out. The hallway seemed to elongate itself as they walked, now arm in arm after Sophia had shown signs of distress.

The clerk at the nurse's station directed the three to room 113.

"Thirteen is a lucky number here in Italy, have faith, Sophia."

The sound emanating from Cardinal Alfonso's room was unfamiliar.

"What's that sound?" Sophia asked. It frightened her, she hesitated outside the door.

"It's a chanting mantra," Lauretta told her. "Nothing to be afraid of, it's from the Zen Buddhists. There's a temple just outside of Trastevere and a Buddhist Temple in the city of Roma. Perhaps the cardinal knows the abbot and he's enacted a healing. They believe in the dynamics of sound repetition; the repetitive chanting is believed to cause vibrations meant to generate restorative properties within the body. We're slowly rediscovering secret mysteries of ancient civilizations that are proving to be beneficial to us."

Sophia and Alessandro looked over at Lauretta with awed expressions.

"How do you know all this stuff, Lauretta?"

"Sophia, I've been alone since you left. Twelve years plus is a long time. I read, I attended lectures, I watched educational television. Something seeped in, I guess. Come now, let's go in. It may be healing for you too."

Lauretta pushed the door open. Sophia stood next to her, Alessandro was behind, he put his hand reassuringly on Sophia's shoulder. Nevaeh remained at the cardinal's side, with her head down, reciting the Zen mantra over and over. Her hair flowed down nearly touching the floor. She seemed unaware of the visitors. When she paused the chant, Sophia called out, "Nevaeh?"

Nevaeh lifted her head and nodded.

Sophia pulled out the necklace that held the ring, the match to Nevaeh's ancient medal.

"Do you have the medal that matches this ring?"

Nevaeh looked over at the woman who was still in the doorway; Cardinal Alfonso opened his hand revealing the healing amulet, "Here it is, Sophia."

Nevaeh fixed her eyes on the cardinal's, he patted her hand, "It's okay, Nevaeh, she's your mother. You can go to her now."

Chapter Seventy-Three

Chris DeMarco should have used the time on the cross-continent flight from Santiago to New York to catch up on his sleep; instead he spent the hours reflecting on the matter of Sophia.

Now, three weeks later, he couldn't shake the jet lag nor the lingering thoughts of her. The truth was, his obsession with her was fueled by guilt. He felt responsible for her, for all of it; he'd been the one to put her in the path of Joseph Morris. Joseph Morris, whom he'd barely known, who'd been a friend of sorts of his older brother. Joseph had been strange back then, aloof, not one of the crowd. Running into a compatriot while in a foreign country gave Chris a sense of home. He'd latched onto Joseph, they'd shared stories of home over drinks a few times.

Joe had already demonstrated an ambitious desire to rise through the ranks of the Church hierarchy, but Chris couldn't help notice his wandering eye. Joe Morris was as glib at flirting as he was at oration. He'd often show up at the bar dressed in street clothes, his religious garb noticeably absent.

Chris felt responsible for igniting the tragic spark that caused Sophia to lose years of her life, to miss out on raising her daughter, and to almost lose her own life. He felt culpable in all of it. He'd longed to be the hero, her hero. He'd attempted and failed to help her reunite with her child, to help her get justice, to help her prove herself credible.

Defeating the most powerful men on earth was like climbing a hill of molasses. For each step he'd taken towards unraveling the plot, he'd fallen back over and over. He'd exhausted all avenues.

Chris had hoped to have taken Cardinal Roselli by surprise in an impromptu confrontation in Chile, get him to turn over the USB, maybe force a confession, but again fate intervened. The cardinal was dead, Lorenzo Mercuri as well, Severino Poverelli had vaporized into thin air. There was no tangible evidence or witness to come forward now to confirm what everyone involved already knew. The pope held all the cards, and he would no doubt hold them close to the breast. The realization that there was nothing more he could do to help Sophia sat uneasily on Chris' shoulders. He knew he had to let go.

Chris hadn't been back to New York in years. He'd worked as a freelance journalist for most of his career. He'd worked, gathering assignments from remote parts of the world, finally landing in Syria working as a makeshift war correspondent in the midst of enemy territory. It had taken its toll. He'd served his time, given his all for his country, and made a journalistic name for himself within the inner circle.

Working for the entertainment magazine had been a frivolous waste of his talents; he'd used his stellar reputation as a tool to pitch the idea of interviewing his old acquaintance now Supreme Pontiff. The assignment sent him back to his beloved Rome and put him face to face with the long-lost Sophia Travato. Now he'd once again distance himself from her, if only his mind could erase the traces.

He rented an Airbnb in Greenwich Village. It was modest, clean with spartan but comfortable furnishings. It suited his purpose for the time being. He rented it by the day, he didn't expect to be in the city for long. He preferred to be on the move, he needed to find a life for himself.

Chris chose the Village because he wanted the distraction of street noise, to hear the frenetic constant commotion of people, mostly kids, ambling about. He looked out the window. It was early August; college kids had arrived already but classes hadn't officially started. They were lazing about in cafés and on park benches in Washington Square soaking up the last days of summer.

The apartment was small but spanned from the front to the back of the small brick building. The window facing the back overlooked a flourishing garden reminiscent of Lauretta's Trastevere terrace. Chris sighed, he could have stayed put there forever. If only things had worked out differently. At this rate, his life would be riddled with regrets. He had to stop, think of himself for once.

He pulled a clean but wrinkled shirt out of his unpacked suitcase. He shook it out. He'd wear a jacket despite the heat and make himself as presentable as he could. His meeting with the editor in chief was scheduled for 11 a.m. He checked the time on his phone; it was only nine, he had plenty of time to mull over what he would say. He'd never actually met the editor. They'd only spoken on the phone and had conducted indirect reviews of assignments via email. Chris was returning empty-handed. For the first time in his life, the story he'd uncovered could not be revealed, not now and maybe not ever. He had no proof of its validity.

He grabbed his messenger bag, put his jacket over the messy shirt, left the apartment, secured the door, and took to the streets. He looked the part of a wayward freelancer. He decided a walk to the Midtown headquarters of the magazine would afford him some time to come up with a reasonable, hopefully buyable excuse to present to the editor. There were no other journalistic human interest stories percolating on his horizon. Chris was tapped out.

Chapter Seventy-Four

The August heat settled over the city of New York in a visible haze. Chris had grown used to heat while living in the city of Rome. He relished in people-watching as he walked uptown. Most were sluggishly lumbering along, stopping every few feet to take a sip from their bottled water. It distracted him from his upcoming meeting, and did little to diminish his fear that he'd be removed from the roster of freelancers and would have to begin again. He supposed he could fashion a fictionalized version of Sophia's tale. He'd have to be creative so as not to land himself in a courtroom full of lawyers working incognito, of course, but on behalf of the current papacy should he cross the line. With time on his hands, he could do it. It might comfort Sophia. Give her some sense of closure. But I need to be free of her, why can't I be free of her?

The offices of *In Conversation Magazine* were located on the twelfth floor of a glass-walled building on 6th Avenue in the heart of Midtown Manhattan. The security guard manning the desk in the lobby checked his ID, looked for his name on the roster of visitors, and pointed to the bank of elevators. Chris found his way up to the twelfth floor. The entire floor was devoted to the magazine. Chris had no idea of its scope. He'd considered it to be in line with other rag magazines he'd seen on newsstands. But in light of the world's obsession with celebrities, he wasn't all that surprised they were successful.

"I'm Chris DeMarco, I have an appointment with the editor." Chris suddenly drew a blank on the editor's name.

"Yes, hello, Mr. DeMarco. Nice to finally meet you. I'm Mr. Halpern's administrative assistant, Joanna Beirnes. He's running a bit late — an unexpected conference call. Some irate low level celebrity is upset about a recent article. A lot of egos run amok around here. He shouldn't be more than twenty minutes. Can I offer you some coffee?"

"No, thank you."

Joanna Beirnes left her desk, and walked over to a locked cabinet. She took out three manila envelopes and handed them all to Chris.

"These were delivered here for you. One arrived yesterday, and the others a week or so ago."

"Really? That's strange."

Chris looked at the return address of the first envelope. It was from a Mary Daniels. He didn't recognize the name. The second was from the colleague he'd sent the preliminary story he'd written as a safeguard for Sophia. His colleague had been sent overseas on assignment to an undisclosed location; he didn't want Chris' work to fall into the wrong hands. The third envelope was from Sophia.

Dear Chris,

I don't know how to properly thank you for all your efforts on my behalf.

I didn't think it was proper to email or text what I have to tell you. The enclosed picture will speak to you in volumes, more than any words could convey. I didn't know where else to send this, I hope it reaches you. I'll be in touch.

Gratefully,

Sophia

Chris turned the envelope over and another smaller one fell out onto the floor. Inside was a photograph. Sophia was breathtaking. She was standing on Lauretta's terrace. The bougainvillea vines in all their splendor monopolized the background. But their beauty paled in comparison to the radiant child. There was no mistaking her for anyone else. The resemblance between mother and daughter was astonishing.

Sophia had not been forthcoming with any details. All Chris' previous mind games whereby he'd put her out of his thoughts were now a thing of the past. He had to know how and where the child was found. Who'd facilitated the reunion? There may be a story still smoldering there somewhere.

Chris turned his attention to the other envelope. It contained something more than a mere letter. It was sent locally. He opened it slowly, thinking it may hold some kind of device. It was a USB accompanied by a letter from Tim Daniels.

Dear Chris,

If you have received this letter then I'm no longer around. I began to fear for my life when Cardinal Roselli discovered I'd bugged his office. I supposed he succeeded in eliminating everyone who could potentially expose his enterprise. In order to safeguard my findings, I gave a USB to Cardinal Alfonso, and I shipped one to my mother here in New York with instructions to send it off to you at your office in New York should I come to an unfortunate end. I'm confident it will prove to be an essential tool in bringing those involved to justice in some fashion and will hopefully help Sophia and Nevaeh to reunite and bring Sophia peace. I hope you tell the story to the world; some may choose not to believe it but it needs to be told.

I ask you not to pity me; I knew Cardinal Roselli recruited me to assist him in his sordid activities under the guises of protecting the Church. I agreed to work for him of my own accord. I was paid handsomely until I could no longer stomach him. The pope is a weak man, if the Church is to survive in the years to come, it must rid itself of all the vipers and those manipulated by them. There are many decent and devoted men still in her service. It's my wish that my efforts will not be proven futile and that you've got an arsenal of evidence in your hands. If anyone can expose the truth it's you, my friend.

Tim

Chris shoved the three envelopes into his messenger bag and headed towards the door. Joanna Beirnes got up from her chair. She hurried behind him, stopping only to adjust her shoe, after her heel snagged on the carpet.

"Mr. DeMarco, wait, what about your appointment?" she yelled after him.

The elevator door opened, Chris stepped in, and as he reached over to press the button for the lobby, Joanna Beirnes put her hand on the door stopping it from closing.

"Mr. DeMarco, Mr. Halpern's ready for you. Where are you going?"

Joanna struggled to keep the door ajar; Chris stared at her, saying nothing. He didn't want to tell her anything, he was grappling with the concept of what he was about to do. Saying it out loud made it all too real. He wanted to forget everything but he couldn't. He didn't want to think anymore, he just wanted to act. He knew he was the only one who could, he needed to leave, and he didn't want to reveal his plan.

"Mr. DeMarco, what are you doing?"

Chris didn't know what he was doing. Was he going to get on with his life, fix Sophia's for the rest of hers, win her love, unravel the Vatican's treachery, and expose it to the world, or do all of it? He didn't know yet. He'd figure it out when he got there.

La fine

Acknowledgments

From inception to publication, *Vatican Daughter* was a labor of love. Despite its dark subject it was exciting to delve into history and put it all together. I am infinitely grateful to everyone who assisted me from start to finish. Thanks to all of you.

Thanks to everyone at Collective Ink Publishing/Roundfire Books who believed in *Vatican Daughter*. To Vicky Hartley, Ben Blundell, and Daniela Norris for your words of encouragement. Thanks to Collective Ink's editorial manager, Frank Smecker, for his unwavering devotion to his authors, especially this needy one. To Elizabeth Radley for the careful spot-on edits and to the rest of the publishing, marketing and publicity team for your efforts on my behalf.

Thanks to Professor David Castriota for lighting the spark that became this story.

Thanks from my heart and soul to my devoted bestie, Karen Poydenis, who read every revision with a keen eye for editing and for her unwavering devotion to my craft.

Thanks to Pulitzer Prize-winning author, Professor David Kertzer, who graciously shared his vast knowledge on the little known historical facts surrounding papal kidnappings.

Thanks to fellow Columbian alumna and award-winning author of *Conjure Women*, Afia Atakora, who I'm honored to call my friend, for taking the time to read and endorse my work with such eloquence. You've been with me from the beginning and I will forever cherish the memories of those early days.

Thanks to the international best-selling thriller writer and historian, Steve Berry, for agreeing without hesitation to endorse my work. I am a forever grateful fan.

Thank you to author, biographer and friend, Tom Santopietro, whose kindness and steadfast advice on all things publishing encouraged me along this journey.

Thank you to all the amazing people who helped me on this writing journey. To Lynn Boulger, and the staff at The Author's Guild for the immense amount of support and advice.

To Pat Rullo, host of the podcast, "Speak Up Talk Radio," for all the support and interest.

To Nancy Bass, owner of the landmark bookstore, "The Strand," for graciously offering her New York City landmark venue without hesitation.

To author, David W. Berner, for your kindness and advice.

To Jane Friedman, John Matthew Fox and book coach, Mark Malatesta, for your tireless efforts helping writers like me navigate the world of publishing.

Thank you especially to my beloved family, Liza, Drew, Grayson, Nic, Amanda, Richard Bristol PhD, Ediss Gandelman, and Lori Massaro for your praise, enthusiasm and encouraging words.

To my chosen family and Peruvian daughter, designer Sivan Lebovich, for your never-ending love, support, and design advice, and to my Venetian daughter, Laura Bertaglia, for sharing your beloved city with me.

Thank you to Dr. Mauro Romita, for your covert support. It was an over the top gesture for which I'm eternally grateful.

Last and most importantly, thank you to my husband, Joe, my best friend, and die-hard supporter in all things. Your love and devotion keeps me going and never allows me the luxury of giving up.

And to my readers past and future, if it weren't for all of you there would be no point. Thank you.

About the Author

Joni Iraci worked as a staff and charge RN in a northern New Jersey hospital, before moving to New York City where she worked as a night nurse at Memorial Sloan Kettering Cancer Center. She subsequently made a life-changing career move when she accepted an offer to work as a staff nurse at Lenox Hill Hospital. It was there where she met her husband; they married and relocated to Pittsburgh for one year to do a fellowship. Returning to New York, Joni helped her husband with his business and raised three children. Once the nest was semi-empty, Joni returned to school to pursue her life-long dream of becoming a writer. In 2013, she earned a BA in liberal studies with a concentration in writing and literature from Sarah Lawrence College; in 2017, she earned an MFA in creative writing from Columbia University. She is a fiction writer. After publishing several short stories in literary journals, her debut novel, *Reinventing Jenna Rose*, was published in May 2019. It has received favorable reviews. It recently won The Firebird Book Award taking first place for women's issues and coming of age, and second place for new adult fiction and legal thriller. It was reissued as a second edition in November 2023.

She has spoken publicly on many occasions, discussing her journey as an adult returning to school, and the trials and tribulations of publishing in your later years. She was invited to talk at Shakespeare and Company and The Strand bookstores in New York City. Along with Hollywood historian and author, Tom Santopietro, she gave an in-conversation talk which can be found on YouTube.com. An interview can be found on Centralvalleytalk.com/BriggsonBooks. Also available on YouTube.com. She spoke about her work on the podcast, SpeakupTalkRadio. She is a retired RN who has completed a novella, completed a third novel, *The Women of the 13th Rione*, which like *Vatican Daughter* is set in Italy, Iraci's home away from home. She is currently working on a fourth novel.

Joni Marie Iraci welcomes emails from readers and is available for speaking engagements be it in relationship to her work or the joys and angst of returning to college in one's older years. She is a freelance writing tutor available to assist college-bound high school students with research, essay writing, and college applications. She worked briefly as an adjunct professor of English Composition. She is a member of the National League of American Pen Women and an active elite member of The Author's Guild.

Note to My Readers

Jmi10805@gmail.com or jmi2118@columbia.edu

I am deeply grateful to all of you for reading *Vatican Daughter*. The extensive research I did while writing *Vatican Daughter* took me down paths I never expected and sparked an intense curiosity to delve further into little-known historical facts pertaining to Vatican cover-ups. For eight years, I did volunteer work for a local church. I witnessed firsthand the blatant hypocritical behavior on the part of the clergy. This along with yearly trips to Italy triggered my "what if?" imagination. A half-page outline sat on the page for several years. In 2019, I traveled back to Italy where I walked 88 miles through Rome and Venice to get the lay of the land. In the midst of the pandemic, I wrote and researched every day for one year to complete *Vatican Daughter*. I welcome contact with my readers. Please follow me on Facebook, Instagram or LinkedIn.

https://www.facebook.com//jonimarieiraciauthor
https://www.instagram.com/jiraci2
https://www.linkedin.com/in/joni-marie-iracib31945129

My first novel, *Reinventing Jenna Rose*, ISBN 979-8986407029, propels the reader on a fast-paced journey through the life of a young girl who's determined to realize her self-worth after escaping an abusive situation. It is a moving story infused with humor, New York City street scenes, and literary references.

As a senior citizen, I am late to the publishing process, and had it not been for readers like you, it is doubtful I would have continued to reinvent myself as an author. I am the embodiment of the adage, "it's never too late."

With gratitude and best wishes,
Joni Marie Iraci

For Further Reading

The Kidnapping of Edgardo Mortara by David Kertzer
ISBN 0679768173

ROUNDFIRE
BOOKS

FICTION

Put simply, we publish great stories. Whether it's literary or popular, a gentle tale or a pulsating thriller, the connecting theme in all Roundfire fiction titles is that once you pick them up you won't want to put them down.
If you have enjoyed this book, why not tell other readers by posting a review on your preferred book site.

The Cause
Roderick Vincent
The second American Revolution will be a
fire lit from an internal spark.
Paperback: 978-1-78279-763-0 ebook: 978-1-78279-762-3

Don't Drink and Fly
The Story of Bernice O'Hanlon: Part One
Cathie Devitt
Bernice is a witch living in Glasgow. She loses her way
in her life and wanders off the beaten track looking for the
garden of enlightenment.
Paperback: 978-1-78279-016-7 ebook: 978-1-78279-015-0

Gag
Melissa Unger
One rainy afternoon in a Brooklyn diner, Peter Howland
punctures an egg with his fork. Repulsed, Peter pushes
the plate away and never eats again.
Paperback: 978-1-78279-564-3 ebook: 978-1-78279-563-6

The Master Yeshua
The Undiscovered Gospel of Joseph
Joyce Luck
Jesus is not who you think he is. The year is 75 CE. Joseph
ben Jude is frail and ailing, but he has a prophecy to fulfil ...
Paperback: 978-1-78279-974-0 ebook: 978-1-78279-975-7

On the Far Side, There's a Boy
Paula Coston
Martine Haslett, a thirty-something 1980s woman, plays hard on the fringes of the London drag club scene until one night which prompts her to sign up to a charity. She writes to a young Sri Lankan boy, with consequences far and long.
Paperback: 978-1-78279-574-2 ebook: 978-1-78279-573-5

Tuareg
Alberto Vazquez-Figueroa
With over 5 million copies sold worldwide, *Tuareg* is a classic adventure story from best-selling author Alberto Vazquez-Figueroa, about honour, revenge and a clash of cultures.
Paperback: 978-1-84694-192-4

Readers of ebooks can buy or view any of these bestsellers by clicking on the live link in the title. Most titles are published in paperback and as an ebook. Paperbacks are available in traditional bookshops. Both print and ebook formats are available online.

Find more titles and sign up to our readers' newsletter at www.collectiveinkbooks.com/fiction